THE UNIVERSE

IS A VERY BIG PLACE

April M. Aasheim

THE UNIVERSE IS A VERY BIG PLACE
Copyright 2013
by April M. Aasheim

Published by Dark Root Press

First Edition

ISBN-13: 978-0615757100
ISBN-10: 0615757103

Cover Art & Design by Shari Runkle

Dark Root Press

Printed in the United States of America

2013

ACKNOWLEDGEMENTS

There are many people I would like to thank: My husband Shawn, for supporting me, inspiring me, and believing in me when I couldn't believe in myself. I couldn't have done any of this without him. My mother and best friend, Shari. She will always be the original Lanie. My writing group: Mike, Thomas, Walt, Becca, Vanessa and Whitney. I am so lucky to have found you all. Julie, for always being there for me personally and professionally. Everyone who reads my blog and short stories. Your enthusiasm for my words keeps me going. The 7/11 man on TV Highway, for supplying me with diet coke at 7 in the morning and only charging me the refill price.

Thanks everyone!

Dedicated to my Aunt Linda
For encouraging me to just be myself
I miss you

ONE

1982

Spring pulled back the flap and peered into the tent. A set of red tapered candles, placed purposely on a trunk in the center of the room, provided enough light to make out the objects inside. There were old books, some heavy with dust, thrown haphazardly across crates on the floor. Recipe cards calling for strange ingredients like cat whiskers and muskrat tails were pinned to the walls. Vials of every imaginable shape and color occupied makeshift shelves along the perimeter of the tent. Their shadows cast long, ghostly silhouettes, lending an eerie credence to the atmosphere.

Lanie could throw a room together in three hours flat.

"Come in Spring," Lanie said, and Spring jumped. She had thought Lanie to be in a trance. The woman sitting opposite her mother gave Spring a scowling look. Lanie charged by the minute and thirty seconds of her time was wasted.

"Don't worry," Lanie told the woman, "This is my babushka and she is learning the family trade." Lanie had on her fake mole, her Russian voice, and perfume three inches thick. Spring felt dizzy as she tiptoed by.

Spring sat down on a large throw-pillow beside her mother and gazed into the crystal ball. Lanie swore she could see the future, but all Spring ever saw was a distorted reflection of herself, taller and skinnier and even more gawky...if that were possible. "Use your third eye," Lanie had told her, but Spring had no idea where her third eye

1

was kept so had to make do with the two she had.

"Will I find true love again?" The woman asked, peering into the ball, hoping to catch a glimpse of what lay ahead for her.

Lanie stared into the glass and said nothing for a full minute; a whole dollar's worth of waiting. Finally, Lanie returned her gaze to the woman. "Nope."

"Nope? What do you mean, nope?" The woman shook her head and her glasses toppled from her nose, landing atop the chest and scattering Lanie's deck of tarot cards. "I paid you good money and you are telling me nope?"

Lanie stood, shook her arms to let the invisible tension loose, and lost her accent. "Look. I don't need a crystal ball to tell me this. You get one chance at true love in this lifetime and that's it."

The woman groped around for her glasses, almost knocking over one of the candles. When she placed them on her stump of a nose, she looked from Lanie to Spring and then back to Lanie. "One chance? That hardly seems fair."

Spring didn't have to look at her mother to know that Lanie was rolling her eyes. Lanie didn't have much tolerance for nonbelievers and even less for those who somehow believed that life was fair. "I don't make the rules, honey. You need to take that up with the Universe."

The woman buried her face in her hands and sobbed. "What am I going to do? I'm 43-years-old. I can't live the rest of my life alone. Oh God, what am I going to do?" Spring wanted to go to the woman and pet her, but her mother didn't allow anyone to touch the customers. Even the sad ones.

Lanie tilted her head and a red curl bounced near her ample bottom. Spring coiled it around her finger and released it, hoping someday she would get a wig as pretty as her mother's.

"Stand," Lanie said to the woman, motioning for her to rise. "It's not that bad. You're still a handsome woman, even if you are teetering on the expiration date. Meet some men at a bar, sleep with a few of them, and then settle down with a nice banker or something. You'll

meet your true love again."

"*Really?*" *the woman looked up, her tear-stained face taking on a look of hope.*

"*Of course. In the next life-time. That will be thirteen bucks.*"

The woman fished around in her purse and pulled out three fives. She handed them to Lanie.

"*Need change?*" *Lanie asked, stuffing the bills into the crest of her cleavage. The woman said nothing and stumbled out of the tent.*

"*Thank God she left when she did.*" *Lanie said, reaching up the back of her multi-flowered house-dress and wriggling around until Spring heard a soft snap. "I had a wedgie so tight it was starting to cut off my circulation.*" *Lanie hooted and took a swig from her closest vial.*

"*What took you so long getting over here, young lady?*" *Lanie asked as Spring rifled through the Tarot Deck, picking out the pretty ones. "How can you learn if you're never on time?*"

"*Got lost.*"

"*The road from the Ferris wheel to my tent is a straight shot. How do you get lost going in a straight line?*"

Spring puckered her lips. "I don't think in straight lines, mama. I think in starbursts."

Lanie nodded. "Just like your father."

"*Mama,*" *Spring said, staring at the Knight of Cups. "I don't think I wanna be a fortune teller when I grow up. I don't like giving people bad news.*"

Lanie scratched her hip through a small hole in the side of her dress. The dress had seen better days, but Lanie would never part with it. "What bad news are you referring to? It's not like I tell them when they're gonna die."

"*You can do that?*" *Spring asked, with renewed awe for her mother. Knowing when someone was going to die was like having a super-power, almost as good as invisibility but even better than flight.*

"*Of course not!*" *Lanie huffed. "That's why I don't tell 'em. Now what bad news are you sayin' I give people?*"

"Do you really only get one true love?"

Lanie squatted down, body parts creaking along the way. "Love's overrated Spring. If you get it once, consider yourself lucky. Life isn't a fairytale, otherwise we'd all have our Prince Charmings."

Spring pulled her pale hair down across her face, shielding herself from her mother. There were lots of boys she thought were cute. She had even let one kiss her. She hoped she hadn't wasted her slot already, before she even turned twelve.

"Stop it. You've got a pretty face. Quit covering it up. It will give you warts. Now go find your daddy and Chloe and tell them it's corn dogs for dinner."

Spring nodded and scampered out of the tent and onto the midway, ignoring the flashing lights and the whirs and whizzes of the rides, and wondering (not for the first time) if any normal families had an extra bedroom and had ever considered adopting a pre-teen girl in need of a good home.

2005

Spring swept through the house, gathering up all evidence of her weekend alone. Sam would be returning from his business trip today and she couldn't endure another one of his 'good-housekeeping' lectures. The kitchen table was littered with candy bar wrappers, pizza cartons, and coffee mugs. Good memories, she thought, smiling to herself as she pushed it all into a giant Glad bag, secured it with a twisty tie, and tossed it onto the back porch. Next she scooped up an armful of dirty socks, hair rollers, and magazines from the living room floor and tottered towards her bedroom, hurling them into her closet. She frowned at the pile that was growing, steadily becoming an entity of its own. She made a mental note to deal with the jumble after work, but as soon as she shut the closet door the mess was forgotten.

Spring did a quick once-over of the bedroom and smiled. Not bad. Sleeping on the couch for the last three nights had left this room, at least, in pretty good shape. A little dusty, perhaps, but the bed was made and there wasn't the usual heap of laundry sitting on the floor. She kicked a few stray shoes under the bed and moved the pillows around to give the illusion she had slept there. Sam believed that only Barbarians and Hippies slept on the sofa and she didn't want to fall into either of those categories. She brushed her hands on her bare legs, satisfied that the place would meet at least precursory expectations.

The phone in the living room rang and Spring paused to listen as the caller left a message. It was her sister Chloe again. "Spring, I know you're there. If you don't pick up I'm going to hunt you down at work and tell your coworkers embarrassing stories about the time we lived in the motel with no water for seven weeks. Don't make me go there. You know I will." Chloe hung up.

"Dios mio." Spring said, slapping her hand to her head and reciting the phrase her homeschool teacher, Sunshine, used to say when the kids were getting out of hand. She wasn't sure how long she could avoid talking to Chloe, but was glad that she hadn't told her sister that she had been issued a cell phone from work. She turned to see the blinking red lights on her alarm clock and her stomach tightened. Despite getting up an hour early and showering the night before, she was going to be late again. She pulled on the floral dress she had worn the previous day, checked for stains hidden among the bouquets of flowers, and shoved her feet into the only pair of shoes that hadn't made it under the bed.

"Hell," she said, running down the hall and searching for her briefcase. She had been so excited about her weekend alone –– the first time in two years she had neither the twins nor Sam to worry about –– that after seeing Sam off to the airport, she had raced back home, clicked on the TV, poured herself a glass of wine, and dumped the briefcase, not thinking about it since. She could almost feel Sam's presence hovering over her, telling her that if she just put things in the same spot every

5

time, this kind of thing wouldn't happen. She pushed him away and tried to retrace her steps on her own. Door. TV. Wine. Bowl of cereal. Aha! She spun around and spied the case and her wallet, huddled cozily on the breakfast counter that separated the dining room from the living area.

"Thank you, Universe," she said aloud, raising her eyes the way her mother did when she was expressing gratitude. "Now if you will provide me with enough money for lunch, I'd be forever grateful." She rifled through her wallet, pulled out one limp dollar bill, and sighed. *The Universe gives what is needed, not what is wanted,* her mother would say.

But I need to eat, Spring thought, wondering if next time she should pray to the Wendy's girl instead. Spring tugged at her dress, willing it to lengthen. Despite her protests, Sam had thrown it in the dryer and it had shrunk above her knees. Her eyes fell to the freezer where her credit card was stored in saran wrap. I could just this once, she thought. Ten dollars won't hurt us too much, especially if it's work related.

It was a tradition for all the caseworkers at *Teens in Trouble* to go to a local Chinese Restaurant on Mondays to de-stress and 'bond as a team.' Although it wasn't mandatory, Jane proclaimed that it was *highly suggested.* Spring was about to seize the card, but resisted. If she broke down first, Sam would feel free to buy all sorts of niceties they couldn't afford. He enjoyed the finer things in life and swore he broke out in hives whenever he had to buy anything store-brand; the decision to stop using their cards altogether had almost sent him to the emergency room. She would just have to buck up, set a good example, and take a can of soup for lunch again. I'm on a diet, she had explained the last time she had taken her own lunch to the restaurant and the ladies politely nodded and smiled. She wasn't sure if she had fooled them before and wondered if they would buy it again. She hoped so. The thought of snooty Suzette offering to pay her way was worse than missing the lunch altogether. As she went to replace the dollar in her wallet, her eyes caught sight of the corner of a picture, hidden behind a stack of business cards.

"Trevor." She said it so softly, barely a whisper, that she couldn't be sure the word had even come out. She had forgotten about the picture, placed there months before, when she had been cleaning out her keepsake box. She hadn't looked at it since and wasn't sure why it seemed to be calling to her now. She traced her finger around the corner of it, biting her lip. Once she had known his face better than her own, but the memory was fading. She tried to mentally draw up his image but it tore apart like old paper. She should just let the memory diminish completely, she thought. Let it slip into that part of the brain where she kept her other unwanted memories. But she couldn't. It was Trevor. She tugged at the photo until it came unlodged. His green eyes smiled at her, teasing her from behind the dark curl that fell across his forehead. "Dimples," she said, recalling how they deepened when he grinned. She swallowed, brushing her thumb across his cheek.

She could throw the picture away now, or better yet, set it on fire. Watch his face melt and rid her of the weight she had been carrying for two years. A cleansing ritual, Lanie called it. That would be best. Besides, if Sam ever discovered that she carried a photo of Trevor Donnelly in her wallet –– and not a single photo of Sam –– he might never forgive her, and she would add another failed relationship to her list. She pinched the photo between her thumb and index finger and tightened her jaw. Maybe tomorrow. She pushed the picture back inside her wallet and hid it once again behind her stack of business cards.

Spring grabbed the briefcase, a can of vegetable soup, and her purse and moved towards the door. No time to reminisce now, she thought, dashing from the house and scrambling down the porch steps into her white station wagon. It was an ugly vehicle, rusted on one side and dented on the other, but it was one of the few things Spring owned outright. Purchased with cash after a brief stint working as The Corn Dog Girl at the State Fair in Pueblo. Popping the clutch into what was left of first gear, she hit the gas and made her way towards *Teens in Trouble.*

Jane's going to be pissed.

Spring steered with one hand, putting on lipstick with the other.

She merged onto the freeway and checked her reflection in the rearview mirror. The result made her grimace. It looked like Bobo the Wonder Dog had helped her with her makeup.

"Really, it's not my fault," she explained to her reflection as she blotted her mouth with the back of her hand. "I'm basically a single parent and I have a lot to do." Her reflection blinked back accusingly, but said nothing about Spring's free weekend. Spring weaved in and out of the few cars on the freeway, changing lanes and narrowly missing a silver Prius. The driver honked, flipped her off, and sped away.

"Sorry!" She called out through the open window, forcing her car into fifth gear. The wagon rattled and coughed like an old man on his death bed, but obliged.

She said a quick thank you to whatever gods governed traffic that she had at least missed rush hour as she zipped past several cargo trucks. *An excuse. I need a good excuse.* Dawdling or easily distracted weren't going to cut it. She sorted through her mental rolodex but came up empty. As far as Jane knew, all her grandparents were dead as well as a few imaginary siblings. She was down to short-term alien abduction or a temporary bout of anthrax poisoning. She saw her exit, veered off the freeway, and careened towards the large brown building where she worked. At the last possible moment she slammed on the brakes, thrust the wheel to the left, and skidded into two empty parking spaces surrounded by potholes. Jane had been promising to fix the lot for a while now, but Spring didn't mind the holes. It guaranteed her a parking spot even when the rest of the lot was full. *Record time I bet!* Spring smiled, but she wasn't sure. Her watch had ceased working earlier; probably a casualty from last night's shower. Sam was not going to be happy. He had just given her a presentation on the subtle differences between waterproof and water resistant.

Maybe Jane's on one of her spiritual retreats. Spring snatched the briefcase and her purse −−the vortex Chloe had called it −− and ran, tripping over her shoes towards the front entrance. She carefully pushed open the door to *Teens in Trouble* and hoped that no one would notice her sneaking in. "Good morning," said Debbie as Spring entered the main lobby. Spring did a quick scan of the area and noted that they were alone. Thank the Universe. Debbie was a new hire, and more concerned with planning her upcoming wedding than reporting employee time card fraud. Spring was safe.

"Morning, Debs," Spring smiled, putting down her bags and raking her fingers through her hair. She hadn't been able to find the brush that morning and had tried her best to work out a knot with one of Sam's shrimp forks. It hadn't worked. "Where is everyone? Kinda eerie."

"Eerie is fine by me. I'd take eerie over the usual jibber-jabber anytime. Especially if it means Jane has something better to do than to ask me to staple things."

Debbie was new to *Teens in Trouble* and did not hide her contempt for being a receptionist.

"Five years in college," Debbie openly lamented. "And twenty-thousand in student loans. Just to be Jane's sock puppet. But I bet sock puppets get better insurance benefits."

Spring admired Debbie's audacity but she could afford to be cheeky. She was about to marry a doctor.

"...I think my hand is turning into a claw." Debbie continued. "Wonder if I qualify for disability?" Debbie winked and continued her task of sorting through a box of wedding invitations, holding each one up to the light to examine something Spring couldn't see. "Oh, that reminds me. Jane wants you in the conference room ASAP."

"Oh?" This couldn't be good. Jane rarely asked for anyone by name. Spring quickly calculated how many times she had been late to work that month and felt the blood drain from her face. "I'm never going to see you again, am I?"

Debbie laughed. "I don't think you have to worry. Jane seemed like she was in a pretty good mood. Hasn't asked me to fax one useless memo yet."

Spring furrowed her brow. Jane Letch was never in a good mood. Ever. She reminded Spring of the Queen from Alice in Wonderland. *Off with their heads!* Perhaps there was going to be a public beheading. That would account for Spring's summoning and Jane's good mood. Spring swallowed, gave Debbie one last look, and proceeded down the hall to meet her fate.

The conference room door was closed but Spring could make out the sounds of muffled conversations and the scrape of moving chairs across the linoleum floor. It sounded like the entire workforce of *Teens in Trouble,* sans Debbie, had gathered inside. Smells of coffee and bacon wafted up under the door and Spring's stomach lurched. She had forgotten to eat that morning. Jane rarely sprang for breakfast and Spring guessed there was slim chance anything was left.

"Serves you right for being late," she chastised herself, secretly hoping that the laws of karma would kick in and that would be the end of her punishment.

Spring cautiously pushed open the door and peeped in. Something serious was happening. The normally disorderly conference room had been cleaned up. Five folding tables, normally used for paper sorting and party planning, had been arranged in a horseshoe formation in front of a drop-down screen. Women sat around the table whom Spring recognized as her coworkers, except for an unknown attendee in a purple suit whose name-tag read MEG. Spring gulped. There had been rumors about 'the poor economy' and 'downsizing' and Spring wondered if her time had come.

"In times like these you need to make yourself indispensable," Sam had cautioned her, but she hadn't listened. Now she regretted tossing aside the *Seven Secrets of Highly Successful People* and its accompanying day planner Sam had given her on her last birthday.

Spring tiptoed in and slipped into an empty chair next to Rebecca, the woman she shared an office with. Rebecca was picking at a hole in her paper plate and Spring noticed that everyone's plates seemed to be cleaned. She picked up a nearby spoon and puckered at her distorted reflection, hoping her lipstick issue had been resolved in the car. Rebecca elbowed her in the ribs and Spring was startled to see that everyone was now staring in their direction. Spring dropped the spoon and it bounced twice, clattering wildly before tumbling onto the floor.

"Spring, nice to see you again," said Jane in a sardonic tone.

Spring swallowed. Apparently her tardiness had not gone unnoticed. A few chuckles from around the table rose and quickly fell, lest they attract Jane's unwanted attention.

Spring was about to respond but Jane continued.

"A few months ago you came up with the idea of adding a mascot to our team to help improve our recognition in the community. Do you remember?" Jane was standing now, twirling a long stick Spring had never seen before. It looked like a cue stick from one of the pool halls her mother used to frequent. Spring squinted to get a better look. Sure enough, the end was tipped in blue felt. Spring wondered which was worse: getting fired or getting hit with the stick.

"Spring?" Jane asked again. "You do remember the mascot idea, right?"

Spring nodded. The idea seemed silly now, created during a weak moment when she was low on blood sugar and watching a McDonald's commercial. "Yes, I remember."

"Well, I discussed it with the board of directors and they loved the idea! So we hired a public relations firm to develop this. What you're about to witness is the fruition of your dreams!" Jane directed the stick towards a closet where toilet paper and ink cartridges were stored. She tapped the door three times and stepped aside.

Nothing happened.

Jane's face reddened and she hit the door again, this time with the side of her fist. A scuttling inside caused a collective oooh around the table and everyone leaned forward in anticipation. The door opened and a pink, pencil-like creature emerged, hopping in the direction of Jane.

"Meet Casey Condom!" Jane waved and the creature bowed clumsily in return, almost toppling over itself. "It's not actually a condom," Jane explained. "It's more like a penis in Saran wrap. But we're hoping people get the idea."

Casey had to be at least seven-feet tall and the color and texture of silly putty. With its scarlet lips and doe-like eyes it had a distinctly feminine appearance. Casey posed on two small ankles garbed in white New Balance tennis shoes.

"What do you think, Spring? This is your baby, after all."

"I think she's finally lost her f-ing mind," Rebecca whispered out of the corner of her mouth. Rebecca was probably right. Ever since Jane's husband had run off with that *two-dollar-Tallahassee-tart* Jane had been doing all sort of strange things. She had stopped shaving her legs, insisted all women in management cut their hair, and no longer allowed employees to discuss soap operas in the break room.

Spring pulled on the ends of her hair, letting the long strands slide through her fingers. "Actually," she said, shifting uncomfortably in her seat, "I was thinking more along the lines of Snuggle the Dryer Sheet Bear."

The lady in the purple suit scowled. With great effort she raised herself from the chair, revealing a body that was as wide as it was tall. Her top lip quivered defiantly and Spring noticed a trace of facial hair around her mouth. She tried to look away but between the giant penis, her crazy boss, and the woman's mustache, there was no safe place to rest her eyes.

"Casey Condom has presence!" Meg said, nodding to the majestic being beside her. "I designed her myself." She reached out to touch the creature but Casey hopped backwards, just out of reach. "This agency has been in the Dark Ages far too long. Casey will deliver your message: *Cover it up or Cut It Out!*" Meg beckoned for Casey to turn around. Sure enough the words were stitched across Casey's backside.

"I thought our message was *Abstinence Makes the Heart Grow Fonder?*" Spring looked around the room at the wide-eyed attendees, most stifling laughs under their hands. She checked the corners of the room for cameras. Surely this had to be a prank.

Jane pointed the stick in Spring's direction, looking down the shaft like she were taking aim with a rifle. "Look. If it were up to me every penis on the planet would be chucked into pile of wood and burned. But some women still find them appealing. We can't stop people from expressing their sexuality, but we can keep them from getting genital warts."

"I'm all for helping girls make informed decisions," Spring began, feeling her voice begin to shake. "I was a young parent myself. But don't you think this is a bit extreme?" Spring's heart was beating so loudly she thought everyone must be able to hear it. She pushed her hands between her knees, feeling every eye upon her. She wasn't the type to make waves, let alone openly challenge one of Jane's decisions. She would surely pay for it.

Jane lowered the stick and cracked a thin-lipped smile in return. "My dear, you haven't heard the best part. Your *dedication* to *Teens in Trouble* has earned you a little promotion. Meg, would you like to tell Spring how she factors into this endeavor?"

"Certainly," Meg tagged on. She leaned forward, resting her stubby hands on the table, and looked Spring directly in the eye. "We want *you* to act as community ambassador for Casey Condom! Take her out and help spread the word. Jane says you will be perfect."

"Me?" Spring asked as Rebecca whinnied beside her.

"Yes." Jane continued for Meg. "I know that you work directly with the girls right now, but I see greater things for you." Jane twirled the stick, passing it from one hand to the next effortlessly, like a majorette twirling a baton. "And the best part is, your schedule can be a little more...flexible."

"What about Sarah?" Sarah had been hired to work with Kimberly in the communications department. This seemed like the job she should have. Jane nodded at Casey, and the condom writhed and wiggled until a messy-haired girl with a large nose emerged from the costume.

Sarah.

"She will be there, too," said Jane. "You girls will make one hell of a team! Don't let me down."

Sarah shrugged her shoulders and stared at Spring in an expression frozen somewhere between horror and apathy. Jane placed the stick on the table and grabbed her stack of notebooks and pens, signaling to everyone that the meeting was over. There were a few stifled chuckles from coworkers as the herd moved out, but no one lingered behind.

Sarah shambled towards Spring, dragging the costume behind her. It looked like melted wax. Spring touched it and quickly pulled away. It felt like those sticky hands her sons won in the gum-ball machines, cold, damp and clammy. "They want us to go to schools, news stations, and community health fairs. They want us to march in parades," Sarah said, gazing out the window into the parking lot. She dropped the costume, and it fell to the floor with a dull thud. "They want us to shake hands with the Mayor."

"Wearing this?" Spring tugged at the ends of her long hair. "I don't understand why Jane's doing this."

Sarah shrugged noncommittally. "I think we're being punished. They haven't said so but it makes sense. Last week I was caught eating one of Jane's yogurts out of the fridge. It was going to go bad. The expiration date said so." She wiped her nose with the back of one of her white-gloved hands and sniffled. "It's not like Jane ever eats anything she puts in the refrigerator anyways."

"That's crazy." Spring said. "Punishing us by humiliating us?"

"Mostly you, I think." Sarah said, nodding towards the heap of material on the floor. "I can hide. You can't."

TWO

1987

"Wake up, Johnny boy." Steve was tugging on his brother's shoulder, jostling him from his dreams. They were good ones, too. Knights and castles and a fire-breathing dragon. John pulled himself upright, feeling the sting of a bladder that had not been emptied in twelve long hours.

"Where are we?" John asked, rubbing his eyes. He climbed from his bunk in the back seat through a small set of double windows and joined his brother in the front of the cab. He swiped his hand across the passenger seat window, erasing the mist that had collected during their hours on the road. Morning was beginning to crack, but even without the full assistance of the sun, John could appreciate the beauty of the view.

"Colorado. I told you you'd like it," Steve said, grinning.

John could make out shapes in the distance and rolled his window down to make sure. Yes. They were real. "Mountains."

Steve laughed and hit the steering wheel good-naturedly with the palm of his hand. "I take you hundreds of miles away from home on your first real adventure and that's all you can say?"

John looked at his brother, his jaw hanging down and he popped it shut before he started to drool. He knew Steve expected more from him, but it had been the only word he could produce. Suddenly John felt like one of the simple kids Pete made fun of. But there were no other words for the wondrous rocks that surrounded him––big, beautiful stones that shot up from the ground and into the clouds, kissing the heavens.

Blue-grey stairways to the Gods. This was the land of storybooks and dreams. Giants might live here. Or goblins. Or trolls.

"Not a cornfield in sight," Steve continued. "Now aren't you glad you came with me instead of spending another year at Camp Carson? You're getting too old for that shit."

John stuck his head out of the car, breathing in the fresh morning air. The feel of it upon his skin as they sped down the highway was like having his soul scrubbed clean. "I never want to leave," he said, wishing he had brought his sketchbook along. He would have to commit the view to memory, as Steve didn't stop long enough for even one Polaroid snapshot. They were on a tight schedule, Steve said, and had to get the truck back by morning. But it was long enough for John to see that there was a big world out there that he knew nothing about. A world beyond Samson, Indiana, cornfields, and Little League baseball. Beyond monster truck rallies and tractor pulls. A world full of magic and adventure.

When he returned home, John decided to build his very own mountain, and after four weeks of moving dirt around with his dad's old shovel, John had built a hill half as tall as himself and four times as wide.

"The only mountain in Samson," his mother bragged to the neighbors over coffee. It wasn't a real mountain, John knew, but it was all he had. And he took to sitting on it with his books and GI Joes until a big rain came that October and turned it all to mud.

"When I grow up," he said to the raven that had settled on an ear of corn in the field before him. "...I'm moving far away from here. I'm moving someplace where I can get out and explore and meet interesting people. I'm moving to a place where no rain can ever wash away my mountain."

"Caw!" the raven answered, gazing across the cornfields.

The raven could fly. It had seen things John had never seen. For a moment he wished they could change places. But the raven flew away and John was left with just his dreams.

2005

"What do you mean you're moving?" Pete was chucking rocks at an old tombstone, trying to dislodge ghosts. Fortunately for the sleeping dead, most of them missed.

"I wish you wouldn't do that," John said. "It's disrespectful."

"What are they gonna do? Haunt me?" Pete laughed but let the rocks tumble from his hand and onto the ground.

John shrugged. A haunting might do Pete some good, actually.

"This place is gonna suck if you go," Pete said, pulling down his zipper, looking for a place to piss. He might have relieved himself on one of the headstones had John not given him the disapproving eye.

John took in the view of the cemetery. He and Pete had been coming here for the last twenty years and it pained him a little to think that those days would soon end. "I have to go. This place...it's death to me. Death to my soul."

Pete laughed. "Death of your soul, man? What the hell have you been reading?" He rubbed his nose with his hand, not caring that he had just held his pecker with that very appendage. "You just need to get laid."

"That's not what I mean."

"Is this about Mara? I told you, it was an accident. You didn't want her anyway. My dick's still burning."

If Pete were any other man in the universe, John would have hit him. Mara had been a girl he'd really liked, but of course, like all the other women in Samson, she had a thing for Pete.

"It's not about Mara. It's about living my life. I'm twenty-six-years-old, living in my brother's old trailer, working a dead-end factory job. I've never been in love. I've never climbed a mountain. And the only adventure I've ever had was getting lost in the corn maze at the state fair."

Pete snorted. "Yeah, that was funny. You cried like a little girl 'til we found you." Pete let out a big laugh and slapped his leg. "You read too many books. But whatever you want, man. I ain't gonna try and stop you from following your *dreams.*"

John found this uncharacteristic display of Pete's humanity creepy, yet touching. The two had grown up together and Pete rarely supported anything that did not somehow support Pete.

"So where you gonna go then? Colorado?" Pete turned his attention on John, his tone more than curious.

John reached into his back pocket and pulled out a small section of the Samson Weekly. "No. There's a recruiter in Evansville looking for people with computer graphics skills to work for a new company in Arizona. I might apply."

"Arizona?" Pete's words were heavy with disbelief. "You know how fucking hot it is in Arizona? Your pansy ass can't take the Indiana summers, let alone an Arizona summer. Besides, thought you wanted to be a real artist, anyway?"

John shrugged. "It's a start and better than sweating away in a factory. And how is it you know so much about Arizona?"

"My cousin lives there. Remember Amy? The girl who finally took your virginity?"

John blushed. Amy had been his first real girlfriend, but before the end of their Junior year her family had moved away. They say you never forgot your first love. Amy had been his only love, if you could call it that. On some especially lonely nights John still thought about her and wondered what she was up to.

"I visited her a few years ago during the Fourth of July. You don't even need matches to start fireworks out there. They ignite all by themselves." Pete laughed again and almost chucked another rock. He caught himself and aimed it at a scampering squirrel in the field instead. Fortunately for the squirrel, Pete had a hard time hitting a stationary target, let alone a moving one.

"Well, it's gotta be better than this. You hear all anyone's talking

18

about lately? Harnessing the power of corn and cow farts to save the world. I want no part of it." John looked past the tombstones, past the gate that opened to the park, past the houses and farms that sat just up the road. In his mind's eye he knew every detail of this town…every house, every field, every signpost. His mother said that someday he would appreciate the security of the familiarity, but he hadn't gotten there yet.

Pete roused him from his thoughts. "Wanna hang out at the VW tonight? Jessica's back from school and I bet she's looking to get lucky. Can't believe she went to an all-girl's college. Anyway, you can have her this time. I think she's bringing a friend." Pete jingled the coins in his pocket and cocked a mischievous eyebrow towards John.

John cringed and shook his head. Pete had been with every girl in Samson. Twice. His claim to fame was that he had, at one time or another, acquired every venereal disease the free clinic could treat, and a few they couldn't. The last thing he wanted was to touch anyone or anything that Pete had laid his penis on. That was another good reason to move away. "No thanks. You can give me the details tomorrow."

"Suit yourself," said Pete, popping open the last of the six pack they had brought with them. "More for me. But remember, man. You can't find adventure. You have to make it."

John nodded, gathered up the empty cans, and made his way home, wondering if his TV would be able to pick up *The Wheel of Fortune* or if it would be scrambled again.

THREE

1997

"Come on, come on." Spring tapped the little white stick against her knees, willing it to change color.

"I don't think that's gonna help," Jason said. He was standing with his back pressed against the door of their stall, looking down at her. She should have stood too. It seemed like a standing occasion. But after she had peed on the stick her knees refused to make the trip upward. They had just ceased to work. "If you keep messing with that stick you might skew the results."

Spring shot him a look. "Since when do you use words like skew?"

Jason released his brown hair from the rubber band at the nape of his neck, only to gather it back up into a small pony tail and secure it again. He had done this at least a dozen times while they had waited for the results. "It's one syllable. Don't be shocked."

Spring looked at the stick again. The little pink cross in the window had darkened, almost to a crimson red. She was not only pregnant. She was really, really pregnant. She thrust the stick at Jason and fell forward, cradling her knees. "Oh God!" Jason went to pat her head but she pulled away. "Please just stop."

He said nothing as he squatted down beside her. She could feel him listening to her, waiting for the sobs to subside. He had no problem fighting her, but he was at a loss when she cried. She took a deep breath to calm herself, a trick Lanie had taught her when she younger. She had suffered anxiety from crowds then, a job hazard for any carnie. "Breathe in, breath out," Lanie had instructed her. "Find your center.

C'mon girl. Stop breathing like you just run a fucking marathon. Slowly. In. out. Release."

Once she had calmed he reached for her hair, letting the baby fine strands of yellow-white ribbon slide through his fingers. She didn't let many people touch her hair, but she let him. "I suppose," she said, looking up at him with red, tear-stained eyes. "...That purchasing a condom from a rusted machine in the lobby of Ed's Guns and Exotic Animal Shoppe was probably not our wisest move." She sobbed and laughed at the same time and felt a long line of snot fall from her nose. Jason grabbed a wad of toilet paper and caught it.

"You don't have to do this alone. I'm here."

Spring felt the wail in her throat and fought it. She was angry right now, and she was afraid she would say something she regretted. "I just got accepted into Arizona State," she said, drying her eyes on the back of her hand. "After three years of struggling to get through Community College so that I could leave this...life behind, things were starting to change for me. Now what?"

"You can still go. This isn't the 50's. Girls go to school pregnant all the time. Even on TV."

"I don't want to go pregnant!" She started crying again and she tucked her face into her skirt, smearing mascara across the hem. He didn't get it. "I wanted to go...hot."

Jason laughed. "Hot's what got you into this mess, my dear. You're too hot for your own good."

Spring snorted and took the tissue Jason offered her. He knew her too well. They had been friends for years, but a few drinks and a slow night slinging cotton candy last fall had changed it all. Now they were bound together, one way or another. As Lanie would say, their fate strings had gotten all jumbled up.

"I got a crazy idea," he said, pulling her up by the arms. He was a good six inches taller than her and smelled like French fries and Old Spice. "Why don't we get married? We've been practically living together in my van for the last 6 months. Why not make it official?"

He pulled her close and wrapped his arms around her. "Just think... you, me, the little Bambino, touring the countryside together. If he's musically inclined, we could start a family band. Be like the Partridges. Only not so gay."

I could, she thought, nuzzling into him. He was safe and warm and familiar. She remembered the day her mother had picked him up on the side of the road nine years earlier.

"Hitchhiking to Santa Cruz," he had said, off to pursue his music career. He never made it to Santa Cruz. Once he learned how much money could be made hustling kids out of their allowances to see The Half-Monkey Lady, he had settled in. That was the way it was here. The Carnival was one big roach motel. You check in, you eat a bunch of crap, and you stay until you die. Very few people escaped. They had intentions of leaving, but one by one The Carnival took them all. Heart disease. Obesity. Drugs. Equipment failure. Most of them dead by fifty. There was no fading gracefully into old age here. You just stopped.

If it didn't take them entirely, it took some of their best parts. Just two months ago, a young man had given up a limb to a roller coaster. He had climbed the steel mountain to fix a dangling bolt when the car ran over his arm. They say he may have saved some people with his bravery. But the papers never heard of it. Bad for business. Now he's quietly employed as the ticket taker at the back of the lot.

"What do you say?" Jason pulled her in tighter. "I bet I'm damned good at changing diapers."

She took a deep breath. Though she cared about Jason, he had nothing more to offer her than his body, his guitar, and the eternal belief that someday he would roadie for Phish. "It wouldn't work," she whispered. "We're too different. And besides..."

Jason released her from his arms and narrowed his eyes, ready to battle. "And besides what? Oh, never mind, I know. I'm not good enough for you." He pushed through the stall door and into the empty bathroom. "Afraid you will end up like your mother?"

Spring lowered her eyes. Yes, she was afraid of that, and why not?

It was a legitimate fear. But there was more to it. She followed him into the bathroom. "We just aren't right for each other Jason."

"Oh, I see." Jason fell forward over the standalone sink, slamming his hands into the mirror. "We were right for each other a few weeks ago weren't we? And even a few nights ago. But not for the long haul. No, Spring reserves that spot for someone more worthy. Am I right?"

"Stop it. That's not fair."

"Isn't it? Don't think I don't know about that little fairy tale you believe in. You get one love in this lifetime and that's it right? Don't waste it on the Ferris wheel guy."

Spring felt her knees give and her stomach roil. She moved back into the stall and fought the nausea. It seemed too early for morning sickness. "Jason, please. There are many reasons we aren't right for each other. You're my best friend but..."

"No, I get it. What could I possibly offer you?" He turned the water on and shut it off again. "I hope for your sake that fairy tales come true. Or you're in for a long, lonely life." Spring heard him pull a paper towel from the chute, wipe his hands, and toss it into the waste bin. "When you decide what you want to do let me know. I will be there for the baby if you decide to keep it. And I hope you do keep it."

Spring listened as Jason stomped across the bathroom and out the door.

2005

Please pick up the boys from school. Sorry. Flat tire. Oh yeah, they have a counseling appointment today. If you take them I'll owe you one.

Jason's voicemail irritated Spring. Jason knew that Sam was coming home today, which was probably why he had conveniently gotten a flat.

She couldn't call Jason back to tell him he should make other plans, either. Jason didn't own a phone.

"Oh yeah, I'm living the dream," she said, clenching her teeth and glancing at the bumper sticker on the car in front of her that read *Casey Condom for President: To Protect and Serve.* The condom was waving and smiling. Spring pulled into the empty parking lot of Cooper Elementary School and cursed Jason for the hundredth time since she had gotten his phone call.

"Mrs. Felding won't be happy," she thought as she raced down the corridor to the twins' classroom. When she reached her destination, Mrs. Felding was holding the boys tightly in the crook of her arms while both children struggled to break free.

"It's about time you got here," Mrs. Felding said, releasing the boys, who immediately began racing each other around the desks. "You're almost as unreliable as the father."

Spring cringed. She was a taxpayer. Sort of. Mrs. Felding could be nicer to her. "I'm so sorry, I had to work late. Long story I'm sure you don't care to know about." Spring scooped the boys up in her arms as they made a pass and headed towards the door. "We're going now. Sorry."

"Ms. Ryan, Jason says you are taking them to the counselor for their attention deficit problem today."

Spring stopped. Mrs. Felding had been harping on her for months now, about the boys' problems in school. High energy. Inability to sit still. Wanting to do things their own way. Though Spring had never attended formal classes herself growing up, it didn't seem like that big of a deal. "I'm no expert but I still don't think we need to involve a counselor in this. Can't we just work this out between ourselves?"

Mrs. Felding crossed her arms and gave Spring a hard stare. "I've been an educator for twenty-seven years, Ms. Ryan, and I have to say these two have the worst case of hyperactivity I have ever seen. And I've seen a lot! I'm going to tell you just what I told their father. If you don't get them some sort of help I will be forced to contact child protective services again and let them know of your parental negligence. Is that clear?"

Spring's throat tightened and she nodded. Mrs. Felding fetched a large spiral notebook from her desk. "I've written up my observations to help expedite the process," she said, shoving the notebook at Spring.

"The whole thing?" Spring shuffled through pages of frantically scrawled notes complete with stick figure drawings.

"If you thumb through it fast enough it becomes a flip book." Mrs. Fielding explained. "That's in case the counselor doesn't have enough time to read it in its entirety."

"Thanks," Spring smiled half-heartedly and slunk out the door.

Spring watched the twins through the rearview mirror. They were identical in every way except for the perpetual cowlick on Blaine's head and the two missing front teeth in Shane's mouth, courtesy of a basketball hucked by his brother. They were thin for their age, almost frail-looking. But looks were deceiving. They were scrappy little guys who had no trouble standing up to anyone if they felt their pride, or their toys, were threatened. It had taken the both of them, but they had even wrestled down Jake Turner, the fifth grade bully, when he tried to load up his pockets with their hot wheels. They had either gotten that from their father or their grandmother.

Spring cringed as Blaine picked at the holes in the knees of his jeans. Jason never paid attention to what he dressed them in. No wonder Mrs. Felding thought they were negligent.

Spring clawed at the side of her face, trying to stave back the itch that was creeping across her head. This was a new development in her body's repertoire of stress management. At least the eye twitch had gone. Mrs. Felding had threatened to call child protective services on her and Jason again. She had done so at the beginning of the year when she thought the boys looked abnormally skinny and were being starved at home. She had done so again around Christmas-time when Blaine had admitted to the class that his daddy's home was sometimes a tent. And again after spring break when Shane had come to school with a black eye, courtesy of a mock sword fight with his brother, but 'highly suspicious' according to their teacher.

Though child protective services did not find any evidence of abuse, it was always on Spring's mind that someday they could snatch her children away. She had seen this happen with some of the parents in the carnival circuit––kids taken away in unmarked station wagons for being dirty or missing school as their frantic parents chased behind, promising to get them back. The memories of childhood friends being snatched up by badge-wearing adults still made her get up at night and check to see if her own boys were still in their beds.

"Shane's making faces at me," Blaine tattled from the backseat. The hair on the back of his head stood up extra high today, as if wanting to call attention to itself.

"Am not, you stupid-head," Shane defended, sticking his Kool-Aid coated tongue out at his brother. Their father was always touting the healing effects of Kool-Aid and often sent the boys to school with a packet for snack-time. He argued that this would give them each a full day's supply of vitamin C, according to the package.

Spring stared in quiet fascination as a French-fry was launched across the backseat, hitting its mark. "Ouch!" Blaine said. "You hit me with the pokey end!"

She parked the car and sat for a moment, collecting her thoughts. "This is how people go insane," she mumbled as something larger and fuzzier flew within her peripheral. When she had counted to ten she turned to give them a stern look. "Boys, *please* be good for Mommy when we see the counselor. Pretty please?"

The twins paused, a ketchup packet poised for assault. "Counselor?"

That caught their attention. They had seen many school therapists during their two years in Elementary School and knew the drill. "I love counseling," said Blaine, the schemer of the two. "They give you candy

26

and toys and you get out of class."

"We aren't in class, dummy," Shane, who loved to be right, corrected his brother, leaning over to stab Blaine with the foot of a G.I. Joe.

"Mommy. Shane's being disruptive!"

"Boys please?" Spring pled, her voice heavy with desperation. She hated bargaining with the twins, but wasn't sure what else she could do. The only punishment that seemed to work on them was Time Out, but they were already buckled in. "If you are good we can go to McDonald's after, okay? But if you are bad then there is no McDonald's. None."

Blaine unfastened his safety belt and leaned over to whisper something in his brother's ear. Shane nodded. "Okay," Blaine said, extending a hand for his mother to shake. "Deal."

The counselor was a prune of a woman who introduced herself as Ms. Droll. Her hair was graying and secured in a neat bun near the nape of her long neck and her skin was the color of skim milk diluted by water. She had the look of something that had been left in the freezer too long. In stark contrast to her own appearance, her office was warm and colorful. The walls were painted a soothing lavender and the windows were large and smudge-free. Smiling pictures of children hung on the wall and classical music played tastefully in the background. Spring sat on the beige couch across from Ms. Droll and nervously tapped her hands in her lap.

"There are some plastic dinosaurs on the floor that you are welcome to play with," Ms. Droll informed the boys, motioning to a small plastic bucket in the corner of the room.

"Yay!" The twins cheered, racing towards the dinosaurs. Spring resisted the urge to remind them that they were toys, not weapons. There was no need to cause Ms. Droll to think of them as violent before she saw the proof.

"Now, what brings you here?" The counselor asked, turning her attention to Spring.

"A car," Spring laughed uncomfortably. When Ms. Droll did not respond she shifted her weight and considered her words carefully.

She and Jason were not the most conventional parents and Spring had learned that some people had trouble with that. "Their teacher wants us to do something about their attention deficit problems."

"I see," Ms. Droll snorted, her long nose twitching. "And what sort of symptoms do they have which would lead you believe they have ADHD?" She glanced at the twins who were calmly debating which dinosaur was the nicest, Triceratops or Brachiosaurus.

"They never sit still. They lose everything. They are impulsive. And they can't focus on anything for very long." Spring felt her face redden. Blaine was giving his brother a hug and Spring regretted telling them to behave earlier. Ms. Droll probably thought she was either neurotic or a liar. Perhaps both.

"And have they been diagnosed?" A smug smile played across her thin lips. "Or is this mother's intuition?"

Spring suddenly realized why some people stab other people with G.I. Joes. It was frustrating to feel that her worth as a parent could be determined in ten minutes. "Their teacher first commented on it, then it was diagnosed three weeks ago by their pediatrician."

"A medical doctor," Ms. Droll snorted. "It figures. They are getting into the mental health field lately. It's a very lucrative field." Spring nodded and Miss Droll continued. "Have you tried anything at home to help them?"

Spring had attempted everything from every parenting book ever written. "I've tried behavior modification and positive reinforcement. Sticker charts. Time outs." *And bribing.* "It just doesn't seem to be enough."

"Ms. Ryan, I've been working with children a very long time and I have to admit, they don't seem hyperactive to me. Not that I don't trust your pediatrician." Ms. Droll wrinkled her nose. "...But I'd like to do a little digging myself before making an *official* diagnosis. If you could step out of the room for a moment, I will have a brief chat with the boys myself. Sometimes children open up more without Mommy around."

Ms. Droll opened the door and ushered Spring out into an overly-air conditioned hallway where Barry Manilow's *Mandy* played on a continual loop. Spring pressed her ear to the door to try and hear something over the music. It was no use. After a few minutes Ms. Droll emerged and the look on her face told Spring that it had not been an entirely uplifting conversation.

"Were they bad?" Spring asked anxiously, peering inside. The dinosaurs had been cleaned up and the boys were grinning mischievously in her direction.

"Children are not bad or good, Ms. Ryan. They are either behaving or misbehaving. As for your boys, they were very well-behaved." Ms. Droll gave them a fond smile and turned her attention back to Spring. "You may return to your children. I will be right back," said Ms. Droll as she vanished down the corridor.

Maybe I should switch schools and doctors, Spring thought, glancing at the exit sign. She wondered if she would appear on *America's Most Wanted* for being a fugitive from therapy. "Okay, boys. New plan," Spring said. "Mama needs you to act normal now. Okay? I know I said no McDonald's if you were bad, but you can be bad. You won't get in trouble. I promise."

"Wait, you told us to be good," said Shane, scratching his head.

"It's a trap!" Blaine accused her. "Don't listen, Shane."

Spring spread her hands, exasperated. "I know what I told you, but now I think Ms. Droll doesn't believe Mommy about your behavior problems. What did you tell her when I was in the hall?"

Blaine spoke up. "That you get angry for no good reason and that Daddy lives in the park."

Spring shook her head and stifled a yelp as Ms. Droll returned. "Blaine and Shane," she said enthusiastically, clapping her small hands together. There was so little skin covering bone that they barely made a sound as flesh hit flesh. "We are going to play a game. All you have to do is draw a picture of whatever you like and I will give you a piece of gum when you are done."

"Not the *Draw Me a Picture* game!" Spring hadn't meant to say these words aloud but they fell from her lips before she could stop them. The twins were masters of *Draw Me a Picture,* having been administered the test by the many counselors that had transitioned in and out of Cooper Elementary since Blaine and Shane had begun school two years ago. They enjoyed toying with their therapists and with each subsequent attempt became more original in their artistic renderings. "Is there any other test we can do? They have done this one before. This one doesn't really test for ADHD does it?"

The lines around Ms. Droll's thin lips deepened, little creeks shooting from a main river. "ADHD is often confused with another disorder, Miss Ryan. These pictures can say what their little mouths cannot." The boys took the crayons and paper and got to work. Spring tried to see what they were drawing but Ms. Droll positioned herself between them, her small frame providing adequate privacy for the boys to create.

Please, God, please. Let them be drawing rainbows and flowers. Puppy dogs and a happy family playing board games. If I haven't called in a favor lately, I need this now.

The twins were deliberate in their work and every color in the box was used at least once. They occasionally glanced at one another's drawings and nodded, confirming to the other that they were on the right track.

"Done," they said simultaneously, and held up their representations for the women to see.

Ms. Droll, seeing the pictures first, staggered back, leaving a space large enough for Spring to peek. The sight turned her cold. Both pieces of paper were covered in dozens, if not hundreds, of sad faces––big, small, thin, fat, red, orange and blue circles with dots for eyes and a turned down line for a mouth. Ms. Droll raced to retrieve her notebook and frantically scrawled away. "I've...never. In all my years.."

She could not finish the sentence.

"You don't think this really represents them, do you? They are never sad. Quick-tempered, but not sad." Spring said. "They are playing you!" Spring gave the boys an angry glare and turned her attention back to Ms.

Droll. "I told you this wasn't a good game."

The counselor regarded Spring. "Miss Ryan. I'm not going to lie. I'm disturbed. I've worked with families for a long, long time and this is a first for me...beyond my scope of help. I'm going to have to find you some additional resources." Ms. Droll snatched up the pictures and began digging through a drawer in a file cabinet. The boys sat cross-legged on the carpet; blue-eyed and innocent.

"Well," said Ms. Droll, rifling through a fistful of pamphlets. "I looked over their school files and there seems to be nothing about depression... but...I'm not convinced. I am also not convinced that there isn't any emotional neglect going on. Normal children do not draw pictures like *this*. I'm recommending that you and the father attend parenting classes and family counseling." She turned and gave them a sympathetic look. "Additionally, based on the recommendations of their teacher..." She tapped the notebook Mrs. Felding had sent over. "...I've decided to put the boys on Ritadate for their ADHD. I'm still not convinced they are hyperactive but let's give it a try. Please take all of this to heart." Ms. Droll handed Spring a prescription and a brochure for a workshop called *Hugs Not Hits*.

"I can't believe you boys did that to me," Spring hissed at them from the front seat. She turned in time to see them pulling plastic dinosaurs from their pockets. "You stole the dinosaurs, too? No McDonald's for either of you. Ever."

"What?" Shane argued. "She liked us. She gave us gum."

"She thinks I'm a child beater," said Spring, running her hands through her hair. "Do you want them to take you away from me?"

Blaine blew a strand of blond hair from his eyes. Spring could see the wheels turning in his head. "I had a friend who went to live with foster parents and they gave him his own room and a bike and took him to Disneyland. Maybe we could get parents like that."

Shane grinned. "Yeah we could get parents who take us to McDonald's *every* night."

Spring tightened her grip on the steering wheel, honking at the car in front of her who sat idling at a green light. "I sacrificed everything for the two of you ungrateful delinquents. I can't believe you would sell me out for McDonald's."

"And Disneyland," corrected Shane.

Spring sat at the dining room table picking at her food. She was not a fan of lamb, but Sam insisted she try it after he spent the last few hours preparing it. She watched him take a bite. He let it roll around in his mouth, chewing several times before swallowing. Each taste was followed by a look so blissful his face could hardly contain it––his lips long and upturned, his eyes rolling back into his head. A look most people reserved for sex. There were very few meats he could eat since he converted to Islam and he relished every one.

"Good?" he asked and she nodded.

"I knew you'd love it," he said, dabbing the linen napkin to his chin. It was pastel green and Spring wondered when they had acquired them. Sam must have snuck in a trip to the mall while he was away on business. She would have to search his closet when he napped to ensure that napkins were all that were purchased. He had a tendency to acquire new, expensive items and never use them. If she were quick she could probably send them back to the store before the labels were off...and the bills were due. She clicked her fingernails on the table and waited until he took his plate to the sink and then she dumped her scraps into her napkin and headed for the trash can.

"Sweetie," he said, glancing at her empty plate. "You don't have to gobble. There's plen-ty." He dried his hands with a paper towel and went to scoop another serving for her, but she caught him.

"I'm stuffed. So, so good." She quickly shook the napkin into the garbage and turned to him, patting her stomach for effect.

"Not too stuffed for dessert, I hope?" Sam's eyes sparkled as he hunched over, holding up one finger to show that he was not done with the surprises. Spring thought he looked a little like the Grinch after he had returned the gifts to Who-Ville. She slumped back into her chair as Sam scurried to the refrigerator and produced a monstrous bowl of brown mud.

"Mocha mousse!" He ladled a blob out for himself and an extra-large helping for Spring. It wriggled off of the serving spoon as if it were alive and knew its impending fate.

Spring wrinkled her nose distastefully. She hated the taste of coffee, its bitterness and smell, but Sam was watching her so she bobbed her spoon into the muck and put it to her lips.

"Mmmm," she nodded again, feeling guilty. Sam tried so hard to instill a sense of 'culture' in her, but her tastes were simpler than his. She couldn't help it. Years of concession stand food tends to do that to you.

"It's wonderful, isn't it Pookie? I learned the recipe while I was away. Mustn't eat too much, though, or you'll get fat."

Spring bristled and thought about correcting him. They had been together two years now and in that time she had never once drank a cup of coffee or gained a single pound. She raised an eyebrow but let it fall before he noticed.

"The boys do okay during drop-off?" Sam feigned interest as he licked the last of his pudding from his lips. What he was really asking was what had transpired between herself and Jason.

"Yep, it went fine. I was so angry with Jason after my date with the counselor today I didn't stick around to talk to him. I dropped them off and ran."

"So," he said, pushing his empty dessert bowl towards the center of the table. "Tell me about your promotion."

Spring snorted. She had given him the rundown on the phone earlier and he had seemed unusually excited. "It's hardly a promotion. Actually, one might call it a demotion."

"But you got a raise, right?" Sam leaned across the table, his eyes twinkling.

"Yes, a whopping fifty cents an hour."

"Not bad," he said. She watched him do the calculations in his head. His face turned a different shade of white when he was working on numbers. "That's twenty bucks more a week, almost a thousand bucks more a year." He tapped the tips of his fingers together and smiled.

"A thousand bucks is not worth my soul," she said, yanking up the bowls and walking towards the sink. She rinsed them out and hoped that it would not clog the drain. She had the memory of a movie Lanie had taken her and Chloe to see as children. Something about a glob of goop that devours everything in its path. She shook the thought from her head.

"But sweetie, it's not like you have to *be* the condom."

"No, but I have to walk into public places holding hands with a penis. A *penis*," she repeated for emphasis. "How would you like to walk down the street holding hands with a vagina?"

"Now that's just silly." Sam shivered. "Vaginas are disgusting. Besides," he continued. "You are doing a good deed for the youth. That's something to be proud of." Sam was holding his head in one hand, propped up on the table, tapping his fingers on his knee with the other. The air conditioner caught what few hairs he had left on his head and they danced in a way that Spring found mesmerizing. Like fairies around a druid ring. She resisted the urge to pluck one. He guarded those last few hairs with his life.

"Meg, the PR lady, even wrote me a song to sing. A rap song." Spring rummaged through her purse on the table, dropping a plastic knife and a yellow crayon which Sam deftly caught before they hit the floor. At last she produced a white piece of paper folded into quarters. "Listen to this...

"*...His name is Casey Condom and he's here to spread
The word about protection, just use your head*

34

Though it feels real good not wearing a coat
Your breasts will leak and your stomach will bloat
So if you're gonna do it, don't be a lout
Cover it up, or cut it out...

"The last line says to lean backwards and cross my arms," Spring added at the end.

"That's actually not too bad. Short and simple. Gets the message across."

"What? Didn't you hear me? They want me to rap!"

Sam took the paper from her, folded it up, and handed it back to her. "You'll do fine, Spring. You always do."

The grandfather clock Sam had purchased at an antique shop struck six. No matter how many times a day that thing went off, Spring still jumped. Before the six dongs had been fully struck, Lanie emerged from the hall, blinking against the light like a groundhog in February.

"What is your mother doing here?" Sam's nails dug into the back of Spring's shoulders.

"I'm sorry. I forgot to tell you earlier...Chloe asked me if I could keep her awhile," Spring said. "You won't even notice her, I promise."

Lanie wandered around the kitchen, arms raised in homage to some god or another. Her black muumuu with its bright purple flowers and her neon red hair gave her a clown-like appearance. "How can anyone not notice her?" Sam said, turning to face the woman. By the way Lanie's fleshy body undulated beneath her dress, Spring could tell that Chloe had been feeding her well.

"Don't mind me," said Lanie, picking up the serving bowl filled with Sam's special mousse. She ran her finger along the inside rim and put it to her mouth. "Yuck. Who the hell eats coffee pudding? I'm a coffee drinker and I don't even eat this shit." Lanie set the bowl down and retreated towards the living room. Six o'clock meant that it was time for her medication and *The Wheel of Fortune*.

"How long?" Sam asked as Lanie flopped into his recliner.

35

"Not that long. Just until she's done with menopause."

"Menopause?" Sam's voice trembled. "Doesn't that take years? Why can't she get her own place?"

"Apparently the carnival didn't provide a very good retirement package. But she did offer to give you free Tarot Card readings for life."

Sam's eyes narrowed as Lanie flipped through the channels. "Can she predict if I will be found guilty in an upcoming murder trial?"

"Sam!"

They watched as Lanie sat in the living room, one hand on the remote control, the other fanning herself. "Oh, Lordy," she grunted. "Why the hell did you pick Arizona to settle in? Arizona is too fuckin' hot. I'm old. I might die."

"Only if we're lucky," Sam said.

FOUR

1984

Lanie stepped outside of the motel room, a steaming mug of coffee cupped between her hands. She took a sip, letting the drink sit in her mouth for a moment before swallowing. It was decaf but it was still pretty damned good.

Lanie inhaled deeply, breathing in the crisp, fall air. Autumn was the very best time of year to be a fortune teller. Even atheists and agnostics came around to have their cards read or their palms glanced over, come Halloween. Good thing, too. Her wig was fraying and she'd need a new one. Maybe something long and sleek this time. Something Cher.

"Morning, gorgeous," said Ernie, closing the door behind him. He was wearing jeans with holes in the knees and his knockoff Members Only jacket purchased at the Asian district in St. Paul. "Let's get some pancakes before the girls wake up. I got something to show you."

Lanie followed leisurely behind her husband as he hustled to the Motel diner: The Blue Moose Café.

"Where we going to anyway?" she said as Ernie opened the door for her. The restaurant inside looked very much like any other restaurant Lanie had seen during her years on the road. Red booths and speckled tables, waitresses in outdated hairstyles, and a jukebox near the entrance that serenaded its guests with Johnny Cash. A few of the roadies whose names Lanie couldn't remember nodded at them as they made their way towards the rear of the place.

"Flagstaff, Arizona, baby." Ernie said as he scooted into the booth.

"Home of the Chipotle tribe. The greatest Indian warriors in all the country. More scalping per square foot there than anywhere else in America."

Lanie narrowed her eyes and leaned across the booth. "Let's make a deal, Ernie. You save the shit for the customers and so will I."

Ernie grinned and snapped his fingers at a nearby waitress.

"So what do you want to show me?" Lanie asked after ordering her hotcakes with extra syrup and bacon. Ernie raised his eyebrows but kept his mouth shut and Lanie was tempted to kick him under the booth. He never gave up his dramatics, even when they were alone. Finally, he reached into his coat pocket and produced a bloated, white tube sock that clattered and clanged when he threw it on the table.

"Ta da! Once again the World's Most Virile Man has come through for the woman he loves. Check this out." Ernest picked up the end of the tube sock and dumped the contents. Ten cent pieces scattered across the booth, some rolling into Lanie's lap.

"You're pilfering from the dime toss, Ernest?" Lanie couldn't believe it. Ernie could be called a lot of things, but she had never thought of him as a crook. A crock but not a crook.

"What? It's not like I'm stealing from the church bowl. These people don't care what happens to their dimes once they toss them into the plates. The only thing they care about is whether or not they win the giant teddy bear. Why do you have to be so negative?" Ernie scooped up the dimes with his right hand and pushed them into his lap. The waitress returned with their breakfasts and gave Lanie a look that said she knew she was going to be paid in change and it wasn't making her happy. Lanie returned the look with a helpless shrug.

"But what about Don? He okay with this?" Don was the owner of the show and had already threatened to give Ernie a booth at the far end of the midway––the worst possible place to have a booth––if he didn't cut out his crap. This was Ernest's fourth booth in the last six months.

"Pfft. I keep the books. It all balances out." Ernie took a bite and considered. "They expect us to take a cut. We're carnies, Lanie. That's what we do."

Lanie straightened up and looked at her husband. She was a gypsy. A witch. A prophetess. She was not a carnie. She finished her breakfast in silence and threw a five dollar bill on the table. "That will pay for mine," she said, rising with the dignity of a queen.

She left her husband staring, and a few of the roadies gossiping.

Lanie walked across the parking lot, weaving in and out of the parked trucks bearing the slogan "The Bob Cat Carnival Show." She waved hello to Maria, the Mexican woman in charge of one of the cotton candy stands who was pregnant with her seventh kid and couldn't find the daddies of the first six. Lanie took out her key and opened the door to room 133, the nicest room in the Blue Moose Motel.

Spring and Chloe were propped up on their elbows, watching The Smurfs on their shared double bed. Lanie huffed, wishing they would take advantage of the free HBO. She worked hard to give them nice things and they never appreciated it. "Time to go," Lanie said, turning off the television. "Take a spitz bath and put on your clothes. We can drive through the McDonald's and pick up Egg McMuffins on the way out of town."

Chloe jumped up and ran to her brown grocery store bag, digging for her favorite jeans. Spring quietly sat there, glaring accusingly at her mother. "But we just got here last night," she said. "I'm not going. I'm tired."

Lanie resisted the urge to roar. She wasn't going to get into this with the girl again. Instead, she grabbed Spring by the elbow and pulled her up onto the floor. "You'd think you'd be excited to see all these new places. Most little girls don't get to sleep in a different room every night. You two are the luckiest little girls in the entire Universe. Right, Chloe?" Chloe nodded and lay on the bed, wriggling into her jeans. She had been making the rounds through the concession stands lately and Lanie hoped she would not need new pants any time soon. "Now hurry up. We have to hit Flagstaff before the snow."

"I hate the snow," Spring mumbled. "When I grow up I'm living in a house where I sleep in the same bed every night and there is never, ever any snow."

"Be boring then," Lanie said. "And see if I care."

<hr/>

2005

Sam was frazzled. "What do you mean you lost your keys again? Didn't you put them in the key cup I made for you?"

Lanie watched the scene from the dining room table as she sipped her coffee. Spring scrambled around the living room, pulling cushions from the couch and flinging them in random directions behind her. Sam followed, dusting off each cushion and placing it back into the sofa.

"No, Sam. I didn't put them in the key cup. I don't even know where the key cup is!"

"You lost the key cup?" Sam ducked to avoid one errant sofa pillow but was hit by another. Spring shot him a look and walked towards the center of the living room. She spun three times, her hair flailing out around her, a pale yellow fan of silk. Lanie missed being that young, when her hair had shone with moonbeams. Too many years of wigs and Ms. Clairol had zapped all of the luster from her own locks. But then Sam said something and the wistfulness was gone. The best thing about being old was that she no longer had to put up with men's crap. Lanie raised her cup to the Universe and slammed it back onto the table with the word KEYS defiantly pointed in Sam's direction.

Sam twitched and Lanie hoped she was about to witness his nervous breakdown. But Spring, in a moment of inspiration, patted the front of her pants and laughed. "I found them! I forgot I stuck them in my jeans!"

Sam wiped his brow in relief and Lanie grumbled, her entertainment over for the night.

"Mom, we're going to a movie," Spring said, kissing Lanie on the cheek. Sam looked as though he might follow suit but Lanie gave him the evil eye and he pretended to tie his shoes instead.

"Okay, you kids have fun."

As they made their way out the door they argued over which movie to see——Spring wanting an adventure flick while Sam hoped for a romantic comedy. When they disappeared from the driveway, Lanie sighed in relief. She took a final swig of coffee and looked at the ugly mug before tossing it into the garbage can. Sam must have taken a ceramics class taught by monkeys. "Alone at last." Lanie wriggled out of her dress and let it fall onto the floor.

Oh sweet freedom! If only Spring and Sam weren't such fuddy-duddies, with their books and their Nationalistic Public Radio, she could walk around naked anytime she wanted. She was going to hate living here, she could tell. This place lacked the freedom that Chloe's house offered. Chloe didn't care if Lanie covered herself in peanut butter and belly danced topless as long as it didn't interrupt her stories.

Lanie pulled off her bra and kicked off her underwear, aiming them in the direction of Sam's bookcase. Her bra draped itself over a copy of Animal Farm and her panties ended up someplace in the Civil War section. Liberated at last, she strutted around the house inspecting her surroundings. Though she had been to Spring's home many times, this would be the first time she was staying.

The house was clean. Too clean. That was all Sam. She hadn't raised Spring that way. Germs were a good thing. They helped the body build immunity against things like the Asian Bird Flu and the plague. It was not only the cleanliness that bothered her. It was the knickknacks. Everywhere. Crammed into every available cubby hole and shelf. Sam was a collector. Of crap. He was also a labeler apparently. Every section of the shelving was neatly titled. She read one: *Bobbleheads of the Great Nihilist Writers*. She leaned in to inspect them. Oh, Bejeezus! The Nietzsche bobble gave Lanie the creeps.

Lanie trotted down the hall to her new bedroom and recovered her fanny pack. She sucked in, fastening it around her waist, annoyed that the little plastic end parts hardly met anymore. From it she produced a pack of cigarettes and a lighter. She almost lit one up but remembered Sam's stupid rule about smoking inside. She curled her lip as she recalled his last scolding, him standing there wagging his finger at her like she was a bad dog that made a no-no on the carpet. She took her smokes and her lighter out to the back patio. It smelled like Sam––cabbage and desperation. Lanie removed the patchouli air spray from her pack, pumped three times, and sniffed the air. Better.

She didn't like Sam. Didn't like his walk. Didn't like his talk. Hated his smell. Come to think of it, there was nothing she liked about the man. His bald, lumpy head with its protruding moles resembled a potato. And he was skinny. God, that man was skinny. How could anyone who ate as much as Sam be that skinny? And he was only thirty-two. At least that's what he claimed. As soon as Lanie learned how to use the internet she would look him up, find out his true age, and tell Spring so she could have a real reason to leave him.

Lanie tapped the ash from the cigarette and watched a bead of sweat glissade its way from her shoulder to her wrist in a slow rolling motion, skirting its way around the hairs that she had only recently acquired. Damned getting older. She was growing hair everywhere, except for the places she needed it, like her head. And the hairs that she already had were grayer than an Oregon morning. The sweat bubble slid across her index finger and plopped onto the cement with a satisfying splat. Though the sun was setting it was still so hot that the sweat bubble sizzled when it hit the ground and dissolved within a few seconds. She was proud of that bead. Well-earned. She looked around, disappointed that no one was there to witness it.

Lanie inhaled a deep lungful of nicotine and held it for five seconds, pretending that she was hitting a bong. The first puff was always the most delicious. It sent tentacles of pleasure coursing through her body, snaking down her torso, spreading into her limbs, fingers, and finally toes. The Surgeon General had gotten it all wrong. Tobacco wasn't bad for you. The Indians smoked it and they were as healthy as the horses they chased the white men on. What was bad for you was the pesticides they put on vegetables. The produce company was using cigarettes as a smokescreen...so to speak. Lanie laughed out loud and took another drag.

Where was she? Vegetables. Potatoes. Oh, back to Sam. The man changed religions as often as most people washed their underwear. A little over eight months ago he had converted to Islam. Now he ran around in baggy pajamas and prayed all the time. Before that he had been a Jehovah's Witness. Luckily he stopped that nonsense when he realized he didn't get birthday presents. And before that he had dabbled in Buddhism. Lanie thought he was going to keep trying until he eventually found one that would allow him into heaven.

"Why in heaven's name are you with him?" Lanie had asked Spring one day while they were out shopping for potatoes. Not only did he look like a potato but he ate them by the bushel, an act that no one found ironic but Lanie.

"After Trevor left I was a mess, remember mother?" Spring answered. "Sam was there for me. And it's nice to feel normal for once."

Lanie huffed. Just because Spring was pushing 30 with two kids didn't mean she had to settle for fall-out boy. As for Sam being normal, well if he was normal then she was Judy Garland. Besides, who in their right mind actually wanted to be normal? While most people spent their lives trying to carve out some kind of individual niche for themselves, Spring preferred to be one of the nameless masses. Poopy.

Lanie inhaled the last wisp of her Winston. The sky was beginning to darken and she couldn't wait for the night to release her from this heat. She'd read somewhere that there were places where night could last for days. Maybe she should move to one of those locations. It might help with the hot flashes. If she ever got a car. She shifted in her chair, lifting a breast to scratch beneath it. A mosquito must have taken a nibble while she had been smoking. A quick movement caught her eye, distracting her from the itch. Across the backyard and over the five-foot wooden fence that separated Spring's home from those behind her, Lanie was pretty sure she caught a human head staring at her. *Why, I'll be,* Lanie thought. *A peeper!* Lanie smiled. It had been a long time since she had been peeped.

Lanie dropped the cigarette onto the ground and watched the ember fade away. It was a struggle to extricate herself from the chair but at last she made it, her voluptuous bottom jouncing as she rose. She stood on tip-toes, craning her neck to see over the top of the fence. The peeper was nowhere to be seen. "He'll be back," she said and fanned herself as she swayed seductively into the house. "They always come back to mama."

Lanie stood beneath the living room ceiling fan, letting the cool air blast over her body. Parts of her wiggled and jiggled, still reacting to the sudden rousting. The sound of a car pulling into the driveway sent her scurrying back into her house dress. "Fuck!" she said, looking around the living room. "Where the hell's my underwear?"

FIVE

Spring barely had the chance to open the door before Debbie handed her a sticky note. Kimberly Welz, the head of the communications department, had summoned Spring into her office. "Good luck," said Debbie. Kimberly was new to management and had already earned a reputation as a pain in the ass. Last week an unsuspecting Fed Ex delivery man had gone in and no one had ever seen him come out. Spring was half-tempted to check the broom closet for bodies, but hadn't gotten up the nerve.

Kimberly's office sat by itself at the end of a long corridor, past the janitor's closet, the copy room, and the family restroom. A world unto its own. Here Kimberly reigned, monarch of none so far. But that was about to change. As Spring crept down the dark hallway she wondered if her insurance covered beheadings.

"Spring, good to see you." Kimberly said, running her fingers through her glistening black hair. Jane had ordered the entire building feng shui'd over the weekend and there were now mirrors everywhere and Kimberly was taking advantage of the opportunity to preen. With the new, energy-efficient, fluorescent bulbs installed, and the walls now pasted with mirrors, *Teens in Trouble* reminded Spring of a carnival fun house, the one attraction she was always afraid of during her youth.

"Yeah, good seeing you again, too," Spring lied. She and Kimberly had started at *Teens in Trouble* on the same day three years ago. In that time Kimberly had been promoted twice. *The quickest rising star in the company*, Jane had quoted in the annual newsletter. During that time, Spring had only managed to bumble from one cubicle by the water cooler to one closer to the main entrance, a godsend on those days she flew in late.

"Sit down, please." Kimberly plopped into her leather office chair and motioned Spring towards an uncomfortable wooden chair on the other side of the desk. Between the women sat a flat-screen monitor and an army of porcelain cats arranged in a neat line, their feline faces turned smugly upwards. "I wanted to talk to you about your marketing plan," said Kimberly, pushing her monitor aside. The cats looked at her expectantly.

"My marketing plan?" Spring was confused. This was the first she had heard of a marketing plan.

"I need you to put together a list of places where you and Casey will be doing community outreach. Churches. Schools. Parades. That sort of thing."

"But I thought you were in charge of that."

Kimberly laughed. "Me? Oh God, no. I've got real work to do. You came up with the mascot idea. You come up with the marketing for it. It's bad enough I have to babysit you."

"What about Meg? Isn't she going to help with this?" Spring began to panic. It was bad enough she would be escorting the condom. She wanted no part in figuring out where to escort him to.

"Budget won't allow for much more with the PR people. Besides, Jane and Meg aren't speaking right now. Lover's quarrel, you know?" Kimberly sighed, twirling the ends of her hair around her fingers.

Despite Spring's dislike of Kimberly, she felt a tremendous urge to touch her hair. It was the most magnificent hair Spring had ever seen—— shiny, lustrous, a black-widow's blue. Spring was sure she didn't use store brand shampoo on her hair. Nothing but salon quality for that bob. Probably no home haircuts either.

"You can get Sarah to help," Kimberly added. "I'm sure she has some ideas."

Spring pursed her lips in agitation. Sarah was the most uninspired person in the company. She could be the spokeswoman for apathy...if she cared enough. Spring sat for a moment, her hands folded in her lap. "You know, Kimberly, I'm, well, happy you all thought of me for this. But...I just...I've been working with the girls now in a support role, and I think I'm doing some good there." Spring closed her eyes, took a deep breath, and let it out slowly.

"First off," Kimberly corrected her. "...I didn't think of you for this. I don't think of you ever. Got that? Secondly, I can't handle you moping around this department. Kimberly-land is happy-land. So take your sad little face and spray-paint a smile onto it if you have to. I won't have Jane thinking it's a torture chamber down here." Kimberly turned her chair away from Spring, towards the large window behind her. "The marketing plan could be fun for you. For once, you get to be the master of your fate. You are being *proactive* rather than *reactive*." Kimberly swiveled to stare at a motivational poster on the wall; a picture of a tree with the words *Give Them Roots* written prettily on the bottom. "I didn't want you here either, my dear. But my hands are tied. This is coming straight from Jane. We have to make it work." Kimberly spun her chair towards Spring and gave her a full once over.

"While we're here, I might as well bring this up." Kimberly stood, moving towards her to inspect her more carefully. "I've been watching you in meetings. We need to do something about your clothes. I know in the counseling department they are a lot more lax about dress style, but here in the *communications department* you have to dress like a professional. You can't wear those rags to work anymore."

Spring looked down at her flowered skirt and brown peasant shirt. "These are not rags!"

"That's debatable."

"What would I wear, then?" Spring saw nothing wrong with the skirt and, in fact, had three more identical to this one. True, the flowers were faded and there was a hole or two where a hungry moth had once fed. But she loved them.

"That's your problem." Kimberly tilted her head and a curtain of hair fell across her eyes, a signal that this conversation was about to end. "And I expect you to have it figured out by the beginning of next week, but here are a few tips. Stop shopping at K-mart. Don't sew your own clothes. And take someone with actual taste with you when you pick things out." Kimberly sat back in her chair, crossed her legs at the ankles, and began typing. "We're done."

"Bitch." Spring muttered as she closed the door behind her.

"No tears?" Debbie asked as Spring re-entered the lobby. The sun shone through the windows, catching itself on the various mirrors and bouncing around in a prism-like fashion. Spring squinted to avoid blindness.

"More like seething hatred. But she hasn't broke me yet."

"That's good. We can't afford another casualty." Debbie pointed to a handmade sign tacked to a bulletin board behind her. *Kimberly Casualties This Week: 2.*

Spring laughed and felt a wave of affection for the woman. Debbie dared to poke the bear everyone else threw honeycombs at. "They are going to make you take that down."

"That's fine. But I will have my laughs till they do, right?" Debbie turned towards the sign and put an x through the number 2 and drew in a large red 3. "For comedic effect," she explained, turning back. "Not that anyone here appreciates good comedy." Debbie capped the marker and jotted down something in her day planner. "Hey, since we're both engaged I thought maybe we could get together soon and talk about weddings and such. Have a girl's night, you know?"

"I'm not engaged."

"How old are you again?" Debbie asked, seemingly mystified.

"Thirty."

"Oh," Debbie said. "Sorry to hear that."

Six

John stood in front of his pickup truck, all his earthly belongings tied up in the truck bed under an old tarp. Before him stood his family and friends––the majority of the community––all of whom had come to say goodbye and to wish him luck in his new life.

"I can't believe you're going," said his mother, grabbing hold of him, her press-on nails digging into his back. Tears ran down her cheeks, etching rivers through her pancake makeup. Standing there before him John realized what a tiny woman she was and he was surprised he had never noticed. She always seemed so big, strong and capable, but as he hugged her goodbye he realized she wasn't Superwoman after all.

"It's not forever, Mom," he said, standing back to look at her. He could see the roots of her hair, grey with the beginnings of grow-out. She spent two Fridays a month at the Samson Beauty Parlor to maintain her natural color, but time was winning the war on her head and it would have horrified her to know.

"I got you a present," his mom whispered in his ear. She presented him with a package wrapped in pink and purple paper, probably left over from his niece's birthday party last week. His mom, a proud Scotch-Irish woman, wasted nothing. No wrapping paper, bow, or even tape was discarded. Each was placed in an old shoe box ready to serve again at a moment's notice. His family had been recycling long before it was fashionable.

"Open it now," his auntie called out from somewhere in the crowd, and his brothers elbowed each other good-naturedly. They were obviously privy to the contents of the package. John smiled and nodded, turning his head away from the sun.

49

"Ah, thanks, Mom. I can never have too many pairs of underwear." John waved the stack of white Fruit-of-the-Looms in the air, bringing laughter from younger members of the crowd and nods of approval from the elders. His mother squeezed his arm.

"That's so in case you get in a car wreck you will always have clean underpants. Read them," she instructed, hiding her mouth behind her hand so that John wouldn't notice her bottom lip tremble. John flipped the pair on top. On the back were the words *John Smith* delicately embroidered in cursive scrawl. "Me-ma did those for you last week," said his mother, nodding to his grandmother in the front row. "Even though she has the arthritis."

John walked towards his grandmother and gave her a long hug goodbye. She broke free and saluted him, assuming he was off to war because that was the only reason anyone ever left Samson. Generations of Samson men had died for the Red, White, and Blue and his grandmother lovingly sacrificed every one of them because that was the cost of freedom. John saluted her back and then he went to each family member and friend, shaking the hands of the men and hugging the women.

"Remember," said his grandfather. "Buy American, vote Democrat, and don't wear colored bandanas or people will think you're in a gang."

John nodded and grasped his grandfather's hand firmly, feeling the heavy veins in the man's thin arm. "I won't forget."

John made it through the crowd, doing his best not to cry. Midwest men did not cry. When he had finished his goodbyes he made his way to his truck and watched as his mother turned away. She had said she couldn't watch him leave. He waved once more and then drove, refusing to look back in case he changed his mind. It wasn't until three hours later at a rest stop that he saw the card on the passenger seat.

Dear John,

You are a good boy. Losing you is like losing my arm. But if you really love something (or someone) set them free. And so I am. Follow your heart. I hope you find your adventure.

Mom.

It was a long, mind-numbing trek from Indiana to Arizona. Traveling as a grownup was not the exciting adventure he remembered from his childhood. His only other trip outside his home state, he had slept through the boring parts while his brother drove. And there were a lot of boring parts. Grain turned into dust, dust into hills, hills into dust again, and finally it all turned into dirt. Phoenix wasn't Colorado, no matter what the job recruiter might have said.

"You like Colorado? You're gonna love Phoenix, Sport. Beautiful landscape. Friendly people. Mountains everywhere, as far as the eye can see. Just don't tell everyone. We like to keep this exclusive."

What a crock of shit.

First off, Phoenix was large, not a nestled little city tucked neatly into the mountain landscape. Phoenix was a sprawling metropolis that ended suddenly, fading into desert nothingness as quickly as it began. It was like something out of a science fiction movie––glistening metal buildings settled uncertainly on a desolate landscape. A lonely, reaching, place trying to make contact with the world, but failing miserably. If the soil were red he might have thought he had landed on Mars, one hundred years in the future.

The people were also strange to him. In Samson everyone looked the same. Jeans. Flannels. Baseball caps. Shorts in the summer. Heavy coats in the winter. Hair a drab yellow or muted brown or a dull red. Facial hair optional.

But here, everyone seemed to go out of their way to be noticed. Dark clothes. Baggy jeans. Short skirts. Piercings. Tattoos. He had counted at least four T-shirts screaming, "Be an Individual!" He shook his head and tried not to make eye contact with any of the strange inhabitants. He had seen enough TV to know that they most likely all carried guns or knives.

After a few hours of driving around––thank God at least the city was on a grid system––John found his apartment. It was a tall, brick structure built in the middle of the city. Probably not more than twenty years old, it had the feel of a building that had survived a couple of wars and prohibition. Another untruth by the job recruiter...*And you'll be living in luxury, a country club like setting on our dime...how many people can say that?*

It felt less like a country club––not that John had ever been to one–– and more like the dog kennel he had worked at as a teenager during his summer vacations.

John unloaded his recliner and his TV from the truck and picked up his keys from the office. The fat man at the desk explained that he did not accept rent after the fifth of each month and that the swimming pool was temporarily closed until the duck situation was under control. With that, John wandered down the empty hallways, searching for the door that would transport him to his new life. He was aware of the echo of his footsteps, his thin shadow cast from the dimly lit corridor, a baby crying behind one of the mystery doors. A wave of homesickness engulfed him and for a moment he wanted to turn and run, back towards his truck and then on to Samson. Screw adventure. That's what books were for. But as he turned to make his escape he spotted the brass numbers of his new apartment: 354.

"Might as well check it out since I'm here," he said, pushing the key into the lock. With one small click and a turn of the knob he entered his new home and his fears subsided. The place was decent inside, if a bit small. Clean. Air conditioned. Newly carpeted. Walls with paint instead of wood paneling or wallpaper. A few appliances he had never seen before, like the hole in the sink that ate things when you flipped on a switch. And a dishwasher. He had never had a dishwasher. Things might not be so bad after all.

He immediately turned on the air conditioner as high as it would go and let the cold air blast over his face. From his third story window he could see the swimming pool directly below, the water an uninviting, inky blue, teaming with birds who must have decided it was not worth the effort to fly north for the summer...not with an oasis such as this in the dessert. Beyond the gates of the pool, roads and buildings grew smaller in the distance until they resembled the world of a toy train set, each mostly undistinguishable from the next.

Among the many establishments, John saw a faint green light a few blocks away. It flickered and blinked enticingly, even in the daylight. The Paradise Pub. Though it certainly did not look like Paradise, it reminded him of the local bars back home. Perhaps his own oasis. The neighborhood was a bit scary to take a walk in that direction, but he wouldn't mind a drive later on.

A knock on the door roused him from the thought. It was the fat man who took the rent.

"Is that your truck out there?" The man walked across the living room to an opposite window and pointed outside to the parking lot.

"...Because I think someone just jacked your rims."

SEVEN

Spring sat at the vanity in her bedroom, working a stubborn knot out of her hair. It was the first vanity she had ever owned, purchased by Sam as a gift when he was out antiquing one day. He was very proud of his purchase and had even rented a U-Haul to bring it back, along with the grandfather clock in the living room. The vanity was a bit ornate for her taste with its scrolled edge work but Sam insisted that all ladies owned such things and so she had acquiesced.

Her room was small, hardly big enough for their Queen Anne Bed, the Goodwill dresser which had been spray-painted white by its previous owner, and the vanity. Sam frequently complained of this, but Spring didn't mind the size of the space. It was a bedroom. In a house. And she had never had a bedroom or a house before. Even if the home was a rental, it was the nicest place she had ever lived.

Spring turned slightly to watch Sam's movements. He had his back to her, swinging his arms wildly like a goose in flight, as he mock-conducted Bach on the stereo. He clutched two dark dress socks in his hands which served as impotent wands, creating small tracers around him. She wasn't allowed to talk during classical music hour, so she busied herself with biting her nails while waiting for the song to end. The problem with Bach, however, was that she wasn't sure when one song ended and another began.

"Sam," she called finally, and he jumped, tossing the socks in opposite directions. He had probably forgotten that she was there. "You said you were going to talk to me. I really need you right now."

Sam lowered the volume on the stereo and opened his night stand, producing another pair of black socks bound together with a rubber band. He sat on the edge of the bed and removed the pair of socks he was wearing and replaced them with the new ones. Sam changed his socks at least three times a day and his underwear twice as often. God didn't like germs.

"What were we going to talk about again? Remind me, Pooks."

"My clothes. Kimberly made me feel like I was a vagabond. I don't see anything wrong with this." Spring pulled at the side of her skirt for Sam to inspect.

"I think you are making a big deal over nothing," Sam said, gathering up both pairs of loose socks. He tossed them into a hamper in the corner of the room. Three out of four of them missed. Sam sighed and retrieved them, dropping them gingerly inside. "It's an old skirt."

"But it's *my* skirt." Spring could feel the words twist in her throat and come slithering out in the form of a whine. "Can't you be supportive? Ever?"

Sam paused a moment, rubbing the fingers of both hands methodically against his thumbs. "You're a beautiful woman. You're about to turn thirty and I think that pisses you off. Maybe it's time to put your little girl days behind you."

Spring spun in his direction and he flinched.

"I didn't mean you were old, Pookie. Or that you dressed like a kid. I only meant, well, that's an ugly dress. Look at it. You're two purple flowers shy of being your mother." Sam stopped, leaving room for Spring to speak. When she said nothing he continued. "A few nice suits. A pair of heels without wedges. Accessories that don't turn your skin green. That's what you need to be wearing."

Spring looked at her reflection again. A barrette dangled from the side of her head. She pulled it out and tossed it in a basket Sam had purchased for her hair accessories. Sam had baskets for everything, including smaller baskets. "I guess you are right."

"Enough of that for now." Sam posed, his back slightly hunched in the manner of a cartoon butler. "I have news. Very, very important news."

"Is everything okay?" When Sam didn't reply, Spring bent over, placing her head between her knees like the stewardess had instructed her to do in case of a crash. "You're sick. Oh God, you're dying!" She glanced from side to side, feeling like she was suddenly caged in. "Cancer? That explains so much!"

Sam groaned. "No, not me. I have a confession, Pooks. I wasn't really away on business. There's no such thing as a Stock Compiling Convention." Sam turned his head and snickered into his hand and then turned back. "I was really visiting Grandma Rosary. She's not doing well. She's on her deathbed."

"No!" Spring looked up and her entire body quaked. Grandma Rosary had practically raised Sam when his own mother disappeared at the age of ten. She was a wonderful woman who had always seemed so healthy and vibrant. How could this be happening? "Oh, Sam. I'm so sorry. She isn't even that old. Well, she's old, but not old, old." Spring lifted her hands to count out the numbers on her fingers.

"Yes, yes, distressing news." Sam waved his free hand. "But that's not all, Spring. She is leaving us an inheritance. A very large one."

Spring stared at him, trying to take in what he was saying, but the words tumbled around in her head like sheets in a dryer.

"Sweetie? Did you hear me?" Sam stood above her, knocking on her forehead with his knuckles. "Anyone home?"

"An inheritance? For us?"

"Yes…provided we get married. She's a God-fearing woman and doesn't want us living in sin." Sam kneeled down before her and looked her in the eyes. "She really, really hates sin."

"Married?" Spring had been living with Sam for a while now, but they had never talked seriously about marriage. Come to think of it they had never talked marriage at all.

"I got a call today," he continued, before she could settle on any one thought. "She loves you, Spring. Once the two of us are married we will get our inheritance and I will be the happiest man on Earth." Sam lifted her chin and pecked her on the lips. He squeezed both her hands in one of his and inhaled, letting it out slowly. "Spring Ryan, I have no ring for you right now, but I will get one. So, will you marry me?"

Spring said nothing. Her mouth fell open and she looked at her feet. How had she never noticed her feet were so big. Practically clown-sized.

Sam lifted her chin again, forcing her gaze. "I will make you happy, Spring. We will buy a house. A real house that you can call your own. No more renting. No more landlords. No more late notices. The boys will be taken care of. And so will your mother. Please say yes."

An inheritance? Buy a house? Married to Sam? It was too much all at once. "I need to think, Sam. Give me a few days. Please?"

Sam sweetened the deal. "And you can quit your job. You can be a stay at home mom or whatever it is you want. No more Kimberly."

The temptation to answer yes was great. Her lips almost formed the word, but before she could make them speak she had a flash of Trevor, of the two of them together. It was a silly thought. She would never see him again. But still...

"Please, Sam. Give me a few days. I promise I will seriously think about it."

Sam's face reddened and Spring couldn't tell if he was angry or embarrassed. Maybe both. He narrowed his eyes and turned from her, storming into the bathroom. Spring heard the lock of the door behind him and the shower turn on. She sat on the bed waiting for him to come out, but he never did. At last she slumped over and sleep overcame her, taking her into a land with no dreams. When Sam finally emerged three hours later, he said nothing to her as he climbed into the bed. She pulled herself awake and crawled under the covers to join him.

"Sam?" She whispered in the dark, but he did not answer and she knew he was feigning sleep.

Spring pulled the pillow over her head. *Where the hell was Trevor?*

Across the hall, Lanie drew a card from the Tarot deck. The Fool, a wandering child about to step over the precipice. Of course. Something was going on with Spring. Again. Every time The Fool came up, it meant another catastrophe for that girl. It had appeared when Spring discovered she was pregnant with the twins, when Trevor abandoned her, and when Sam had stepped into her life.

Lanie reached into her Crown Royal pouch and pulled out a palm full of vials. She squinted at each of the labels and wondered where she had put her reading glasses. More on intuition than certainty, she opened one that contained a crystalline, glitter-like substance and sprinkled the dust upon the card. "For protection," she said, staring at the ceiling.

She knew the Universe could read her heart but she wanted to leave nothing to chance.

Spring was allowed to work off-site in order to develop *the marketing plan,* likely because Kimberly was still using her office as a place to store office supplies.

She looked for a parking space in the back lot of Paradise Pub. Though Kimberly had insisted she could work remotely, she hadn't specified a location, and a bar was probably not what she had in mind. But Spring needed a drink. And badly.

At last she found a narrow space between two large trucks. She carefully wrenched her way in until she was uncomfortably sandwiched between the two. Seeing that there wasn't enough room to open her door, she made one final reversal and her body went cold as she felt the crunch of her bumper against the metal of a vehicle behind her. She turned to look. Sure enough, her car had collided with a roving black truck. Spring bit her lip and carefully inched herself forward, hoping that the glaring indent in the driver's side door had been imprinted there by some other bad driver long ago. But the man who emerged from the truck, flailing his arms, made it clear that this was a new injury.

"Oh God!" Spring said, jumping out of her vehicle. "Are you okay?"

The man paid her no attention as he surveyed the damage to his pickup. It was an older model but appeared well taken care of, except for the large rip cut into its side. Spring took a quick glance at her car and was relieved to see that it looked fine.

"What the hell did you do?" The man turned to accuse her. His hair was the color of wheat and he was wearing a blue flannel shirt that probably doubled as a jacket in colder months. He crossed his arms and awaited an explanation.

"I'm sorry." Spring wasn't sure what she was supposed to say. She had been involved in several near-misses, but had never had an accident. "I didn't see you."

"Didn't see me? You didn't see me? Oh, that's a laugh. I'm driving a truck for Christ's sake!" The man shook his head in disbelief, straw hair falling over his forehead. "I've had this truck since I learned to drive. It was my father's. My *dead* father's. Is everyone in this city hell-bent on destroying it?" He kicked his tire with the heel of his foot to illustrate his frustration.

"What do we do?" Spring spread her hands.

The man looked at her purse. "Gimme your phone." He lunged forward but Spring held tight.

"What do you want it for?" Her heart was racing and she wondered if this were all a ploy to mug her.

"To call the police and report this. And we should call our insurance agencies. Hope there's long distance on that. Mine is back in Indiana."

Spring flexed and unflexed her fingers. *Police? Insurance agency? Had she paid her insurance premium?* She wracked her brain, doing a mental scan of the bills that sat unopened on the table. She had only been able to pay half of them that month. Was the insurance bill among the lucky few?

"Do we have to get the police and our insurance companies involved? Can we work this out ourselves?" Spring shuffled from one foot to another, pleading with the man. He narrowed his eyes and leaned back against the dented side of his truck.

"I don't know. I'm not sure how much this will cost." He turned his head to look at the damage and grunted through his nostrils. "This is just great," he said. "My first day in Phoenix and I get hit by a crazy lady with no insurance."

Spring tore open her purse and searched every pocket. A pair of old sunglasses, a green sock, and three Christmas photos of her Aunt Loraine's dog fell to the ground. Finally, she found her Hello Kitty wallet. "I have forty-three dollars and twelve cents." She thrust the money at the man. "I'm good for the rest. I promise."

The man turned to regard her. His eyes ran from the top of her head to the bottom of her feet. It wasn't a very promising appraisal. She was about to hand him the phone and begin her new life as a convict when he grabbed the money.

"I guess we could work something out." He shoved the money into his front pocket, leaned through the window of his truck, and produced a pen and paper. He scribbled the name 'John' on it and a number and handed it to Spring. "Call me."

"Wait a second!" Spring slapped his hand away. "Just because I hit your precious little truck doesn't mean I'm going to have sex with you."

John laughed. "I'm not letting you off that easy, lady. Trust me. This truck is worth more to me than a few hours with any woman, let alone a lunatic. I could get that back home far cheaper."

Spring felt her face redden. "Well, then...I'm not going to date you either. I don't date jerks."

The left corner of John's mouth turned up in what Spring guessed was a smile. "You watch a lot of movies, don't you? Again...not worth the trouble. Call me and we can set up a payment plan after I get an estimate."

Spring nodded, torn between gratitude and indignation as she took the slip of paper. "Thank you. Sorry about the jerk comment. You really are nice." She reached to hug him but he put his arm out in a halting motion.

"I'm not that nice. I'm just tired. It's been a long day. Think I'm going to have my beer at home instead." With a final shake of the head, he entered his truck and drove away. Spring hoped the scraping sound she heard as he pulled out was a preexisting condition. She took the sheet of paper, folded it twice, and placed it in the pocket of her wallet where there had once been money. She grabbed her things and trudged inside. Near the rear of the bar she spotted a small round table and seated herself. "Hi, honey I'm home."

She took a deep breath and surveyed the place where she had spent so many hours––the place she had not been back to since Trevor disappeared. But it seemed so necessary lately, to reclaim her past, to return to the scene of the crime, to figure out what had went wrong. She stirred uncomfortably on her stool, scratching at an imaginary itch.

Maybe this was a mistake. She tried to ignore them, the ghosts that lingered here, but the flashing Budweiser sign above the bar, the smell of ash and beer, the old juke box by the bathroom that played their song, *Bad Moon Rising* (red flag!), were all reminders of her past life. *Why did I come here, anyway?* she wondered, chewing on the ends of her hair. Phoenix boasted many bars, most far nicer than this one. But something had pulled her back this day, some quiet insistence of the Universe that turned the steering wheel into the parking lot and tapped out the words to Debbie and Sarah as she texted them on her cell phone.

"Having anything, hon?"

The waitress, perhaps a decade older than Spring, had the look of a woman who had lived a lot of years in a short amount of time. With her hair bleached to a crisp white, her lips varnished to an apple red, and blue eyeshadow that extended from lash line to brow, she reminded Spring of Old Glory, now more old than glorious. Spring immediately wanted to know her story. Had she had dreams once, too? Maybe she would have been a singer. A writer. A counselor. Or maybe some guy with a big smile and empty promises had ripped her heart out and she had stumbled into this bar and found absolution in serving drinks to strangers.

"Well?" the waitress inquired, flicking the head of her pen to a pad to indicate that she was in a hurry.

"I really shouldn't. I'm on the clock. Well, not really on the clock. We don't punch in, actually. It's more an honor system thing, which I owe a huge karmic debt to already. But I am technically working right now and I'm not sure what our policy is on drinking during work hours." The waitress shrugged and turned to go. "Wait. Piña Colada. With whipped cream. And pineapple." The waitress nodded without writing it down, and turned to leave. "Oh, and a cherry. Two. Please. Cherries, not Piña Coladas. That would be pushing it and probably *would* be against employee regulations."

When the waitress left, Spring realized what a stupid idea this had been. Whatever force was at work with her subconscious was not a very helpful one. Did it really think this would cure some old wound and release her from Trevor's psychological hold? That everything would finally come full circle and all the rest of the stuff Lanie preached about when there wasn't anything good on TV? Maybe it wasn't too late. She could pack up her stuff and run. Quit work. Leave Sam. Start a new life somewhere.

Where?

Someplace exciting. Istanbul. She could be a belly dancer. Did Istanbul still exist? Or was that Constantinople? Was she too blonde to be accepted into the belly dancing culture? Too old to learn? What about the boys? They'd probably be bad for business.

The waitress returned with a sad-looking drink and sat it down apologetically in front of her. Spring took a sip and looked across the dark room at the bar. Third seat from the left. That was where he was sitting when they had first met. She had been standing in line, getting a drink. The bartender, a young braless woman, was ignoring her in favor of the men she was sure would tip more. But Trevor had caught the bartender's attention for Spring and had helped to get the drink. He even paid for it.

"Thanks," she said, slurping up the thick cream through the straw. "I don't think she liked me."

"I don't think she likes anyone, really," he said, smiling. A wicked smile. Clover-green eyes shadowed by lush, black lashes. Dimples. White teeth. A bad boy smile. He was cotton candy, caramel apples, and saltwater taffy, all rolled up in one. Spring had seen boys like him before, those she knew she should stay away from. Heartbreakers. She was about to retreat back into the crowd, disappearing before he could spring the trap. But he smiled again and there was no turning back.

"Name's Trevor," he said, extending a hand. He had an accent. Irish maybe? Spring balanced her drink in her left hand and shook with her right. Someone bumped into her from behind and she spilled her Piña Colada down the front of her dress.

"Oh no," Trevor said, taking a napkin and dabbing it on the spill. When he got to the place where he knew he shouldn't dab anymore, he blushed. Spring laughed.

"It's okay, Trevor. My dignity was gone long ago." She took the napkin from him and finished the job. He ordered her another.

Instant chemistry. He gave her his stool and they spent the entire evening together, closing down the bar. When it was time for her to go home, he called her a cab but took her number. They became inseparable. Together they were like two kids, laughing, giggling, sharing secrets. Three months of that. Movies. Bars. Late night dinners. Mad sex. And then it was time for him to leave.

"I want to go with you," Spring begged him. "Don't leave me here, please."

"We hardly know each other," Trevor answered, kissing her as they lie in bed on his last day. "It wouldn't work."

"What do you mean, we don't know each other? We've spent the entire summer together. You told me you loved me!" Spring sat up, wrapping the sheet tightly around her body. "I can't believe you just said that."

Trevor looked at her, seemingly confused. "Spring. You know I care about you. It's been fun. Can't you leave it at that?" His tone was pragmatic. Before she could respond he softened. "I'm sorry. I've got to go to New York for a while, then abroad. We'll stay in touch. Email. Phone. Whatever. True love takes time. If it's meant to be, it will be."

She pled with him. Cried. Begged. Threw herself in front of the door as he tried to leave. She did all of those things she knew women shouldn't do to hold on to a man. But it made no difference. And when he was gone, he was gone. Not a call. Not a letter. Not a forwarded joke in her junk mail. Every day she waited, certain he longed for her in the same way she longed for him. But no communication was made. She tried to console herself at first by saying he must have died (surely better than being a deserter) but a quick Google search assured her that he was still alive. The jerk.

Spring wondered if she had misread it all along. In her head it was perfect, and nobody walks out on perfect. She spent countless hours scanning her memory banks, replaying every moment, every scene. What had she missed? A word, a nuance, a shrug, a disagreement. Somewhere in all the fragments was the answer.

Sometimes she would think she'd have it, the a-ha moment. But nothing ever really made sense. She'd throw the memories up in the air and see where they'd land, a puzzle with some pieces facing in at times, some turned upside down, and some completely missing. She'd move them around, the best she could. Remember when he gave you that bizarre look when you mentioned you wanted to go on a road trip? Recall the way there was a pause that time at dinner when you said you absolutely loved shrimp? Remember that weekend you couldn't reach him and he said he was camping? He even came back with scratches on his arms where he had to cut through some nasty bushes. Remember those times the phone would ring at random hours and he wouldn't answer it, claiming the calls were from anxious telemarketers?

Remember...

"Must be some drink," said a voice.

Spring looked up to see Debbie and Sarah with an armful of packets. She had almost forgotten they were coming to help. She wanted to stay inside her head and luxuriate in self-pity. She scratched at an eye that was beginning to twitch, but nodded amicably.

"Get any work done while we were prostituting ourselves for the silent auction?" Sarah laughed, but there was an edge to her voice. Jane had her on the phone all week, soliciting donations from local businesses. The silent auction was only one of a dozen fundraising events Jane conducted each year, though no one ever knew where all the money actually went once raised.

"Only if getting tipsy counts as work." Spring dropped her eyes, feeling guilty. "Sorry."

Sarah smiled. "It's okay. This job blows. Drinking is the only thing that helps."

Debbie put the folders on the ground and fished into her large black bag for something else. "Look what I got." Debbie passed around ivory cards with purple lettering that read: *Welcome to the Hitchin'*. A farmer was tying up a mule to a wagon. "This is Jack's idea of a wedding invitation."

Are you supposed to be the mule or the wagon?" Spring handed back the card.

Sarah choked on her beer.

"Gah. Can you believe men?" Debbie stuffed them back into her bag. "Serves me right for marrying a guy from Wyoming."

"I guess we should discuss work," Spring said. "In case Kimberly wants a report."

Sarah bit on the tips of her fingers where her nails used to be. "You know that woman wants me to throw condoms at the Memorial Day parade downtown?"

"You have to do the parade? In May? In Arizona? In that costume?" Debbie almost fell out of her chair with each realization. "What the hell is wrong with her?"

"Don't get too cocky," Sarah said. "I heard you might get the honor of joining us."

Spring's phone buzzed and she looked to see that Sam had left her a voicemail.

Sweetie. Bought a cappuccino maker for you! Was not cheap...but only the best for my Pooks! Kisses!

She turned off her phone and sighed.

The waitress returned, handing Spring a bill. "Want me to add anything else?" Spring wanted another drink, but she resisted. "No. Thanks. One is all I can afford." The waitress smiled and walked away. "I shouldn't even have the one," she said to the two girls seated with her.

"I can buy the next," Debbie offered, digging into her purse.

Spring shook her head. "No. I'll be fine. I only need to pay a few bills, get Mom her meds, pay off some auto body work for a complete stranger and develop a sudden love for cappuccino." Spring shook her cup, letting the ice melt before taking the final swig.

EIGHT

1983

"There he is!" The fat boy who never ironed his shirt and smelled like gasoline, pointed. The two boys beside him followed his gaze and Sam knew he had been spotted. For a moment he wasn't sure if he should run, or stand and fight.

Sam did the calculations. There were three of them, each weighing twice as much as he did. He could probably outrun them, but they were not weighted down as Sam was, with necessary items like books and ballet slippers. Still, it might be his only chance.

"Get him," the pasty one said.

Sam thought his name was Lewis but he wasn't sure. Though he had been classmates with the trio for most of his life, nothing had ever inspired him to learn what they were called. Uncivilized apes did not deserve names.

Sam took off running, zigging through a swarm of students in white shirts, navy pants, and plaid skirts. He passed Mary Jane Drinsel and gave her a quick smile, but she turned away from him, as most of the girls at St. Mary's did. He took no heed of it and continued his escape, feeling the heat of the three dirty thugs behind him. Sam thought about ducking into the bathroom, but realized if they found him there he'd be cornered. Besides, the bathroom smelled. Bad. Sam made it a point to pee right before school and to hold it until three p.m. so that he would never have to endure the unsanitary conditions of the St. Mary's urinals.

Bump. Bump. Bump. Sam turned his head. They were closing in on him. Sam thought about throwing his copy of Anna Karenina at one of the boys, but he wasn't going to lose a prized book, even if it meant taking a beating.

The hall had cleared as students settled into their classrooms. The exit sign was straight ahead and Sam pushed through the double doors leading out onto the blacktop. But the boys continued their pursuit.

"Step on a crack, break your mother's back," Sam said, aiming for every tear in the asphalt.

This, however, took up precious time and he could feel the energy of the boys behind him. It took his entire will to ignore the cracks but there were more important things to consider at the moment. Sam noticed a pair of tin trashcans and rushed towards them. Nimbly skirting around them, he pushed the bins over with his right hand and sent them rolling in the direction of Lewis and pals. He listened for the crash of their bodies as they fumbled over the receptacles but was dismayed to hear nothing but their heavy breathing and the steady pounding of their puffy feet.

These things never worked out in life the way they did in his story books.

"This is it," Sam said, hoping they would choke him, rather than beat him to death. If he was going to die today he wanted to die clean. He stopped and waited for his demise.

Dong! Dong!

Sam turned his head in the direction of the bell and a building came into view. A colossal, brick monstrosity that caused the hairs on Sam's thin arms to rise up in protest. A place more horrible than the boy's bathroom. The Chapel.

He felt one of the boys tug on his elbow and he realized he had no choice.

He changed direction, running towards the bell as fast as his long, tired legs would carry him. In a leap of faith he vaulted the three stairs and pushed open the great wooden door. Sam thought he heard Lewis yell, "No!" but wasn't certain. His heart was beating too loudly.

When he caught his breath, he turned to look at his pursuers. He was dumbfounded to see that they stood immediately outside but would not cross the threshold into the church. The boys waited a moment and, seeing that Sam was not going to emerge anytime soon, stomped their feet, called him a queer, and left.

Sam had only ever been inside the chapel when he was forced to by his grandmother or the nuns. But here, alone in the chapel with nothing but stained glass and music, he found it to be a much different place. It was sanitary and quiet, even more so than the school library where he usually hung out.

"Sanctuary," he said, and it all made sense.

From that day on, Sam took to retreating into the chapel whenever he needed an escape. He could spend hours lying flat-backed on the wooden pews with The Hardy Boys or Sherlock Holmes and nobody bothered him. In fact, his teachers seemed to approve and Mary Jane Drinsel actually smiled at him one day as he left the Cathedral. And on those rare days when he was without reading material, he even perused the Old Testament that the church was kind enough to provide him with.

2005

"Is it our week again?" Sam was grilling turkey hotdogs on the back patio. He was wearing his new apron and chef's hat combo, purchased from the Eddie Bauer store during his last mall outing. Spring sat on the patio chair beside him, rummaging through a bag of potato chips like a puppy looking for a lost bone. She had this annoying habit of only eating the ones that were curled or folded. Sam sighed, wishing she would use the chip bowl he had made for her in week two of his ceramics class.

"Yes, Sam," she finally spoke when she found the perfect chip.

It was folded over like a taco, and she popped it into her mouth and immediately began searching for the next. "It's our week again."

"But why tomorrow? Why can't Jason follow the rules? Sunday through Saturday. That is what it says in the custody agreement."

"He asked me if I could have them an extra couple of days so that he could take a trip to the botanical garden." Spring tossed the bag onto the ground and Sam bent over to snatch it up. He folded the top and fastened it with the chip clip he stored in his apron pocket.

"You mean the one he grows in his backyard?" Sam snorted. When Spring didn't respond he realized the joke might have been funnier if Jason actually *had* a backyard. "But really, he isn't above the law. You should bring that up in court."

Spring held her ground. "He asked me, Sam. And they are my kids. I love them." Spring stood, crumbs falling from her dress, and stomped into the living room. Sam decided it was a battle not worth fighting. He would simply remind her of his concession the next time he wanted something.

Sam turned off the grill and placed the hotdogs on the plate. They looked sad and shriveled and for a brief moment he missed pork. Still, it was a small price to pay to enter Paradise, where the women behaved themselves. It could be worse. He remembered his stint as a Buddhist. He hadn't fared well on the Himalayan diet of yak butter and grass. He took the hotdogs into the kitchen and set them down on the counter. Not quite hungry, he left them to wither, picking up a new book he had acquired in a hard-won eBay fight. It was leather-bound and he held it to his nose a moment, taking in its scent. His fingers pulsed around the spine and his grip tightened. There was nothing sexier than opening a brand new book.

Sam wasn't ashamed to admit that he loved books. In fact, he loved books more than he loved people, and definitely more than he loved animals. The only thing he loved more than books was Allah, for it was Allah who created the great minds that created great books. Sometimes when Spring was asleep he would wander around his den and run his fingers along the spines of all of his books. Hundreds and hundreds of beautiful books. He felt like the Count from Sesame Street as he touched each one. "One book...two books...three books...(pause, cue lightning bolt)...three beautiful books! Ah-hah-ha!" There was so much knowledge sitting on those shelves that he could get drunk thinking about it. If he could absorb every bit of information from every one of his books he could control the world.

Sam cocked an ear, listening for Spring. She must have disappeared into the bedroom. He trotted out to his lawn chair. A breeze brought the scent of the book back up to him and he squirmed in his chair as he recalled one particular memory, the evening Spring was gone all night with her sister for a girl's night out. He was alone in the house. The lights were low. Bach was playing on the radio. He felt that familiar longing and pull in his trousers.

He checked to make sure the driveway was empty, that she hadn't forgotten anything. Seeing that the house was clear, he tiptoed to his den and pulled a book from his shelves. His hands slid over it, his fingers trembling at the feel of leather beneath his palm. His thumb fell into its grooves and bumps and dents, and he moaned with each new crevice he explored.

"Economics in a New World," he shuddered. He held it to his cheek for a long, delicious moment.

And then he licked it.

"Oh God." He was going to the Muslim equivalent of Hell for certain. But he didn't care. His tongue forked out, digging into the gold lettering inscribed by some master. The taste of it was so strong, so primal he thought his pants would burst. He ran to the bathroom with it and locked the door. Spring knew nothing, of course. By the time she had come home the book had been replaced and she was none the wiser.

"Now those little bastards are going to be touching my books again," he said, imagining them sweeping into the house with their tiny, sticky hands, defiling everything he held sacred. He tasted the acid that bubbled up from his esophagus and took a swig of cold coffee to wash it away.

Sam wondered why, in retrospect, he had decided to keep his relationship going with Spring after he learned about *The Twins*. They were five-years-old when he met her, and when she mentioned she had boys that age he almost thought it was sweet, until they descended upon their home like the hounds of hell. They were loud. Hyper. Twitchy. Always doing stuff. Always talking. Always getting into everything. Touching things with filthy hands. Fiddling with things that shouldn't be fiddled with. Arguing over everything.

The worst part was that Spring always took their side. Always.

"Pookie, the boys were touching my books again. Can you tell them not to?"

"God, Sam. They are kids. You'd think you'd want them to be interested in reading."

They'd stand there, grinning at Sam, smug little *Omen* children waiting to push him over the banister. The only reason Child Protective Services didn't take them was because no one would have them.

Sam was getting upset thinking about it. He looked at the title again. *Secrets From the World's Best Day Traders*. His hand shook. But Spring and Lanie were both home. He gave the book a promissory peck. Another time.

Nine

Lanie took a stroll around the neighborhood, a nice walk to do her heart and lungs some good. She puffed on her cigarette as she took in the scenery––pretty, cookie-cutter homes with neat lawns and gingerbread shingles. In the window of each home she saw faces––mothers, fathers, children. Most looked happy and content. It made her want to gag.

"Maybe I've stayed in one place too long," Lanie said, nodding at a young couple pushing a big-headed baby in a stroller down the sidewalk. "I could look up some of the old gang, go back on the road." Lanie tried to remember where she put her address book, and then realized it didn't really matter anyway. None of her old friends had permanent addresses.

How do they live their lives like this? The same people and places day after day. Don't they lose their fucking minds?

A stray cat meowed and Lanie leaned over to scratch it. The cat hissed and Lanie backed off. Too bad, she really would have liked a familiar.

As she rounded the corner she kept her eyes open for what type of people might live on the other side of her daughter's fence. There were three houses that might all line up to Spring's backyard, and Lanie stepped lightly as she approached the trio of homes. In front of the first were two red bikes, probably belonging to children. In front of the second was a fixed up hot rod, probably circa 1960 something. And in front of the third stood a young man cleaning out sporting equipment from his garage. Lanie smiled and waved at him. He paused a moment, looked behind him, and waved back. Then he hastened into the house.

The sky was beginning to darken.

"Fucking global warming," she grumbled, sucking in the last puff of her cigarette before tossing it on the sidewalk. "...Making the days short like this."

She was about to turn the corner back to her own street when she saw movement behind her from the middle house. She turned in time to see a middle-aged man with an impossibly thin frame jump into the hot rod and zoom away. He had a long, hookish nose and not a hair on his head. The gleam of the waxing moon hit his scalp in a familiar way. Like an eagle. A majestic bald eagle, she thought, and almost skipped home.

"How well do you know the neighbors?" Lanie asked, opening the door. Her daughter was wiping her brow with the hem of her dress.

"I can't talk now, Mom. Look at this!" Spring slammed a stack of envelops onto the table. Lanie picked up the top one. Someone had drawn a bright, red, frownie face in sharpie on the cover of it, with an arrow pointing to the words Cancellation Policy.

"My insurance is cancelled. Great huh? And that's just the start of it. The landlord wants to charge us one hundred dollars more a month for you to live here. I thought I told you not to tell anyone." Spring looked exasperated and Lanie wondered if she was having problems with irregularity. She had something for that, but decided not to bring it up yet. Timing was everything with these types of issues.

"I didn't tell anyone." Lanie said. "I got ethics."

Spring gave Lanie a full once over. "I guess it's pretty tough to hide you." Lanie watched as Spring tore the envelops into a dozen tiny pieces and emptied them into the garbage can. Obviously she did not want Sam to find them.

"Well, if you'll excuse me, I gotta go take a crap. I wouldn't plan on going in there for a while if I were you. Just giving you fair warning." Lanie popped a prune in her mouth and thought if she timed it right she wouldn't have to wait on the pot but a minute or two.

"When...if...you ever get done, I could use your help, mother. The boys will be here tomorrow and I want the house clean." Lanie watched as her daughter wiped the table with one of Sam's socks.

"They live half the month in a van with their unemployed father.

This is fucking Nirvana as far as they're concerned." Lanie paused, feeling the pressure of the prunes settle in. "Why the hell do the courts allow that, anyway?"

Spring shrugged. "I think he's sleeping with one of the social workers again. I can't figure out why else they'd let him keep shared custody."

Lanie licked her lips. She knew why. "Jason has a way about him. Even I've felt his sex appeal."

"God, mother!" Spring frowned. "But I have to agree with you." Spring leaned back against the counter and wiped the sock to her forehead. "I think Jason is going to try and get more child support. He says his restless leg syndrome makes working impossible."

Gurgle, gurgle, thump, thump. The prunes were knocking. But Lanie wasn't about to leave her daughter feeling unsupported. "What? That's nuts! The whole court system has gone to hell, I tell you. They should make that man get a fucking job. Perry Mason never would have allowed this."

Spring groaned. "I'm not about to have the Perry Mason argument with you. Again."

"You could turn him in for selling dope," Lanie suggested, hoping to draw the conversation to the close. She looked fleetingly down the hall in the direction of the toilet.

"He doesn't sell. I don't even know if he uses anymore." Spring searched the entryway closet, and Lanie watched as she moved her collection of boas from side to side. "Do we own a vacuum?"

Lanie leaned back and laughed. "Where do you think I buy mine from? You think I put a rolling paper under my pillow and the reefer fairy pays me a visit each month?"

Spring gritted her teeth and stormed towards Lanie. "If you ever, ever say those things in front of Sam, the boys, or the social workers who pay me those lovely visits, I will boot you out so fast you won't have time to wipe the scuff marks from your butt."

"It's for medical use anyway. It's not like I'm doing it cuz I like it."

Spring looked at her sideways. "Insomnia hardly qualifies as a medical emergency. If you wouldn't play video games all night you might sleep."

Lanie crossed her arms and stared at Spring. "What crawled up your butt this morning? Sam still not giving you any?"

"No, but that's not my problem." Spring looked at the wastebasket with the shredded letters. "Things are difficult right now, Mom. My life isn't turning out anything like I planned."

Lanie looked from Spring to the *No Smoking* sign Sam had scotch taped up on the kitchen wall. "Whose is?" she asked and trotted to the bathroom.

TEN

It didn't take John more than one full week to realize that coming to Phoenix had been a mistake. The employment application ad had been misleading.

"Artist, my ass," he said when he discovered his job would be airbrushing off the wrinkles and veins of women who modeled in the penny saver ads. His artistic talents were being wasted. To compensate, he tried his hand at painting in his apartment at night. But everything he created was flat and uninspired. Not much better than his pictures of corn. What he needed, he decided, was a muse. But muses were few and far between in this oven city and he considered, not for the first time in the last seven days, going back to Samson.

"You could always look up Amy," Pete suggested helpfully on the phone. "I hear she's single again. At least get laid while you are choking on the heat. Kind of like a souvenir."

"You do realize that's your cousin?" John asked, too tired to even be disgusted.

Pete chuckled on the other end.

"Give it a few more weeks and see what happens. You were so sure about going. I'm sure whatever you are looking for is bound to pop up sooner or later."

John heaved an agreement into the receiver and went back to watching the cartoon network.

He had been certain at the time but maybe he had just been crazy.

Spring was summoned to Kimberly's office the moment she arrived into work.

"Don't hate me," Debbie said, handing her the neon pink post-it note. "...I'm just the messenger."

Spring entered the room and was relieved to see that Sarah was also there. Kimberly stood akimbo before her, like the warden of a POW camp.

"First things first," Kimberly said, never taking her eyes from Sarah. "Jane wants you to come up with an act to perform at the city centennial. Something lively and relevant. Maybe a dance."

"A dance?" Sarah's thin knees clattered together. She looked at Spring for support.

"Kimberly," Spring said. "Sarah can hardly walk in that thing, let alone dance."

Kimberly gave Spring a wan smile and tapped her chin. "I'm thinking..." She paused. "...Fred and Ginger."

"Fine. We'll figure it out. Can we go now?"

Sarah looked paler than usual. Spring touched her arm and noted that it was warm.

"Not yet. These promotional videos need to be delivered to all the VIPs in Phoenix. Today." Kimberly picked up a stack of DVDs from her desk and divided them between Spring and Sarah.

"VIPS?" Spring held up a DVD. On the cover was a cartoon depiction of Casey in a ten-gallon hat. In rodeo scroll were the words *Cover It Up or Cut It Out, Cowboy.*

"Business owners. CEOs. The Mayor."

Spring tried again, hoping Kimberly had a pragmatic side. "Can't we mail them? It will be cheaper in stamps than in gas."

"Jane believes that personally delivering them will help establish a bond with the community. Going as Casey is a good political move."

"As Casey?" Sarah's eyes widened with disbelief.

"She doesn't look like she's feeling good." Spring said, looking at her friend. "Maybe it's not a good idea to put her in the costume today."

Kimberly surveyed the woman. "If she is healthy enough to eat that entire box of donuts I saw her inhaling earlier, she's healthy enough to do her job." Kimberly pointed towards the door indicating that the discussion was over.

Though it was only May, the heat was unforgiving. Sarah panted as they carried Casey out to the car. "I don't think I can do this today," Sarah moaned. "I'm not sure what's wrong but I haven't been feeling good all morning. My stomach hurts and I'm peeing so much I should be wearing diapers."

"Maybe you should use a sick day and go home," Spring suggested.

"I can't! I've used all my sick days. And I wasn't even sick."

Spring stood in the parking lot wondering what to do. Putting Sarah in that costume would be dangerous. "I could wear the costume," she said, swallowing.

"What?"

"I could wear the costume. You can drive your car and I can be Casey." Spring bit her lip before she could take back the offer.

"Thank you!" Sarah said, relief rolling over her face. "I would have puked if I had to put it on today. It stinks inside. Like kitty litter that hasn't been scooped in a week."

Sarah's car was small and Spring felt claustrophobic. Sitting in the passenger seat in full costume, she tried to breathe in as much air as she could. But each inhale only succeeded in shrink-wrapping the material tighter onto her body. Sarah flipped through a variety of channels from rap to country as she sped down the highway towards their first destination.

"Ever wonder about life?" Spring asked, trying to push out her words through what she guessed was the mouth hole.

"You think too much," said Sarah, lowering the volume on a country song Spring had heard many times before, but never knew the name of.

"Thinking leads to expectations. Expectations lead to disappointment. Better not to think."

Outside the car she watched the metropolis whiz by. The city had grown a lot in the last few years. Smaller towns had melted together making it one massive landscape of adobe dwellings and superstructures. They were on their way to their first location, a private gym that Jane thought might play the videos while its patrons exercised.

"I hope this place has a bathroom. I need to pee again," Sarah said as she pulled into a long curved driveway surrounded by beautiful landscaping. A large sign with fancy black lettering announced *Members Only*.

Spring laughed and shook her head. "I guess the Universe has a sense of humor."

"Yeah," Sarah said, nodding to a curious woman who walked by. "A very mean one."

ELEVEN

1984

Spring glanced nervously behind her, sure that she would see the disapproving stares of her parents. All alone. She let out a relieved breath. Time was short. Someone would soon notice that she was not manning her booth and her father would be scouring the fairgrounds looking for her. But she had to see it. Her first close look at a real school.

Spring pressed her face into the chain link fence that separated her from the buildings on the other side. She could hear children laughing, talking excitedly, being told to line up for lunch. "Pizza day," a woman said. She could see artwork taped on the windows, testimony to the learning that occurred inside. She imagined the boys and girls with their crayons and glue sticks, making holiday decorations for their families. For their homes. It made her stomach swim.

A little girl ran out of the main building and towards a smaller one, but upon catching glimpse of Spring, changed direction and skipped towards her. Spring was about to run but her curiosity was far too great to leave.

"Hi," said the girl. She was wearing a purple jumpsuit and two ponytails secured by fluffy pink pompons.

"Hi," Spring said. "I like your jumpsuit." Spring reached through the fence to touch the material. It was soft and warm. Corduroy, like Daddy's jacket. Spring wanted to climb the fence and play with the girl but she didn't dare. Her mother was against public education.

"Thanks!" The girl beamed. "I like your dress too. All those flowers. Where did you get it?"

Spring paused. Lanie had made it. Lanie made most of her clothes. "At the mall. I had an Orange Julius, too." Spring had never been to the mall but had seen a few on the TV

The girl nodded. "Where do you live?"

Spring paused again. No one had ever asked her that question before and it made her nervous that she did not have an answer. She concentrated and thought for a moment. "In a castle on a hill. You can come there sometime if you want."

The girl laughed. "You're funny." She reached through the fence and touched the ends of Spring's hair. "I wish I had your hair."

Spring had heard that from some of Lanie's friends but never from another little girl and it made her happy.

The girl said, "I gotta go now. I'm supposed to be getting a Band-Aid from the nurse's office." She raised a leg and Spring winced at a small scrape on her knee. "Bye." The girl skipped off and Spring watched her disappear, pigtails flying behind her. She wished she could take her hand and go with her.

"What are you doing?" Spring jumped at the sound of her sister's voice. "Daddy's been looking everywhere for you. He says he's gonna use the belt if you don't get back to the booth. Show's starting in a few minutes."

"Can't you be the headless girl for a change?" Spring hated that job. It was a silly trick done with mirrors and nobody really believed it. She had to lie very still while people poked at her arms and tummy and tried to make her laugh or moan. Spring gave her sister her best pitiful look, hoping it would awaken something soft inside of her.

"No," said Chloe. "I'm too pretty to be headless."

Spring shoved her hands into her large pockets and followed, casting one last glance behind her at a school where a little girl with a purple jumpsuit was eating her lunch.

Spring returned home to see a familiar white van parked in her driveway. Jason leaned against it, snapping his fingers to the music of the Grateful Dead. Sam glared through the living room window and Spring thought if he concentrated any harder either the glass, or the vein in his right temple, would explode.

"Oh, fuck. I didn't think you'd be here yet."

Jason nodded. "Maybe you should get a calendar."

"Maybe," she sighed, looking around for the twins.

"I need to talk to you when you get time," Jason said. One leg was bent, propped against his van. The other rested on the ground. His hair was bound at the nape of his neck by a rubber band probably stolen from somebody's newspaper. His skin was tanned and his lazy smile was as intoxicating as ever. Even after all this time she could still feel herself give way to his maleness.

"I have time now," Spring answered, looking up and down the driveway for signs of her sons. "Where's Blaine and Shane?"

"They went to go see their grandma," Jason said. He pulled himself upright and whispered conspiratorially. "Between you and me, I think your mother has finally lost her fuckin' marbles. But we all knew that was coming, didn't we?"

Spring panicked. "Why? What did she do?"

"She answered the door naked. And you know me. I'm no prude." Jason scratched at his left arm. "But you might wanna tell the old lady to put some clothes on before she goes scaring the neighbors."

"Is that what you needed to talk to me about? Aren't you used to seeing naked people in that commune you live in?" Spring tried not to notice the pale hairs on his arms or the shadow of stubble across his jaw line.

Jason reached through the window and turned down the volume on his radio. "I think I'm gonna need more child support," he said. "The boys are starting to eat a lot."

"God. I knew it! I give you most of my money as it is. What do you spend it on?" Spring crossed her arms. "Maybe I will try and get full custody this time."

Jason seemed undisturbed. "You can try, but I think the arrangements are fine. If you think about it, seriously think about it, you will too. You get your freedom half the month and you get to play mommy the other half. Everybody wins."

Spring was annoyed. "I do not *play* mommy. I *am* their mother, Jason."

Jason shrugged. "Yeah. Whatever. But I know Nancy-boy in there isn't going to be thrilled if you have them all the time, is he?"

Spring glanced at the window and saw Sam's bare head still watching. "That may be true, but he knew this coming in. The boys need stability. That's what everyone needs."

Jason laughed. "You move in with the little yuppie man and suddenly you're Donna Reed. I remember where you came from. Do you?"

Spring looked towards the horizon but all she could see were the rows and rows of tract homes in the subdivision. The only thing that set one house apart from the next were the cars in the driveway. "I'm not that girl anymore."

Jason let that go. "Anyhoo, how did their appointment go last week? We never really talked about it. Their teacher says unless they get treated for their attention deficit disorder they won't be going to the second grade. Wonder where they get that from?" Jason raised an amused eyebrow.

Spring stuck her tongue out at Jason and he laughed, throwing back his head. The sun hit the little hollow of his neck and Spring had the urge to bite it. "It cost a hundred bucks." She decided to bring up the medication, parenting classes, and child protective services at a later date.

"No problem. I will try and spange some money together. Please try and keep them off the drugs. I hear they are bad for you." Jason made a kissing gesture, and swung open the van door. "Girl, it wasn't that bad. Us. Right? Better to eat Top Ramen every night than to live with Ichabod Crane here, I'd think." He closed the door and smiled at her through the window. "We didn't have a lot. But we had fun."

Spange, that was a word she hadn't heard in a long time. Most people didn't even know what it meant. It was homeless-speak for panhandling. Spring watched as Jason pumped on the gas several times and turned over the engine. The van coughed a few times before roaring to life. She nodded goodbye and turned to see Sam disappear from view. From inside she heard his voice. "No! No boys! For the love of God. Not Dickens!"

"You did what?" Sam threw his arms in the air, trying to make sense of what Spring was saying. He had originally planned on lecturing her about the evils of spending so much time talking to Jason, but in light of this new information, he figured it could wait.

"I threw away the promotional tapes Kimberly gave me to deliver." Spring's hair hung in her face and she was wearing one of those dreadful floral numbers with a hole in the armpit.

Sam cradled his head in his right hand, fighting back the impending migraine. "But why?"

"I couldn't do it, Sam. Do you know what it's like to trip and fall face first in City Hall while wearing a penis outfit?" When Sam said nothing, Spring stamped her foot. "Well, do you?"

"Settle down, Pookie," he said. "I'm concerned about you is all."

"People were laughing at me and the secretary at one of the places on Jane's *list* called security on me. She thought I was offering her porno!"

Sam snickered and made his way towards the dresser where he kept his Midol. "That does evoke quite an image. Still, that doesn't give you the right to destroy work property. Where did you toss them?" He popped two of the pills and swallowed without water. He never understood why Midols were marketed for women when they cured absolutely everything.

Spring glared defiantly and Sam wondered if he should offer her a couple of the pills, but thought better of it.

"I dumped them in the bin behind WCFG."

"Gah! The TV station!" Sam stumbled back and clutched his chest, feeling the pain in his head travel down his left arm into his heart.

Spring plopped down on the bed and started to cry. He sighed and sat down next to her and waited for her sobs to subside. "I don't think Kimberly will find out. Sarah and I made a pinkie promise." Spring held up her little finger which she had curved into a hook to show the seriousness of their pact. Spring laid her head on his chest and even though he was still angry he put his arms around her.

"What's done is done. I only hope you don't lose your job."

"I know Sam," she said.

He patted her head and squeezed her extra tight. "On that note," he said, pulling away from her. "I got a surprise. I went shopping."

Spring looked confused. "Shopping?"

"Yes, for you!" Sam felt under the bed for the silver bag he had stashed earlier, and handed it to Spring. "I made a special trip to The Career Outlet this afternoon!" He watched as she lifted each piece of clothing out of the bag and scowled. He held his tongue but when she balked at the silk scarf he could refrain no longer. "Try them on first," he encouraged, ushering her into the bathroom. After a short while she emerged in her first outfit. What an amazing transformation.

"Sweetie, I know looking nice is new to you but it's good for your job."

She was sitting on the edge of the bed in a grey suit and silver heels. Her décolletage peeped out and Sam went into the closet and pulled out a burgundy camisole.

"Try this with it. It will bring out your skin tone."

Spring looked up at him, dark circles under her eyes. "This isn't me." She lay back on the bed, rumpling her new suit. "This isn't me and I hate it!"

"Sweetie, come on. It's just a suit. It's not like you are wearing a clown costume or something." He flinched as she rolled back and forth on the bed, wrinkles imbedding themselves deeper into the fabric. If she

86

took it off and hung it up now it could probably be salvaged without a trip to the dry cleaner.

Spring popped back up and shot him an accusing look. "I know it's just a suit, Sam. But it's not me! I didn't get into social work to wear navy suits and silver heels. I did it to help people."

Spring was such a drama queen, always making a big fuss over nothing. He sat down on the bed beside her and smoothed the top of her hair. *Would it kill her to keep the conditioner on the entire three minutes the bottle recommends?* "It will be okay, Pookie. I promise you."

Spring turned to him, her blue eyes moist. Her bangs were askew and Sam resisted the urge to fix them. Maybe he could trim them when she went to sleep. "Do you love me Sam?" She tilted her head to the side.

"Of course I do, Pookie. That's why I want you to look and feel your best. And this suit is going to be exactly the thing you need to do that."

Spring sighed but said nothing.

Sam watched as she hung her clothes. *Who uses metal hangers anymore?* His penis twitched as she held up her new khaki slacks and button down blouses. Now, if only he could get her to cut her hair. Something short and sporty. Maybe a Dorothy Hamill. He waited until all of her clothing was secured in the closet, and decided that now was the perfect moment.

"I want to make you happy, Spring. I want to buy you a house. I want you to be able to quit your job. I want to..." Sam cleared his throat. "...Take care of your boys and your mother." The last word hurt but he kept his face steady and his voice from cracking. "I want to marry you. Please say yes."

Spring didn't say a word. Sam waited for a long, anxious moment and tried again. "Think of how good it would look to the state if the boys were in a stable home, Spring. There's no way anyone could take them from you with me as their dad. I'm the most respectable person I know." Sam straightened an invisible tie. "Bankers don't lose their kids."

At last Spring nodded. "Yes."

"Oh Pookie!" Sam was so relieved he thought he might pass out.

"Thank you! Thank you so much. I'm getting married. There's so much to do. We have a wedding to plan. Oh. And don't worry. I'm going to get you a ring, even if I have to work overtime for a month straight. You've made me so happy."

Spring stepped out of her suit and pulled her ugly dress back on. "I'm glad Sam. I'm going to go help Lanie with dinner now. What shall we have?"

Sam looked at her and crossed his arms playfully. "Sweetie, I think we both know what I want." He gave her his sweetest smile and even tried for a dimple.

"Mashed potatoes and gravy?"

Sam winked. "Now hurry, snookums. I have to do my prayers. And you know God doesn't like it when women or dogs are in the room when I'm talking to the big guy."

"You mean Allah." Spring corrected him.

He was in such a good mood he didn't even mind her correction. "Whatever. Now go make us some dinner." Sam pecked her on the cheek and watched her leave, listening as her footsteps disappeared down the shag-carpeted hall. When he was sure she was not in range, he closed the door and very quietly turned the lock. He opened his arms wide and threw himself on the bed, kicking his legs in the air like an overturned bug. What joy!

Their two years together were finally paying off. Two years of listening to her whine, telling her she looked pretty, and teaching her how to be a lady. She was going to marry him and he would come into his inheritance. He only had to ensure that nothing happened between now and the time of the nuptials.

He surveyed her closet, twisting his face at her rows of flowered dresses that were hanging alongside her newer clothes. He saw the way men looked at her when she wore them. It was the very reason the Creator commanded women to cover up from head to toe. "Virtuous women don't get raped," he tried to explain to her one day. "Because they show modesty and help men to avoid undue temptation." She had

88

scoffed of course, and refused to try on the head covering he had picked out.

"I could toss them," he said to himself as he moved the hangers back and forth across the rod. He imagined them in a large barrel, set alight. A good old-fashioned dress burning. But he didn't. He wouldn't risk unnecessary drama right now. Maybe they could slowly disappear, one short dress at a time.

How much longer do I have? Sam returned to the bed and did the math. A few months, maybe. Grandma wasn't going to hold out much longer. He reached under the bed and pulled out a copy of *Contemporary Bride* magazine. He lay on his stomach, his ankles crossed, and flipped through the pages. Too bad it wasn't Fall. An autumn wedding would have been nice.

"Soon, soon, very soon," he said as he caught his reflection in the vanity mirror. His nine little hairs perked up and he smoothed them back into place, running his hand along bumps and ridges. "You're a good-looking guy," he said, smiling and his reflection nodded back.

TWELVE

"So what exactly is it we are working on today?" Debbie asked when they had settled in at their table at Paradise Pub. Spring was still without an office and Sarah's cubicle was hardly big enough for Sarah.

Spring unloaded a box filled with bumper stickers that read, *Casey the Condom for Mayor. Let's Keep Our City Safe.*

"We have a parade to attend," Spring said. "Kimberly wants to make sure we know exactly what we are doing before we arrive. Come up with a *game plan.*"

"Lame," Sarah said, doodling on her napkin. "Who came up with this crap?"

"Rumor is Jane was sleeping with the PR lady," Debbie explained. Debbie, who had been working there the shortest amount of time, somehow had all the dirt on everyone.

"Look at these!" Sarah squawked, holding up a black T-shirt for the others to see. Written across the front in bold white letters were the words *Teens in Trouble* and on the back of the shirt TiT Patrol. "I call dibs on the penis suit."

"It's a job," Spring said, inspecting the T-shirt. "As long as they are paying me I don't care what I have to do."

"What a liar," Sarah accused. "You cared yesterday when I was carting you around Phoenix in the rubber suit. And I've heard you talk to the kids when you were a counselor. You care deeply."

Spring snorted. "Same as you."

Sarah leaned over, staring into Spring's eyes. "Do you really think I'm here because I care? I'm here because my husband is *finding himself,* which is code for unemployed. My mother knows Jane——God, I don't want to think how––and she helped get me the job. That's the only reason I'm here."

Spring folded her arms. "You're depressing me. Thanks."

"We could always work on the condom dance spectacular," Debbie offered in reference to Kimberly's suggestion of something Fred and Gingeresque. "To further push us over the edge. If we get a vagina costume we could do a splendid rendition of *anything you can do I can do better.*"

"This is what I say," said Sarah. "Let's eat lunch, have a drink, and check out the guys that come in here. Nothing to plan. I get in my costume, I toddle down the road throwing rubbers to the local youth, and you hold my hand. Meeting adjourned."

"Sounds like a plan," said Spring. She was getting a migraine and beckoned for the waitress.

"Let's talk about weddings." Debbie bounced on her chair. Spring thought about how pretty she was when she was excited. "A little birdie told me you are officially engaged," Debbie said, winking at the bread wrapper twisty-tie Sam had wrapped lovingly around her finger. "How are your arrangements going?" Debbie's brown eyes were large and curious. Sarah tilted her head to listen.

"We haven't made a lot of plans, in all honesty." In all honesty, Spring hadn't made any plans, but Sam had been thinking of all kinds of ways to torture her in the last 24 hours. *"Pookie what do you think about feathers on the bridesmaids' dresses? You know, like swans. They can move around in a circle and we can run through them. Wouldn't that be pretty? Pookie, what if I wear a top hat? Wouldn't that be nice? Maybe we could do your hair up real high, so we'd match. Pookie, maybe we could have a potato bar. You don't see them at weddings much, do you?"*

"We haven't set a date. I don't even have a ring yet." Spring removed the twisty and tossed it on the table.

Sarah narrowed her eyes. "There are worse things than not having a ring. Trust me. Like walking in on your mother giving your first husband a hand job."

"Ewww," Debbie said and Spring laughed.

"Listen to this. When I marry Sam, my name will be...Spring Wayne."

"That's hilarious!" Debbie howled, causing a few of the guys at the bar to look in their direction. One of the men, a good-looking, dark haired fellow, looked hauntingly familiar and for a second Spring thought she was seeing a ghost. Her knees began to shake and her hands trembled on the table. Maybe she was.

"That man over there at the bar. I think that's Trevor."

"Ooooh! Ex-boyfriend Trevor?" Sarah asked.

"Yes. Hide me. Quick." Spring reached down to pull a packet from the box to shield herself, but she over-guessed the reach and fell, crashing ceremoniously onto the dirty floor.

"I ain't gonna serve you if you can't handle your alcohol," said the waitress, dumping off the drinks they had ordered, two Piña Coladas and a Seven Up. Spring looked over at him again and sure enough he was staring at her.

"You!" he said, setting down his beer and leaping from stool. Trevor. Her Trevor. He was even more beautiful than she remembered. Rocky Road ice cream after a month of dieting. When he reached her he took her hand, helping her up. "My fucking God. How the hell have you been?"

Two and a half years," Spring shook her head in disbelief as she sat in the passenger seat of Trevor's car. She had her seat pushed back and her legs propped up on the dashboard as Trevor fiddled with the radio, settling on a station that was playing old British punk music.

"Yeah, crazy huh?" He turned to face her, lazily stretching his lightly muscled arm with the beautiful dark hairs behind her head. His jade eyes took her in. "You look great, by the way. Really, really great."

"Why didn't you tell me you were going to be in town?" Spring demanded, pulling her legs back and placing them on the floor. "It's not like you don't know how to reach me."

"I figured I'd give you a call when I got here. Wanted to surprise you." Trevor took her right hand in his, and put it to his lips. "Besides, a girl like you must have a boyfriend. Didn't want to make the old man jealous."

Spring lowered her eyes. He was right, of course. Sam would have flipped out.

"I've thought about you a lot," Trevor said, the warmth of his breath still on her fingers. "Every day in fact."

Spring met his eyes. Mere mortals should not possess eyes like these. It was the sexual equivalent of a nuclear bomb. "You could have written. An e-mail. A letter. Anything." Her lips pushed out, and she fought for control over them. She would not be a drama queen in this moment. When she had brought them back into submission she took a deep breath and continued. "I would have waited for you. I would have done anything for you."

The song on the radio ended and another, even more obnoxious tune, began. Something about frequent masturbation and pissing on authority. Trevor lowered the volume and pulled Spring closer to him. She breathed in his familiar scent, taking her back to a kiss two years ago. "I'm here now. And unless I miss my guess, you aren't married. Yet." Trevor leaned over, his warm breath falling on her face, stirring a wisp of her hair. He kissed her softly on the tip of her nose. "I missed you, babe. I missed you a lot."

Spring cupped her hand over Trevor's chest. The thump-thump-thump of his heartbeat flooded her with almost-forgotten memories. Lying in bed with Trevor on a Sunday afternoon as they planned their day ahead. Him telling her he loved her. That they would never be apart. Until...she swallowed the thought. She wasn't going to let it ruin this moment. "How long are you here for?"

Trevor's brow furrowed. He had three new lines etched in his forehead since last she'd seen him. "A few weeks, maybe a month. I'd love to see you some, if you have the time."

"I will make time," Spring said. Trevor went to kiss her and she fought every instinct she had, scrambling out of the car before she did anything else she would regret.

"How will I find you?" Trevor asked, rolling down the window.

Spring glanced at the Paradise Pub sign. It blinked at her with its fluorescent green scroll. It was lit up even in the daytime. "Don't worry. I know where you will be."

"What do you mean Trevor's in town?" Lanie furiously shuffled her deck of tarot cards as she sat cross-legged across from Spring. She laid out the cards before her in the spread of a Celtic cross.

"He's here. I talked to him. I sat with him in his car."

"That's great, honey. Now you can leave the spud dud and get on with your life."

"Mother. He's here. That doesn't mean he wants me."

"Oh, he wants you. I know it."

Lanie turned over the first card. The Fool. She sighed and patted Spring's hand. "Well, that's you. Now let's see what, or who, crosses you at the moment." Lanie flipped over the next card: The Devil. She laughed.

"Too bad there's not a Mr. Potato card. But this one is easy enough."

"Just read them, mother. We don't need your comedic interpretations."

"Fine. Say, whose the man that lives behind you. The attractive, mature man."

There's a mature attractive guy behind me? Where have I been?"

"He's thin. And doesn't have much hair."

"Sounds like Sam." Spring snickered and stopped. She really had to stop making fun of her fiancé like that.

"Definitely not Sam." Lanie scolded her. "An older man, with a less lumpy head."

"You mean Mr. McClure? Mother, he is not attractive. Have you had your eyes examined lately? He looks like a pod person."

Lanie sighed. "I was just wondering. Okay. Your past. The Lovers Card. You with the higher arcana. Can't you ever stay out of the higher Arcana?"

Spring shrugged. Though she had watched Lanie read cards her entire life, she had little more than a basic grasp of the art. She did know that the tarot deck was divided into two distinct parts, the higher and lower arcana. The higher arcana cards were supposedly more important or pressing. "I don't know. I have no idea how these things work."

"Well, you know what The Lovers card is, too. I don't have to go explaining it. It's obviously referencing you and Trevor."

"Can't we skip to the end? Do we really need to know what my thoughts and feelings are, or what I was eating for breakfast last week?"

Lanie leaned over, studying the cards and Spring noticed she was remarkably limber for a woman of her age and girth. "Would you skip to the end of the book without hearing the story?" Lanie flipped more cards over, muttering to herself. Spring saw several she was familiar with, and a few she had never seen. "Well, Jason is in the picture. The Moon. Might give you a bit of trouble as usual, but nothing you can't handle. But still, I'm not sure what this all means. You have plenty of men around you. But nothing is really happening."

Spring exhaled. "Sounds about right."

"Must be bad karma from another life," Lanie scolded her.

Spring watched as Lanie turned over the last card. Lanie gasped and clapped her hands. "Finally. A minor arcana card. But since it's in the final position it's a big one."

Spring looked down at the spread. The Knight of Cups.

"Looks like there's another man in your life now, Spring. And I'd say from the looks of things, he is here to shake things up a bit."

"But I don't know any other men."

"Doesn't matter. He knows you."

THIRTEEN

Sam and Spring had taken the boys to Chuck E. Cheese and Lanie had the house to herself. She put on some music, some good music, not that classical crap Sam listened to. Santana's Black Magic Woman.

"God, I miss the 70s," she said as she gyrated around the living room. "Those were the days."

She twirled, liberating her body from her dress and underwear, kicking her clothing into Sam's recliner.

"Woooo!" She let the music take her, rolling her head and swinging her hair the way the girl did in that movie about strippers she had watched the night before on pay-per-view. "Mama needs a drink." She danced her way towards the kitchen, past the large glass door that led to the back yard.

And there he was. Her peeper! His little head hovered between the slats of the fence. He saw her, blinked, and scurried away.

Lanie's smile snaked across her face. "Like what you see, big boy?" She fanned herself and shimmied. "Yeah. You know you do. You know you do."

The sound of the car pulling up in the driveway sent Lanie running to her muumuu and scampering back to her room. Didn't anyone stay out late anymore?

Sam held the door open and two little blond boys wearing T-shirts that said *Wasting Away in Cabo* and *Miss Pac Man for President*

tumbled inside. Spring followed, shaking her head.

"How the hell does anyone get kicked out of Chuck E Cheese?" Sam demanded, slamming the door behind them. The boys disappeared down the hall as Spring hung up their baseball caps.

"I don't know. They are special I guess." She smiled at him, trying to lighten the mood, but he wasn't going for it.

"Only your kids could turn Whack-A-Mole into a felony offense. Have you thought about what a good paddling would do for them?"

"Spanking? Sam, are you crazy? They're a bit rambunctious but not worse than the kids I grew up with. I don't think they need to be spanked. It's not in their best interest."

"Well, it might be in mine." Sam walked over to the sofa and flopped down. Picking up the remote control he scanned the channels, settling on the Shark Week Marathon on the Discovery Channel. He smiled and folded his arms behind his head.

"I could make it up to you," Spring said. She walked towards Sam, obscuring his view of the TV. She rolled her hips and touched her lips with her fingertip the way the lady did in that movie Lanie had her watch last evening.

"Pookie, you are in the way," Sam whined, straining his neck to look around her. Spring took a sudden step forward and snatched the remote control from his lap. With one quick click, the shark and scuba man disappeared. "They were about to eat the guy in the wetsuit," Sam moaned.

"You know Sam, call me crazy. But isn't it strange to you that we never have sex?"

"We have sex. Remember Easter?"

How could she forget? He had come to bed dressed in bunny ears and a cottontail, fastened to his bottom with safety pins.

"Sam, I can count on my two hands how many times we've had sex over the past year. Nine times. That's less than once a month. Doesn't it bother you at all?"

Sam looked around, his eyes widening. "Shhh. Lanie and the boys will hear. Do you want that?"

"Lanie is the one who brought it up to me, if you want to know the truth. She wonders why she never hears anything coming from our bedroom. I tried to ignore her, but she is right."

Sam stood his ground. "Damn it, Spring. There are a million other more pressing matters in the world than food and sex...the only two things you seem to care about." Sam surveyed her waist as if to point out that her vices were beginning to show.

Spring gaped. Sam's face softened and he patted the couch beside him, beckoning for her to join him. When she crawled up beside him he tenderly pushed the damp hair from her face.

"Sweetie, listen. We need to talk," he said reassuringly, as she sipped on the diet soda Lanie had left on the coffee table. "Lately, I'm getting the feeling that the only reason you are with me is for my body."

Spring choked, spitting soda all over herself and Sam. "I'm sorry you feel that way," Spring said, holding back the laugh. Sex, even at its best, was lukewarm with Sam. He was so fussy about the way it was executed and he had so many rules.

Rule 1: One must always wear a condom, maybe even two. They did not even have to be the good condoms, such as those that were lubricated or ribbed for her pleasure. In fact, the less money spent on the quality of condoms, the more money that could be spent on important things like mochas and books.

Rule 2: Foreplay is a myth created by a matriarchal society to enslave men. Those days have passed. Get used to it.

Rule 3: One must never kiss one's partner anywhere below the neck. Ever. You could touch someone below the neck, if you must, but your hands must not linger on any one body part for more than say, 30 seconds. You were being timed.

Rule 4: The missionary position is your friend. Learn to love it. Experimentation is bad. Woman on top is heretical. God might come and smite us right in the midst of lovemaking for even thinking of this maneuver.

Rule 5: The bed only. Enough said. Refer to rule 4.

Rule 6: Forget any semblance of after-play either. Or snuggling. Immediately after sex the male must rise, steal the blanket, and shower profusely until all evidence of physical intercourse has been washed away. Then the male deposits blanket back down on the bed for the female, and sneaks quietly into the study to read before going to sleep.

"Spring, honey, are you understanding what I'm trying to say?" Sam was waving his hand before her eyes, trying to bring her back. She had gone to that place she went whenever he was trying to explain anything important to her.

Spring nodded.

"What did I say, then?" He quizzed her.

Spring knew the answer by heart, even if she hadn't heard the speech today. "That lately you think I just want you for sex. And that makes you feel dirty and disgusting and demeaned. That I should be focusing my energies on more important matters. That sex is trivial and only for people with no will power and no ambition. And should only be used for procreation."

Spring tilted her head and looked at him for confirmation.

Sam tightened his lips and smiled. It was strained. "Well, most of what you are saying is true Spring, although I may have said it differently. The Lord wants us to have sex but only when we are married, and we are not married yet. If you do not have sex within the sanctity of marriage then you are saying to God that He did not know what is best for us when He laid down the laws of marriage."

Spring thought for a moment. "Do you think there's any chance that God might be a She, Sam?"

Sam seemed taken aback as if she had said the most blasphemous words that had ever been uttered. Then, slowly he smiled. "You are so funny, Pooks! You almost had me. Give me a hug!" He took her in his arms and patted her head reassuringly. "There, there, it will be okay. We will get married soon. I have a date picked out now: July 21. Then you can use my body whenever you want!"

Spring allowed herself to be hugged a moment more, and then released herself from his grasp in time to see a blur pass in the dining room. Two boys chasing each other using their fingers as guns and wearing their grandmother's underwear as face masks.

Fourteen

It was John's first outing to a real grocery store. Back home there had been only one place to shop, Earl's Beef and Hardware. Where back home there had been a church on every corner, here there was a supermarket. It seemed these people had traded in God for convenience. John had driven around the city aimlessly until he finally settled upon this one. It wasn't as newfangled and shiny as most of the others, which was why he chose it. He was getting darn tired of shiny.

Even this store felt overwhelming. The fluorescent lights gave shoppers a stark, zombie-like appearance. They stocked food here he had never seen before. He imagined his family would get a good laugh at some of it. Like pot stickers. That was a warning if ever he heard one.

Finally he found his comfort zone in an aisle filled with boxes of macaroni and cheese and canned chili. And then he saw her. The woman who smashed his truck. She was hard to miss. She ran past his aisle many times, dodging carts, skirting children, pushing through families. She reminded him of the White Queen from *Alice in Wonderland*...or was it the Red Queen? Running fast, yet getting nowhere. Her arms were full sometimes and empty others. He caught glimpses of her expression as she passed his aisle, a strange combination of panic and sweetness. He wondered what it was she was looking for. Finally, she ended up in the canned foods aisle with him. This time her arms were empty.

John tried to study her discreetly, his head bent over the cart while his eyes glanced up from time to time. She was scanning the aisle, her right arm raised and her index finger pointed. She seemed to be using it as a divining rod; it led and she followed, pulling her towards something, finally resting on a can of tomatoes.

"Ah, here it is," she said out loud, and John could see the smile on her profile. "I must have been planning to cook spaghetti for dinner."

John scratched his head and studied her more. Even beneath her sack of a dress he could tell that she was petite and curvy. The material hugged the roundness of her front and back yet fell softly away from her middle. Her arms and legs were tan, a natural tan, not like the girls who visited the salons back home. Her skin was clear. Her lipstick smeared out slightly over her full lips as if she had tried to apply it correctly but was in too big of a hurry to be bothered with precision, like a school child that refused to color in the lines. For some reason this appealed to his artistic nature.

"Spaghetti," she said. "I'm making spaghetti." She turned to him and smiled.

"Yes, I heard," John replied, shoving his hands in his pockets. He wasn't sure what the proper response to a statement like that was.

"You see, I lost my list," she explained, holding out her empty palm. "And I couldn't remember what I had wanted to eat for dinner."

"Oh?" John lowered his eyes. She had not recognized him yet, and he wanted to keep talking to her before the realization struck. "Couldn't you have decided once you got here?"

"Hmmm," she pursed her lips together and her eyes drifted down the aisle. "I hadn't thought about that. Maybe next time I will."

The woman looked in John's cart and gasped. It was a familiar sound from all the women he had ever known. His diet consisted entirely of hamburgers, frozen pizzas, strawberry milk and fruit cocktail. John waited for her to snicker or to point out the value of a vegetable. But she didn't. She simply looked up at him and grinned. God, what a smile. He scanned her hands for a ring, and seeing none, reminded himself that he was angry with her for not contacting him about his beat up pickup.

"Well, it was nice meeting you, um..." She paused. "Did you tell me your name? I'm sorry. If you did, I forgot." A rosy color washed over her cheeks.

"I'm John," he said. "John Smith."

"Oh my God!" She dropped her can of tomatoes and John bent down to pick it up as she rifled through her purse. After several minutes she produced a piece of paper and read the name. "Fuck, me." She slumped back against the aisle behind her, sending three cans of ravioli crashing to the ground.

"I was going to call you. Honest. My life has been crazy. I'm so sorry. You haven't called the police yet have you?"

"Well." John crossed his arms and shook his head. "...Where I come from, a person makes good on their word."

The woman continued to rummage through her bag. "I don't have any money. I have a credit card. And two packs of cigarettes for Lanie. You don't smoke do you?" She pushed the cigarettes in his direction and he nodded that he did not want them.

"What can I do?" The woman tilted her head, shuffling from one foot to another. "If you need your tarot cards read I know someone who will do it for free."

John blinked and decided not to ask what a tarot card was. "Look. I'm not calling the police on you. You seem like a nice person and I still think we can work this out. I got two estimates. Both were around eighteen hundred dollars."

"Eighteen Hundred dollars?" The woman's jaw dropped and her left eye began to twitch. He had seen this same expression when the local judge had ordered Pete to undergo his third paternity test of the year. "Where am I going to get eighteen hundred dollars?" Her eyes moved up and down the aisles as if bags of money might suddenly fall from the sky.

"Give me your name and number. I will call you and you can pay me a little bit each week. Okay?" He tried to sound reassuring. She paused and nodded, relief spreading across her face. He handed her a pen from his back pocket and she scribbled her name on the back of a receipt from her purse. *Spring Ryan.*

Of course a girl like this would have a name like Spring.

"I'll be calling you," he said, handing her back the can of tomatoes. She took his offer and he felt a small shock as he touched her. "I hope your spaghetti turns out good."

"Oh, it won't. I spend most of my cooking time with a broom handle aimed at the little button that turns off the fire alarm. But you have to try. You never know how things will work out unless you try." She took the tomatoes and smiled apologetically once more. Then she walked down the aisle and disappeared. John had half expected her to fly. Even though he had only talked to her for a few minutes, he knew that she was nothing like the people he had known back home. He looked at the name and number scribbled haphazardly on the receipt, and then folded it up and placed it in his wallet.

John went home and made himself a burger on the stove top. He did the math over and over again in his head. He finally decided on a figure. If he asked her for 20 dollars a week he would see her for a total of 90 weeks. He turned on the TV and watched Cartoon Network, one of the hundreds of channels his new cable service offered him, and fell fast asleep in his recliner. His dreams were a mixture of things, images from back home, the people he had met at his new job, and a pretty, blonde woman whose hair hung in her face and who could not remember what she wanted to eat for dinner.

Spring was still shaken from her run in with John Smith. Phoenix was such a large city that the possibility of meeting him there, miles from the scene of the crime, seemed incredibly slim. Of course, Lanie believed that there were no coincidences. "It's fate," she'd say, shaking her cigarette. "You got karma you need to pay back. You can't run from karma. Trust me, I tried."

"How was your trip to the grocery store?" asked Sam, tapping his foot and looking at his watch as she stepped through the door.

"It was good," Spring replied, unloading the tomato sauce and diet coke from her bag. She read Sam's face. It was the same look he gave her when she forgot to shave her legs.

"You didn't want spaghetti?" she asked.

"You were gone for over an hour and all you got was diet soda and a can of stewed tomatoes?" He rummaged through the brown paper sack to see if he had missed something.

"Oh, I didn't mean to be gone that long," she said. "It took me awhile to remember what we were having for dinner."

"Pookie," he said, drawing out the word. "We were going to have meatloaf and mashed potatoes and gravy tonight. Remember? I mentioned that to you this morning before I went to work." He picked up her cellphone from the table and handed it to her. "And if you'd remember to take this little gadget with you, we wouldn't have these problems."

Spring gritted her teeth. Maybe Lanie was right. Maybe Sam *was* an alien from the planet where potatoes were extinct, and so he was eating as many as he could before he was beamed back up. "We had mashed potatoes last night. We always have mashed potatoes."

"That's because mashed potatoes are good. That's why everyone in America eats them. I know you grew up kind of...different...but *normal* people eat mashed potatoes."

Spring shot Sam a look but he didn't seem to notice. "I guess I can use the tomatoes in the meatloaf."

He gave her a quick hug and kissed her forehead. "Thank you. I really do appreciate it. Now I'm going to go read in the bathroom for a while. Let me know when dinner is served."

Spring began defrosting what she hoped was ground beef in the microwave. It had been in the freezer for so long she couldn't tell anymore. She shrugged. Once it was in loaf format it probably didn't matter what it had begun as.

"I don't know why that man wants potatoes for every G-damned meal," Lanie said, materializing from nowhere. "No wonder he's so G-damned unhealthy looking. Anyone who lives on nothing but tubers is going to get sick." Lanie pulled the peeler from the gadget drawer and stabbed at the eyes of the potatoes as if they belonged to Sam.

"Mother," Spring said, rinsing each potato that Lanie peeled. "You don't need to concern yourself with what Sam does and does not eat. Let me worry about it."

"You're getting sick too," Lanie said. "You keep losing weight. And another thing," Lanie continued. "How the hell can you love a man who doesn't eat pig? Pigs are nature's perfect animals. Who the hell doesn't eat pig?"

Spring rolled her eyes. They had been over this before. "It's for his religion, mother. He can't."

"Well I don't see why Muslims can't eat pig. Seems silly to me. How long is he going to keep praying to Allah anyways? I thought he'd be through with this phase by now. I'm not trying to tell tales out of school..." Lanie leaned in conspiratorially. "But are you sure he's practicing his religion right? Some of the things he does seem...odd. I'm pretty sure Muslims don't need to shave their underarms to enter Paradise."

Spring shrugged. "When it comes to Sam, I'm not sure of anything."

"He should be a Krishna. At least he wouldn't have to shave his head," Lanie snorted. When Spring said nothing, she changed the subject.

"Heard from Trevor lately?" She asked, placing a pot of water on the stove.

"Not this again," Spring whispered, looking around to see if they were being watched. "If Sam hears you talking about Trevor, he's not going to let you stay here."

Lanie tossed all four potatoes into the pot. "It's your house too, missy. He might pretend to be Mr. Fancy Britches, but I know how little bankers make. Remember, I was married to one."

"He was a bank *robber,* mother, not a banker. And a bad one at that." Lanie pretended not to hear. "Anyways, Sam still pays half the rent. And he doesn't like for me to talk about Trevor."

"That's because he's jealous of him. He knows he ain't got dick on Trevor."

"Mother!"

"It's true," Lanie said. "If you faced facts you'd know I was right."

"Trevor left me. Remember? You're the one who said you get one chance at true love."

Lanie slouched and Spring knew she had her. "What about Jason then? You didn't love him but at least you got laid."

"I can't believe you'd rather have me shacking up with the tilt-o-whirl guy than with Sam. I'm not you, Mom."

Lanie huffed. "How are we supposed to make gravy?" she grumbled, rummaging through the spice shelf. "You have no seasonings at all."

"With this." Spring foraged through a cupboard, tossing aside cans of creamed corn and pumpkin, and produced a packet of instant gravy mix.

"Does his majesty know you use this stuff?" Lanie asked, dumping it into a saucepan. She added water and stirred, scraping a metal spatula across Sam's nonstick pan. Spring snatched the spatula away and offered her a plastic spoon.

"No, and he won't, either." Spring shot Lanie a warning look.

"So the gourmet doesn't know you been feeding him common fare. Shocking."

Spring swallowed. There was no perfect time and this was good as any. "I got even more incredible news. Sam asked me to marry him. And I said yes."

Lanie dropped the saucepan and gravy splattered across the kitchen.

FIFTEEN

"I'm going to see Trevor," Spring told Debbie and Sarah as she raced through traffic on their way to the event. "Am I being dumb?"

Sarah leaned over from the backseat. She was wearing the condom costume, which produced a weird waffling sound as the latex met the leather of her car seat. Her voice was muffled but Spring could make out most of what she said. "If––love––Trevor––you––talk to––him." Sarah exhaled and sank back into her seat, fanning herself with her gloved hands.

Spring accelerated, barely missing a minivan that was teetering into her lane. "Fuck my life."

Debbie spoke. "Spring. Honey. Look at you. You're nice. You're pretty. You're a hell of a lot of fun. There are going to be so many men who want to be with you. Honest. Have you considered that neither one of these guys are the right ones for you?"

This was an easy statement for Debbie to make. Debbie probably had her pick of men with her quirky good looks, sense of humor, and her upper-class background. "No offense, Debbie but your parents were wealthy. You get to marry pediatricians or podiatrists or whatever the hell Roger is." Spring smiled in Debbie's direction to let her know that there were no hard feelings. "I'm the child of traveling scam artists. What kind of man wants a woman like me?"

Debbie patted her hand. "A man who wants an adventure."

They arrived at the event and parking was a nightmare. People had lined up with chairs and sleeping bags the night before to reserve their spots for the parade. Cars were crammed into every available space. Teenagers held up signs that read *Parade Parking Five Bucks*. Spring handed one of the girls a five dollar bill and was escorted to a small lot four blocks from the main route.

"It's hot in here!" Sarah said, her voice a series of broken words through the costume. Spring felt bad that she had to endure that.

"At least you aren't part of The TIT Patrol," Debbie said, pulling at her shirt. "You think this is Jane's way of recruiting more lesbians?"

Spring and Sarah laughed as they unloaded the back of the car. "How'd you get roped into this, too?" Spring asked Debbie.

"I'm being punished, I presume. About a month ago I asked Jane—— in public——why a vegetarian like herself would carry a leather purse. Ever since, she has found new and entertaining ways to get even. Last week she had me calling local salons to try and wrangle free bikini waxes for a silent auction she is going to put on. Apparently not that many places are willing to wax hoo-has for charity."

"You wanna hold Casey's hand, or throw rubbers?" Spring asked as they made their way towards the start of the route. Sarah hopped uneasily beside them. A young guy smirked at the trio as he passed.

"I'll throw the rubbers," Debbie said, snatching the box from Spring. "I might even let you two walk twenty paces ahead of me," Debbie grinned teasingly.

"Gre mel fjos soolw I see," said Sarah.

Spring stopped and turned towards her friend. "What?"

"Neber-mean," replied Sarah, which Spring interpreted as never mind. She held her hand tighter and proceeded into the crowd.

John looked out the window. The sky was the color of washed denim, a noncommittal blue interrupted by splotches of blanched white. Below, the streets were packed.

John had never seen so many people crammed into one small area in his life. This made the Black Bird Festival back home seem puny. He thought about painting the scene but the figures below churned and squirmed in and out of view, refusing to stand still for his creative energies to capture. John was about to shut the curtains and give his full attention to the TV when he saw her—Spring Ryan, the pretty woman who owed him money. She looked to be holding hands with a giant, pink pencil as she navigated the street. He grabbed his shoes, slipping into them without bothering to tie the laces, and tumbled out the door. Even in the heat, it might be a good day for a parade after all.

The parade was a three-mile jaunt downtown. Traffic cops had closed off the entire road except to event-goers and concession stand vendors. Spring gripped Casey's gloved hand tighter as they maneuvered through the crowd. "You gonna be okay?"

Casey nodded, folding her whole body in half. Some younger kids who were laying on their mother's lap laughed. "That's obscene," said the mother and Spring smiled apologetically, scooting around her.

"I can't believe this many people care about Memorial Day," said Debbie, lifting her legs to avoid stepping on an old man snoozing in a lawn chair. "I don't even know what Memorial Day is for."

Spring surveyed the other participants. Most were veterans or somehow tied to the military. They wore their uniforms and donned swords and carried flags while the high school bands played patriotic songs. Some poor soul in a giant hotdog costume schlepped by and exchanged sympathetic sighs with Casey as they passed one another on their way to their designated spots.

"We don't belong here," Spring said as they found their space. They were shoved in between the Widows of the Korean War, and a group of Vietnam Vets who were discussing a possible connection between Hillary Clinton and Agent Orange. One widow turned on a boom box they were dragging in an old red wagon, and began a series of twitches and jolts. The others joined her, singing, dancing, and clapping along to *The Boogie Woogie Bugle Boy of Company B*. They walked, rolled, and hobbled forward, waving and smiling to the crowd.

"Ladies, meet your future." Debbie nodded and Spring gave her a warning look. "What? It's not like they can hear us."

A parade official motioned them to begin.

"Okay, our turn. Let's go Casey." Spring took Sarah's hand and led her down the street. Sarah took baby steps in the costume, supplemented by periodic hops, but they did not seem to be making much progress. Spring could smell the vets behind her.

"We are slower than the grandmas," Debbie complained.

"Can you move any faster?" Spring asked Sarah. Sarah paused and responded with an affirmative bobbing motion. Some teenage boys on the sidewalk made lewd comments and Debbie whacked them in the head with well-aimed prophylactics.

The going was slow and sweat beaded on Spring's forehead. She couldn't imagine how poor Sarah felt inside the thing.

"Okay," Spring said. "We have to get through this once. Then we protest. Take it directly to Jane if needed. One parade. That's it." Sarah sped up, almost tripping over her Keds. Spring held on to one of Sarah's hand and placed the other on Sarah's back for support. "Good job, Sarah. We're getting there." The road was sticky as the tar turned to mush under the heat of the sun and the girls slogged towards their destination.

"Crisis, ladies," Debbie alerted the others. "We are running out of condoms."

"Already?" Spring had packed at least 500 into the box that morning. "How did that happen?"

Debbie's face drained of color. "I left the box unattended for a minute. I think the grannies or the vets may have helped themselves."

Sarah chortled in the suit, flapping her arms out to the side in a penguin-esque fashion. Spring patted her back. "We'll be okay, Sarah. Conserve your energy."

A marker on the road announced that they had made it to the one-mile mark. "One down, two to go," said Debbie and the others nodded. Sarah's breathing was becoming raspy and Spring was getting worried.

She could see a water stand up ahead but wasn't sure they would make it that far.

"I think we need to rest," Spring said, looking around for shade. Alpine buildings lined the street but it was still early and shade was scant.

"I don't think we are allowed to rest," said Debbie, handing Spring a piece of stationary from Kimberly's desk with the words *Screw This Up and Die* written across it in angry black letters.

"How you doing, Sarah?" Spring asked and Sarah responded with a weak thumb's up. Two children emerged from the crowd to give Casey a hug, sending Sarah sprawling backwards.

"Get out of here," Debbie hissed, catching Sarah before she hit the ground. In front of them the widows danced. "I can't believe the grandmas are outlasting us."

Sarah said something but Spring could no longer make out any words. They came out crooked and pinched. And then she fainted.

"Sarah!" Spring fell to her knees beside her friend and tapped on her cheek. "Do you hear me? Sarah? You okay?" Spring climbed on top of Sarah and tried to peer at the girl's face through an eye hole. All she saw was darkness. "I think she's got heat exhaustion. Someone call 911." The vets scratched their heads and searched their pockets but the quick-thinking widows began yelling into their Life Alerts for assistance. There was a ripping noise near Sarah's feet and Spring turned to see a man tearing open the costume from the bottom end with what she guessed was a Swiss-army knife. He cut up the costume until Sarah's face was revealed. Her skin was red and her eyes were closed but she was still breathing. Spring heard a siren and saw firemen weaving through the crowd, making their way towards the women. One fireman finished removing the costume and called for a stretcher. "We are taking her to the hospital. Can one of you come with?" he asked.

"I'll go," Debbie volunteered. She leaned over and whispered to Spring, "I'll make sure she is okay." Before Spring could process what had happened, Debbie and Sarah disappeared in the truck.

"Thank you," Spring said to the man as she picked up the costume and pulled it in the direction of her car. The man nodded and picked up the other end and followed. "I can do it." She turned to let him know that it was okay and was surprised to see that it was John Smith. "What are you doing here?"

"I saw you from my window upstairs." He nodded to a tall grey building a block away.

"You saw me?"

"I can see the whole road from up there. You guys were kinda hard to miss."

Spring blushed. "You came for your money. Of course."

John shook his head as they hefted the costume into her back seat. Sarah's perspiration had weighed it down considerably, like a plastic kiddie pool that had not been fully drained. "That's not why I'm here. I wanted to see you."

"See me?" The words confused her. Why would he want to see her if it wasn't for the money? She was about to ask when her cell phone rang. It was Kimberly's number from the office. Just her luck.

"I better be going," Spring said, closing the car door as she got in. John stood motionless, watching her. "If you want, I can give you a check. Please don't cash it for a while?"

"Nah," John said. "But if you don't pay up I'm gonna have to keep stalking you. You never know where I will turn up next."

Spring tilted her head but said nothing. She drove away wondering how she was going to explain this to Kimberly, and if Sarah was going to be okay. She would go to the hospital now to check on Sarah and deal with Kimberly on Monday.

"I just have to get through a few more months of this," she said to her bedraggled reflection in the rearview mirror. "And then Sam will get his inheritance and life will get easier."

Sixteen

"Are they supposed to look like that?" Spring studied the boys who sat propped up with pillows on the couch, watching their third straight hour of *Murder She Wrote* with Lanie. Their mouths hung open and their eyes were frosted. It had been four hours since their first dose of Ritadate.

"They're fine," said Lanie during the commercial break.

Sam thumbed through a copy of *Pride and Prejudice*. "You worry too much, Pookie. Relax and enjoy the peace and quiet for a change."

Spring was torn. While half of her was glad they were no longer looting, pillaging, and starting small fires, the other half worried. "Maybe the dose they gave them was too strong." She read the bottle of Ritadate and shook her head. "Side effects include drowsiness, depression, loss of appetite, loss of self-esteem, feelings of inadequacy, and diarrhea."

"Loss of appetite?" Lanie stood up and snatched the bottle from Spring's hand. "Very interesting."

Spring offered the boys one last worried glance. "Mom, can you watch them for a while. I want to go meet Chloe."

Lanie nodded, still reading the bottle. "I think I'm coming down with some defective attention problems, too," she said as Spring slipped out the door.

"So what's up?" Chloe was sipping on her Diet Coke, clicking her long fingernails against the cheap plastic of the table. Chloe was so pretty and exotic-looking, favoring their father, that Spring sometimes found herself envious of her sister. With her high forehead and propensity towards curves, Spring took after Lanie and shuddered when she thought what the future held for her.

"This has been a really bad day." Spring scrutinized the menu, unsure of what to order. She was torn between a hamburger and a club sandwich. "A really bad life, actually."

Chloe stretched her arm across the table and gently took the menu from Spring. "I know. I saw the news."

"The news? What news?"

"Well, Rob and I were having sex on the couch and all a sudden he starts cracking up. 'What's so funny?' I asked, and he's like, isn't' that your sister giving CPR to a penis?' And sure enough, it was."

"I was on the news?" Spring felt her face redden.

"It was quite inspiring, really, and gave me some ideas on what to do for Robert." Chloe smiled and patted Spring's hand reassuringly. "Oh, It's not that big a deal. Everyone gets fifteen minutes of fame."

The waitress came to take their orders. Her face looked like one of Ms. Droll's inkblots. "What'll it be, ladies?" she asked.

"Two pork chop platters, mashed potatoes, spiced apples." Chloe ordered, handing back the menus. The waitress scribbled in her pad and plodded back to the kitchen, her white shoes squeaking with every step.

"I hate mashed potatoes," Spring moaned, stirring her soda with her straw.

"The condom gonna be okay?"

Spring nodded. "I think so."

"So, what else is going on? I know you didn't call a meeting just to discuss work, amusing for me as it might be." Chloe caught the eye of a rugged cop sitting at an adjacent booth. She pushed out her chest in his direction and he smiled.

Spring strummed her fingers across the table and waited for her sister to turn her attention back to her. "Trevor is in town."

"No way! Spring, that's great. Did he come back for you? You guys gonna finally get together?"

Spring's shoulders rose then fell. "I wish I knew. I only saw him for a few minutes and I haven't had time to process it yet. My life is a blur right now." The waitress returned with the two plates. Spring grimaced at her potatoes but picked at them anyway.

"You only live once, Spring," Chloe said, raising her fork to her mouth in a toast. "Live it up."

"There's more. Sam is going to inherit a lot of money if I marry him."

"Really?" Chloe said, shuddering. Her bosom jiggled enticingly and the policeman next to them noticed. "He would have to inherit fucking Fort Knox for me to marry him."

"I'm not like you, Chloe. You take risks. I can't."

"And why is that, sister of mine?" Chloe asked Spring. The waitress returned to their table with a receipt she handed to Chloe. "Look at this," said Chloe, waving to the cop. "That nice man paid for our meal and left me his number."

"Fantastic," said Spring, wishing that she could use her feminine wiles the way Chloe did. Things came easy to women like that. "Maybe I don't take risks because I'm the oldest. Adler's theory of sibling birth order."

"Bullshit! Save that mumbo jumbo for your work, will you? Spring, I'm gonna tell you something I should have told you years ago. I didn't because once you know, I will no longer be able to manipulate and exploit you for my own personal gain."

"Wow. How did I luck out and get you as a sister?" Spring worked her fork against the rubbery pork chop on her plate, trying to saw it in two. When she realized the futility she picked it up with her fingers and gnawed on it, glad that Sam wasn't around to witness this public display of barbarianism. "Now, what is it you are going to tell me?"

"Your problem is that you don't stand up for yourself. You let everyone walk all over you and make decisions for you."

"Do not."

"Really? Did you tell Trevor that you wanted more of a relationship than one based on booze and sex?"

"It didn't seem important until he was leaving."

"Did you tell the counselor you didn't want the boys medicated? Insist that they try alternative approaches for their ADHD?"

"No."

"Tell your boss where to shove that penis?"

Spring sighed. "No."

"Tell me you wouldn't take mama? Or that you wanted to order for yourself?" Chloe raised a perfectly groomed eyebrow at her, her lips forming a wicked half-smile.

"Okay, I got it. I'm a doormat. What am I supposed to do? I can't change my nature."

"You are too nice, my dear. Nice girls become everyone's bitch. You have to learn to *be* the bitch. I can teach you." Chloe grinned.

When Spring said nothing her sister continued.

"...You gotta make a stand, Spring. Figure out what you really want out of life and take back control. Until you can do that, you are always going to depend on someone else." Chloe paused, giving the cop one last sideways glance as he waved goodbye to her. "For now, I think you need to do one thing." Chloe purred, her eyes lighting up like embers on the log of a dying campfire.

"What's that?"

"Get laid, preferably by someone who doesn't come to bed in animal costumes." Chloe wriggled her nose and made bunny ears with her fingers over her head.

Spring turned her head to tune her out, as thoughts of Trevor's warm, naked body washed over her. What she wouldn't give to feel that way again.

Spring drove home, one hand on the steering wheel, the other dialing Trevor's number. A lazy voice on the other end answered.

"Hello?"

She was surprised. In the two years he had been away he hadn't picked up the phone when she had called once. She was sure the number had been changed. "Trevor...it's me."

"Hey! What are you up to beautiful?"

"I don't have much time. Can you meet me tomorrow? I need to talk to you."

"Okay. Sure. Where? When?"

"Paradise at six tomorrow."

"You got it, gorgeous." A pause. "I'm free tonight, too, if you wanna come hang out for a while."

For a moment she thought about going to him, driving dangerously fast, ignoring stoplights. She took a deep breath.

"No, not tonight. I wish I could, trust me. But I can't."

"Okay. Tomorrow then at Paradise. Wear something sexy."

Spring had it all worked out. She was going to the grocery store while Lanie watched the kids. If she was quick she could grab what she needed and still have enough time to see Trevor afterward. Sam was out at the bookstore so she scrawled him a quick note and left it on the kitchen table.

"Mom, watch the boys for me?" Lanie looked up from her video game and gave her a thumbs up. The boys lay with their heads on her lap while Lanie punched furiously on the controller buttons.

Spring had thought about it all night. Her one chance at true love was not gone. Trevor had come back into her life and she would make it right this time. As she pulled into the parking lot of the grocery store she looked down at her dress and wondered if she should be wearing something newer, but Trevor had always said he liked this dress.

She would make Sam a special dinner of meatloaf to soften the blow. Explain to him that while she was fond of him, she was destined to be with Trevor. Sam had to understand. He would want her to be happy. A sign at the butcher counter read *Ground Beef - 99 cents a pound. Limit one pound per person. Does not have to be consumed on the premises.*

The line was long and she sighed impatiently.

She felt a slight tap on her shoulder and she turned to look behind her. Dressed in a plain white T-shirt and faded blue jeans was John. "Always in a hurry, aren't you, Spring?"

"Are you following me?" Spring began rifling through her purse, searching for her cell phone. "Isn't this about the time a woman is supposed to call the cops to let them know she has a stalker?"

John shrugged his shoulders. "Suit yourself. I'm sure they'd *love* to hear our story." His eyes sparkled and Spring resisted the urge to sock him in the jaw.

"I told you I'd pay you weekly. You do realize it hasn't been a week, right?"

"Well, technically it's been several weeks since you ruined my vehicle. Do you know how hard it is to pick up chicks in a jalopy like that?"

Spring snorted, ready to leave when he spoke again, his voice an octave softer.

"Believe it or not I have better things to do than to follow you all over Phoenix. Ever consider this might be fate?"

"It *would* be my fate to have a bill-collecting stalker," she sighed.

"Well, Spring Rainbow Ryan, there are worse fates, I think."

Spring took a step back. "How did you know my middle name?" He really was a stalker. Maybe he had a trunk full of heads somewhere.

"Either I'm a magician..." He waved his hands in the air mystically. "...Or you were on the news."

Spring glanced from her left to her right. Several other people were looking in her direction. A few were whispering. One was blatantly pointing.

"See," John said. "You are a celebrity."

Spring stumbled and clutched her cart. "I feel dizzy all of a sudden."

"Next," called the butcher. Spring regained her balance and moved forward. John watched her and she felt a strange, tingling sensation. "What can I do you for?"

"A pound of ground beef please."

"It's ninety-nine cents today." The man smiled approvingly. He scooped his gloved paw through the meat and set exactly a pound on the scale. "Do I know you?"

"I don't think so."

His bushy brows knit together while he studied her. "You sure? I know I seen you before."

Spring heard John begin to speak but stomped on his toe before the words came out.

"Ouch," he said, laughing. "Why are you hurting me?"

"I know. You were on News at Noon! You're the young lady giving CPR to that penis." The butcher's eyes lit up with recognition. He rang the little bell on his counter three times. "Hey, boys. We have a celebrity here! Can I get your autograph?"

Spring left the line without her purchase as the other shoppers watched her flee.

"Some people like to be famous," said John, catching up to her. He handed her the ground beef, neatly wrapped in brown paper.

"I'm not talking to you. You were gonna rat me out."

John laughed. "No. I wasn't. But it was kinda funny to watch you squirm a little."

Spring grabbed a small bag of potatoes as she passed through the produce section. John kept pace with her step for step. "You should be leaving me alone. Can't you see my life is screwed up enough without some kid following me around pointing out what a freak I am?"

John blinked. He reached for her wrist, but she shook him away.

"Hey, I'm not a kid. And I never thought of you as a freak. I'm just not used to talking to beautiful women."

Spring stopped but he was already on his way out.

"Take care, Spring." His plain T-shirt and his plain jeans disappeared from her view, and for some reason she was a bit sad to see him go.

He called me beautiful.

Looking at her watch, she noticed it was ten minutes until six and Trevor would be waiting at the bar. She raced towards self-checkout with her bag of potatoes and a feeling that some part of her had been lost.

When Spring arrived at Paradise Pub it was ten minutes after six. Not only was she late to see Trevor, her time was also limited, as Sam would surely start to wonder where dinner was in a few hours. She looked at her reflection in the side-view mirror. Her time at the parade had given her a hint of a tan. Her lipstick was perfect, and her hair was combed and smoothed. For once she wasn't a total mess. A good sign. Before leaving the car she changed from sandals into her silver heels and tucked some Kleenex into her bra.

The place was dark, kept dim so customers could forget about time. It had been over two years since she had been here on a Saturday evening, but it was like she had never left. The two pool tables in the far corner were occupied by men in faded jeans and tight T-shirts, blue collar guys, complaining about work, lack of overtime, and the impending recession. Young women in restricted clothing with flesh spilling out in obvious places chatted up guys old enough to be their fathers. Neon signs advertising every known beer company winked erratically around the room, like uninspired Christmas tree lights. The juke box was playing a combination of country music and classic rock. The rest of the world might pass, age, change, decay, but here in Paradise Pub things always stayed the same.

She saw him before he saw her. He was engaged in an animated conversation with a man occupying the next stool. She took a deep breath and made her way towards him. She placed her hand on the back of his shoulder, and he turned towards her, beer frothing at the sides of his lips. She resisted the urge to lean over and lick it off.

"Hello beautiful!" He raised his mug to her and elbowed the guy next to him in the ribs. "This is the love of my life I've been yammering on about. Isn't she gorgeous?"

The guy nodded and sipped on his drink while Spring tried to control the vicious thumping of her heart. *The love of his life?*

Trevor patted the empty stool beside him and called out to the bartender. "Piña Colada for the lady, please. Two cherries. Pineapple. Whipped cream." He turned to Spring. "I miss anything?"

Spring couldn't speak, but she managed to shake her head.

"Good. And keep them coming."

"I can only have the one."

Trevor frowned. He leaned over and brushed the hair away from her ear and whispered, "Hope you aren't planning on leaving early. I got all night."

Spring closed her eyes and tried to picture Sam. "I don't have much time. But I needed to see you. Can we go to a table for a moment?"

Trevor raised an eyebrow at his friend, who nodded that he would survive a few minutes alone. Spring took his hand and led him to a small table in the far corner, away from the crowd. Their table.

"So what's on your mind, beautiful?" Trevor walked his stool close to Spring's, and she could feel his warm breath on her neck as he spoke. He was studying her, moving his eyes across her body like she were an undiscovered island.

"Why are you here?" Her knees were weak. Her body was reacting in strange ways. She had forgotten what he could do to her.

"Because you told me to be here." He winked and took a long swig as he hailed the waitress and motioned for another.

"No. Why are you here in Phoenix?"

Trevor nuzzled her neck and Spring closed her eyes. Sam. Sam. Picture Sam.

"There are some things I couldn't stay away from." He placed his hand on her knee. "I miss the desert. It's so...warm here."

Spring took his hand and placed it over her heart. *Tell me you love me*, she thought. *Love me and I will take the boys and we will run away together. I just need to hear it.*

Instead he grabbed her boob. "Honk, honk." He squeezed and Spring pulled away. "Oh, come on. What's with western girls? Don't they have a sense of humor?"

Her face tightened. He stopped moving and looked at her, a look Blaine or Shane had given her when they knew that they were in trouble but were going to try and sweet talk their way out of it.

"Trevor. Do you love me? Is that why you are here?"

Trevor sat and thought for a moment. He pursed his lips together and looked up at the ceiling fan. Spring dared not breathe while he considered his answer. Finally, he sat his beer on the table and took both her hands in his own. "Yes. I love you. I've always, always loved you."

She knew it! He had come back for her. She reached over and hugged him, both arms firmly securing him, pulling him into her body. Their lips met. For the first time in a very long time she was happy. Wonderfully, deliriously, deliciously happy.

"Oh God, Trevor. I knew it. I knew you couldn't leave me."

Trevor nodded his head and kissed her. Her lips. Her cheeks. Her forehead. Every inch of her face. His lips were so warm. "Yes. I love you."

Spring squeezed him tightly, feeling his heartbeat beneath the thin cotton of his shirt. Their beats synced up. "I don't believe this. It's amazing. I'm so, so happy." She wiped her nose on his shoulder and pressed his cheek to hers.

"It's okay, beautiful," Trevor said, pulling her head into his chest and running his fingers through the back of her hair. "I'm here now. Everything will be fine."

Spring collected herself and sat back. "I'm gonna tell Sam. Give me some time. I will tell him as soon as I can."

Trevor smiled. "Who's Sam and what are you going to tell him?"

"My fiancé. I need to think. I've got to go now." She looked at her watch. "When can I see you again?"

"Anytime you want. I'm always here." He opened his arms wide.

"I'm always here."

Spring dabbed at her face with a napkin and rose from her stool. "I love you. I'm so happy, Trevor. So happy." She kissed him on the cheek and gave him a final hug. "I will call you in the next few days. I promise."

Trevor lifted his mug to her and his eyes followed her as she went out the door. She blew him a quick kiss and ran to her car. It was getting dark. And Sam would be hungry.

Trevor stretched and returned to his seat by the large, bald man that had been nice enough to buy him a round earlier. "Hey Paul," Trevor called to the bartender on duty. "Another one, please."

The bald man next to Trevor wiped his mouth with the back of his hand. "Nice ass on that one. I wouldn't kick her out of bed."

Trevor furrowed his brows in an attempt to figure out who the bald man was referencing. "Oh, the girl that just left? Yeah, she's cool. Likes Piña Coladas. I never forget a drink."

The bald man nodded and Trevor stared at his reflection in the Miller Lite mirror across the bar. His hair had thinned some since last he had seen that mirror and he tried not to think about it. A memory dropped into his brain and he caught it before it scurried away. "She wasn't bad in the sack either, come to think of it." He lifted his glass and took a drink, swashing it around in his mouth before swallowing.

"Fuck, man. You East Coast boys get all the good shit."

Trevor shrugged and took another drink. "After a few of these they all start to look the same."

"Yeah. I hear that, man. I hear that."

SEVENTEEN

Spring woke up to the sound of Jason honking the horn. It played La Cucaracha. She blinked twice and looked over at the digital clock on her night stand.

6:15 on a Sunday. She was going to kill him.

Sam was up, sipping coffee in the kitchen. He liked his quiet Sunday mornings, reading the newspaper and listening to something called 'The Whipper Wills,' and would be annoyed to have it interrupted. Spring scrambled out of her sheets and felt around the floor with her toes for her robe. Finding it, she pulled it on and headed out to see Jason.

"What are you doing here so early?" she demanded as she opened the door. He was leaning against the doorframe, perfectly white teeth peeking out from a lazy smile, his sandy brown hair loosened from its normal pony tail. He smelled like incense and sex.

"Nice to see you too," he said, tracing her cheek with his index finger.

The intensity of his raw masculinity gripped her. Even when she hated him the sex had been good. Behind her she could feel Sam's eyes watching them. She tightened her robe and stepped outside, closing the door.

"I thought I'd take the boys to the zoo."

"Jason! You do realize it's supposed to be over 100 degrees today, right?"

"Not in San Diego." He grinned, deepening his dimples. Spring wondered how many women had fallen prey to those dimples. The itch was coming back.

"Okay. It's your week. I'm not gonna argue with you about things like...well, like your van breaking down in the middle of the trip. Or the fact that they have school tomorrow. Nope. You do what you think you must."

Jason winked. "Thank you. I appreciate it."

"I should warn you about the boys. They might not be acting like their old selves."

"What do you mean?" Jason set his jaw and leaned forward, a look of concern crossing his face.

"Well, the counselor recommended, among other things, medication for their hyperactivity."

"I thought we agreed there would be no medication. Why didn't you let me know?"

"Because you have no phone!"

Jason closed his eyes, putting his fingers to the sides of his temple, pushing in. "God. Jesus. I don't want my kids doped up. You know I'm against that shit."

"Jason, I was there, being made to feel like a total failure of a parent while your children ratted me out for everything I've ever done in my life and many things I haven't. After all the inquisitions we've had from the state over the last year you should be glad we still have children."

Jason shifted his weight to the other foot and stared off to the side. "I hate this. I fucking hate this."

"Well, you tell Counselor Klink then. Anyway, let me go get the boys." Spring did not invite him in. Sam wasn't thrilled when Jason roamed about the house. Jason liked to touch everything, including Sam's books, and comment on them. *"Banking for Dummies?* If I ever find *Sex for Dummies* I will send you a copy, Sam."

"Boys, Daddy is here. Get up. You are going back early today." The boys stirred in the double bed they shared. Spring could see their ribs through the thin cloth of the pajama material and flinched. The boys roused and obediently dressed and combed their hair. Mindless zombies on cruise control. Spring grabbed their bottle of medication and ushered them out to the front porch.

"Mommy's gonna miss you boys." She reached down to give them each a kiss on the cheek. It was a strange feeling when they stood there, not protesting her maternal affection. A pang of guilt shot through her like a bullet.

"They are fucking amoebas, Spring. What the hell were you thinking?"

"Don't blame me, Jason. You're the one who set this whole thing up."

Jason lifted each of the twin's arms high into the air and let them drop. Their arms flapped down towards their side, making loud thwacking sounds as they landed.

"Here is their medicine. I gave you half and put the other half away so don't worry about bringing it back. Please make sure they get no more than one pill each per day."

Jason placed a firm hand on each of their heads and steered them in the direction of the van. They slogged to their seats, not even arguing about who would get to ride shotgun.

"I guess we will see how it goes. The zoo should be easier, anyway. But not as fun."

"They want us to go to parenting classes," Spring called out as Jason buckled them in. "I'm not sure exactly how that would work. But unless we want to see Blaine and Shane living in the hills with rich parents who take them to theme parks, we need to figure it out."

Jason waved her off dismissively.

"See you next week," Spring said to her boys who stared vacantly past her.

Jason sped out of sight, Jerry Garcia serenading him out of the cul de sac.

She was about to go into the house when she saw her neighbor, a scraggly, middle-aged woman whose cataracts were so bad her eyes took on a misty river effect. She called herself Mistress Zara. Rumor had it that she had lost her young son to a car accident years ago. Lanie claimed that Mistress Zara was a witch, and not the good kind either, and gave her the stink-eye every chance she got. Zara's house was painted purple and she had socks hung on her trees like ornaments. The housing association had issued her countless warnings but as far as Spring knew no one had the gumption to do anything more. This morning Mistress Zara was racing down the road on a large tricycle chasing a cat.

"There are some strange people in the world," Spring said to herself, then went inside to have Lanie read her tea leaves.

Spring was guilty of something. Lanie could smell it all over her. It was thick as caramel and twice as sticky. Her thoughts were confirmed when Spring suggested she and Sam take an outing to Sam's favorite bookstore.

"I can have anything I want Pookie?" Sam scratched his head in disbelief. A smarter man would have figured out that this was a payoff for something, but without a book to tell him what to think, Sam was out of his league.

"Yes, Sam. Anything." Spring took her credit card out of the freezer while Sam salivated, rubbing his spindly hands together. Finally, they left, and Lanie could think about her plan. Though Spring insisted there were no peepers in the neighborhood, Lanie had been around the block a few more times than her kiddo and knew a peeper when she saw one. Lanie held up the red-lace lingerie set she had purchased at the fancy underwear store. It had set her back an entire social security check, but to catch a cat, sometimes you had to parade around like a mouse.

"Thongs should stay on feet," Lanie huffed, shaking her buttocks to release the strand of material that had wedged its way between her cheeks. Too bad they didn't make these in Dr. Scholl's. She sucked in her gut, donned Spring's silver heels, and sprayed on some of Sam's perfume.

"Come to mama," she cooed, positioning herself in the lawn chair enticingly.

What Lanie would do with the peeper should she actually catch him, she wasn't sure. She would worry about that when it happened. The sun dipped below the palm trees on the horizon and her eyelids grew heavy. She wasn't sure when she had fallen asleep, but when she woke up, the daylight had shifted into a grey nothingness. It was cooler out at least, though not by much. Lanie checked the back yard for peeper tracks, but seeing none, sighed, and stood up to go back in.

And there he was. His head popped up, then disappeared, a gopher in its hole. *The pervy little bastard.* Lanie was on him. She raced across the yard, feeling the heavy weight of her breasts pull like two cannonballs as she made her way to the back gate. She heard a thump from behind the fence and scrambled to unlatch the gate door in time to see him get up and dart away. Lanie had been correct. It was the attractive man with the hotrod that lived behind them.

"Wait!" she called, but he vanished down the alley, disappearing into the encroaching darkness. She saw the pale silhouette of his smooth head, but then it too faded away.

Lanie smirked, fingering the lace on her undies. *What nerve!* She marched to her yard, latched the gate, and headed back inside. As she entered the living room she heard Sam's nasal voice.

"Spring. For the sake of all that's good and holy, make your mother put on some clothes."

Lanie shot him a dirty look and strutted to her bedroom. She had an admirer. He didn't.

What did he know anyway?

Kimberly was waiting for them on Monday morning. Spring entered her office to see her face pinched and the toes of her black shoes scuffed.

"You made a laughing stock of this organization," Kimberly said, her mouth opening extra wide with every word. "Have you seen the headlines of yesterday's paper?" Kimberly thrust a newspaper at the trio and Spring read the words, *Condoms Not Safe For Everyone to Wear.*

"It's not our fault," Debbie said, looking Kimberly in the eye. "You sent us out in 100 degree heat and put poor Sarah in a wetsuit and you expect that everything is going to go okay? You're lucky there's not a lawsuit."

Kimberly glowered across the desk. She was not Debbie's direct boss and so held no power over her. But she could still torture the other two. She snapped her finger and pointed at the door, indicating that Debbie should go. Debbie gathered her things and spoke to Spring and Sarah.

"Remember, ladies, it's just a job." Then she left, slamming the door behind her.

When Debbie had left, Kimberly turned her full attention to the Spring and Sarah. "What have you girls to say for yourselves?" Kimberly had her elbows on the table, a sharp pencil held tersely in her right hand. When neither girl spoke Kimberly launched it across the office. It sailed like a rocket, grazing Sarah's hair on its way towards the wall behind them. Both girls flinched and Sarah trembled, huffing laboriously in her chair. Spring wondered if she were having an asthma attack.

"Kimberly. Are you losing your mind?" Spring looked at the small dent in the wall where the pencil had made contact.

Kimberly picked up her stapler and Spring raised one arm over her own head and the other over Sarah's. Kimberly clucked. "What babies you girls are," she said, lowering the stapler and pounding it into a stack of papers on her desk. "What? Did you think I was going to throw this at you?" A small dimple punctuated the end of her cat smile.

"...What we need to do," Kimberly went on, stapling papers like it were the most important task that she had ever undertaken. "...Is to decide how to deal with the situation. You made me look bad. And I can't have that." Kimberly slammed her fist into the stapler. "I've worked too damned hard...done too many things...to let the two of you louse it up."

"It wasn't our fault," Spring repeated, looking to Sarah for support. Sarah had her face buried in her hands and wouldn't look up.

Kimberly wagged a finger in Sarah's direction. "Out of here. I will deal with you later. I want to see Spring. Alone." Sarah scrambled to the door, giving Spring an apologetic look before disappearing into the corridor.

"Oh, dear God, you're gonna kill me, aren't you?" How would she do it? Pencils. File Folders. A computer monitor. Could a person die of paper cuts? She wondered how creative Kimberly could get with the office supplies.

"God, no. Have a backbone woman. But we do need to talk. You put me in an embarrassing predicament. And you owe me. Big."

"I owe you? What do you want?" Spring didn't understand.

Kimberly sat for a long moment, her lips puckered as she appraised Spring."Your hair."

"My hair?"

"Yes. What are you deaf as well? I-Want-Your-Hair."

Kimberly sat on the edge of the desk, one toned leg crossed over the other. When Spring said nothing Kimberly rolled her eyes and fiddled with her temples. Spring watched in horror as Kimberly peeled the hair from her head like the shell from a hard-boiled egg.

"You're bald!"

"No shit, genius." Kimberly positioned her bob back into place. "It's a condition I've had since I took some weight loss drugs that may not have been FDA-approved. And if you tell anyone you will be very, very sorry."

"But why me? You don't even like me." Spring tried not to stare at Kimberly. She felt like a gazelle in a lion's den.

"Dunno. Always wanted to be a blond I guess." Kimberly reached across her desk, fiddled in a drawer and produced a pair of scissors. "We can rubber band it off and cut across the pony tail. You can say you donated it to those sick cancer kids."

"You can't have my hair!" Spring tucked the ends of her hair protectively in her collar and backed away.

"Give it some thought. I'll even throw in an office," she said, tossing the scissors back in the drawer. "I might even be able to wrangle you a raise. Let's just say, Jane does anything I ask."

Spring shook her head. "You're a sick woman. Sick."

"Suit yourself, Miss Ryan. But know this; you are digging your own grave."

Spring ran for the door. "Sarah won't give you her hair, either," Spring hissed as she opened it.

Kimberly shrugged. "Like I'd want that mop. Please."

Spring left the room to find Sarah waiting on a seat right outside the office.

"How'd it go? Still have your job?" Sarah looked up nervously at Spring.

Spring contemplated telling Sarah, but decided against it. "Let's say I will probably be looking for another job very soon."

"Oh, God. I can't wear the condom outfit without you, Spring." Sarah was visibly panicked and Spring thought she might pass out again.

"I think you're off the hook for a while, Sarah. John sliced it like a fish to get you out of it."

"John?"

"No one special. Just a man I know from the grocery store."

"I'm not going back to that crazy woman!" Spring was adamant as she threw dishes into the sink. Sam studied her from the dining room table, scratching his chin while she worked.

"Now, Pookie. You gotta stay. At least until you find another job." He chewed on the eraser of a Number 2 pencil thoughtfully, contemplating their options. His eyes widened in an epiphany. "Maybe you can work with me! I'm looking for a personal assistant."

Spring thought of an existence where she had to choose between being bald in a condom costume, or one as Sam's personal assistant at the Islamic Banking Institute. All roads led to hell.

"I tell you what I'd do," said Lanie who was busy playing with a wind-up pig in the living room. Ever since she had seen a program on

TLC, she had been on a pig craze, insisting they needed one in order to be prepared for the end times to come. She had purchased a mechanical one to convince Sam and Spring how cute they were, but had only succeeded in annoying them instead. "I'd put a curse on her. Put her in the freezer."

"Mother. Stop it. You're the one who goes on and on about karma, and then you say things like that."

"It's only bad karma if they don't deserve it," Lanie hissed, scooping up the pig.

"In the freezer?" Sam scratched his head.

"You make a likeness of the person who has wronged you...like a voodoo doll. I make mine out of socks. Then you throw it in the freezer. Their life pretty much sucks after that. They get all skinny and lumpy." Lanie gave Sam a knowing smile.

"I don't think Allah would smile upon that," Sam said. "In fact, I think he'd be pretty pissed about the whole thing."

Lanie snarled. "Yeah, but he doesn't mind you having five wives? Some god."

"You two, stop it." Spring readied herself to stand between them.

"Maybe you could give her half of your hair," Sam said. "It's not like it wouldn't grow back. Did she mention what kind of raise you'd be getting?"

"Oh, you'd love that, wouldn't you baldie?" Lanie hissed. "Misery loves company."

Sam was about to say something cutting. Spring could tell by the way the ends of his lips twisted up in disdain. But before he could speak there was a knock on the door. The three looked at one another, and Spring went to answer it, expecting to be greeted either by a salesman or a Jehovah's Witness. But the man at the door was neither seller nor preacher. In fact, he was a pleasant looking man with wheat-colored hair, pale blue eyes, and faded old jeans.

"John. What are you doing here?"

EIGHTEEN

John Smith had not intended to stalk the woman.

Though she seemed to haunt his thoughts every hour of every day, he was not the kind that followed women home, however attractive they might be. But when she came into the pub Friday night, immediately after seeing him at the store, his first guess was that *she* was stalking him. Or at the very least paying off her debt. Of course, the very next thing she did was to advance towards the pretty boy at the counter and his hopes disappeared as quickly as a drop of water on a hot frying pan.

"It figures," he said to himself. No girl as pretty and as interesting as Spring would be chasing after him. It was just like home.

He drank his beer slowly, watching the scene. They moved from the bar to a corner table. She looking worried and talking excitedly. He looking horny and amused. She talked quickly and the pretty boy watched her, cracking a smile now and then and copping feels when he had the chance. And then she left. He wondered where she had gone and why pretty boy was not going with her. But pretty boy seemed to forget Spring the second she was out the door.

This disturbed John. How could anyone forget a woman like that? She was unlike any of the women he had grown up with in Samson, Indiana. And as far as John could tell, unlike any woman out here in the hot lands as well. As John got up to take a leak he noticed something under the table where Spring had been sitting. Something shiny. He left a few bills on the table for his tab and walked towards it, looking over to make sure pretty boy was not watching. He wasn't.

There on the floor where her feet had dangled lay a small diamond earring. He could have returned it to her at work. He still had the name of her organization, courtesy of a rubber thrown at him by a twitchy girl. But he wanted to see her alone, and soon, and with a little help from the internet he found her address and worked up the courage to go to her house.

"John," she said, surprised, looking behind her to see if anyone had followed. "I promised I'd call you. Couldn't you give me a few days at least?" She tried to shut the door but he wedged his foot in quickly.

"I'm sorry," he said, wishing he hadn't alarmed her. "I found this at the bar on Friday and I knew it belonged to you."

Spring took the stud and held it in her hand, looking at it like she had never seen it before. Recognition registered in her eyes and she grinned at him. A large, Disney Princess grin.

"You are returning this to me."

Behind her, two figures moved. A large woman with clown-red hair and a stick man without any hair at all. Both stood on tiptoes, craning their necks to see who was at the door. The large woman barreled forward, shoving Spring out of her way. When her eyes took him in she smacked her lips like she were about to have dinner and smiled.

"Who's this?" the woman asked, rubbing her hands.

Spring looked up at the woman, who stood a good foot taller, and stammered. "He, he is a guy I know from the grocery store. John Smith."

The woman extended a fleshy hand towards John, and instead of shaking it, yanked him indoors. "I'm Spring's mama, Lanie. Glad to meet you. We could use an attractive man around here." John caught the cutting look Spring gave her mother when she invited him inside.

It was an open space. The dining room, kitchen, and living room were delineated only by a small bar and floor coverings. And it was bright. Every bulb in the place was lit. John squinted as his eyes fought for adjustment. The thin man advanced and John offered his hand.

"You must be Spring's father then."

The man turned a shade of red John had never seen before and John knew that he had been mistaken.

"No. I'm not Spring's father. I'm Spring's fiancé, Sam Wayne."

Lanie snorted as she retreated. "As if I couldn't do better than this jackass."

For a minute John could think of nothing to say. He had been sure the pretty boy was her boyfriend. He forced himself to say the words. "Nice to meet you, Sam."

Sam appraised John in the same manner Pete appraised his competition at the bars. After a moment Sam smiled and shook his head. For once John was thankful for his nondescript looks. Sam didn't view him as any threat at all.

"Why don't you have a seat, John?" Spring motioned towards a chair next to her at the dining room table. Sam did not look pleased as John settled in beside her.

"So, sweetie. Where did you say you know John from?" Sam skillfully delivered three glasses of soda to the table, followed by three neon bendy straws, and sat himself on the other side of Spring. Spring dipped a straw into her drink and took a long sip before answering.

"The grocery store. We both shop at the Food Fortress."

Sam lounged lazily in his chair, propping his head in his clasped hands. "No little woman around to shop for you, eh? Now that's too bad. Every home needs a woman. It's in the Bible and the Koran. Of course, sometimes more than one woman in those days." Sam laughed. "Oh, but who would want all that trouble? One female in the house is more than I can handle." Sam gave Lanie a disdainful sideways look that she didn't seem to notice.

John nodded and said nothing. The soda was flat but he drank it anyway. The three sat in such complete silence that John could hear the tick tock of the grandfather clock which looked strangely out of place in this fluorescent cave.

"He found my earring," Spring finally spoke, smiling sweetly at Sam. "At the store. Wasn't that nice?" She looked at John, her eyes begging him to confirm the story. He nodded in agreement.

"Sweetie. Why would you wear your diamond studs to the grocery store? You know those are for special occasions only." He leaned over and patted her head. Spring looked down at her hands on the table but did not answer. "Not a big deal," Sam picked up again. "Just remember. Diamonds are forever, but only if you don't lose them."

"Got it," she said and laughed a nervous laugh. "It's my first pair of diamonds. Sam bought them for me on a business trip to Mexico. I'm still learning to take care of them."

Sam elbowed John. "Good deals down in Mexico if you know who to talk to. Don't suppose you've ever been south of the border?"

John shook his head that he had not, and Sam continued.

"Well, let me know if you ever plan to go. I can tell you where to get the best prices. The trick is to haggle. If you don't haggle you're gonna get screwed. It's public knowledge. And don't let those little kids with the big weepy eyes selling chicklets fool you. They rake in the dough. A few American dollars will buy them a month's rent in one of their huts."

Spring's face reddened and John changed the subject. "So how did you two meet?"

"Us?" Sam sat up and puffed his chest out. "I saw her wandering around a book store. She had just been dumped and was looking for a book on healing. Poor thing, couldn't find the non-fiction section, let alone the self-help books. There's irony there." Sam looked at Spring and gave her a soft pat on the knee. "I guided her to my personal favorites. The rest is history."

Lanie snorted but Sam ignored her.

"...How about you two? Tell me about your cute meet."

"Our cute what?" Spring asked, knitting her eyebrows together.

"The cute way you two met in the grocery store. It happens in all the best movies and stories." Sam leaned forward, meeting John's eyes. John felt immediately uncomfortable.

"It wasn't that cute. We just happened to be in the same checkout line. She dropped an earring and a business card. And I tracked her down. Not much of a story."

Sam scrunched his lips together, analyzing the story. "Well, I can see Spring dropping things. It's not that cute, you're right." He leaned over and squeezed her. "Maybe I should accompany you shopping more, my dear. Just to make sure you don't lose anything else." Sam walked into an adjoining room and returned with a book. *The Art of War*. He sat it on the table and opened it up to a random page, reading to himself. When he caught John staring at him he closed the book. "Sorry to be a bad host," said Sam. "But I've been itching to read this book all week." He tapped his fingers on the table as he studied John.

"It's a good book," said John, and Sam looked incredulous.

"No offense, but you don't seem like the reading type. I'm a knowledge fiend. Knowledge is the only thing that matters. It's all I live for."

"I'm an artist myself," said John. He searched his pockets until he found the business cards he had recently purchased from Kinkos announcing that he was starting his own business. He offered one to Sam. "I used to read more, when I was a kid. Now, I just can't find the time. Reading takes away from real life."

Sam furrowed his brow, creating a deep V in his forehead. "An artist huh? I don't suppose you live in a van?"

Lanie returned from the living room cradling something that looked like a rat. John steeled himself against the rodent, not wanting to give Sam any further ammunition.

"John. Have you ever thought about owning a pig?" Lanie asked as casually as if she were commenting on the weather. She slid into the chair next to him and tossed the creature onto the floor. John was relieved to see that it was nothing more than a windup toy. She then produced a brochure which took up most of the table.

"Mother!" Spring said. "Don't do that to the guests."

"It's okay," John said, patting Spring's hand. He could feel Sam's eyes burn into his skull. "No. I've never thought of owning a pig. Should I?"

"She likes pigs," Spring explained. John felt the warmth of her breath on his neck and it sent shivers down his spine. She could like flying monkeys for all he cared, so long as Spring would continue to sit near him. "She is trying to convince us to buy one as a pet, and then when Armageddon comes we can eat him."

"That's horrible" he whispered as Lanie pointed out the pros and cons of each variety of pig.

"Don't worry, it will never happen. We can't afford Lanie, let alone a pig."

"I heard that," said Lanie, wadding up the brochure when she realized that no one was paying attention. "You just wait till the end days, then you will wish you would have listened to me!"

"You have an accent," Sam said, breaking into the conversation. "Where are you from?"

John chewed on the bottom of his lip. Small talk was not his forte. Back home everyone knew everything about him and he wasn't used to explaining himself. "Samson, Indiana. I came out here for work."

"A Midwesterner!" Sam seemed genuinely delighted. "Aurora, Illinois," he said, tapping his chest in a 'Me, Tarzan' sort of way. "But I've been to Samson. Shithole of the world. Bet you're glad to be out of there."

"Sam!" Spring's jaw dropped in disbelief.

"No, he's right," John said, before a fight erupted. "Not much going on in Samson. But my job didn't end up working out, so I might end up going back."

Sam nodded and smiled.

"It is still rude," Spring said, and went back to her drink. She dipped her straw into her soda and blew bubbles the way John had done as a child with his chocolate milk. Without saying a word Sam reached over and took the straw from her and set it out of her reach. Spring extended her bottom lip but said nothing.

"Here, take this one." John handed his bendy straw to Spring and she smiled widely in return. The look Sam shot him let John know that he had crossed the line.

"It's getting late," said Sam. "Spring needs to get up early."

John looked at the clock behind him. It was almost eight.

"Yes," said Spring, rising from her chair. "I have to do my homework and go to bed or I won't get to go to prom."

John forced a laugh, but he was glad to be told to go. Why had he thought coming here would be a good idea?

Sam draped his arm protectively around Spring's shoulders. "I'm sure a bachelor like you has better things to do than to hang out with us old folks, anyway."

"Old? You can't be a day older than twenty-six," said John.

"Twenty-six?" Sam straightened. "Some people say I look young for my age, but I assure you I haven't seen twenty-six in quite a while."

John grinned, nodding to Spring. "I meant her."

Sam gave Spring a playful squeeze. "Spring will be thirty in a few months. All downhill from there. Right, babe?" Spring cringed and sunk in his grasp.

"Thirty? Wow. Well, you look great," he said.

Spring looked as if she wanted to run.

"...I mean really, really great."

"Especially after she popped out them twins." Sam patted her belly. "She still has a little work to do but she'll get there. I'm working on a fitness plan for her."

John felt his fists tighten and he did his very best not to punch the stickman. He felt he better go before he did something stupid.

"Well. Nice meeting you, Lanie and Sam. And good to see you again, Spring. I uh, well, goodnight." John turned towards the door and let himself out.

He drove home, listening to the country music station. Spring was thirty-years-old, had twins, and was engaged. He scratched his head curiously.

"I'm a long way from Indiana," he said.

But no one answered.

"He's cute," said Lanie that evening, when she and Spring were alone on the back patio. Sam had gone to bed early with one of his migraines.

"He's just a guy I owe money to."

"Aren't they usually supposed to pay you?" Lanie laughed at her joke and stopped when she realized Spring didn't find it funny.

"Mother. Please. Besides, I have a man. Two. Maybe."

"So that means you talked to Trevor?"

"Yes. We talked some at the Pub Friday. That's where I lost the earring." Spring looked down at her hands to avoid Lanie's questioning eyes.

"What did he say? Does he want you back? Does he have a guest room?"

Spring laughed. "Always thinking of me, aren't you, Mom?"

Lanie huffed. "What's wrong with me wanting a cut of the action? After all, I gave you life. And excitement."

"Yeah," Spring said. She looked out at the stars visible even with the glare of the city lights. It was one of the reasons she loved Arizona. When she was a kid and every town looked like the next at night, she remembered passing through Arizona with its millions of stars. "Years of living as a carnie would certainly seem exciting."

"They were!" Lanie defended herself. "How many other girls do you know that got tutored by a bearded woman?"

Spring had to laugh. "Well, Mom, you got me there. I can safely say that I don't know anyone else who had the fortune of that experience."

Lanie took a long puff on her cigarette and Spring watched the orange ember trace a trail through the dark. It was a wonder the woman wasn't carting an oxygen tank around by now.

"Mom. Was I that bad of a kid?"

Lanie did a double take. "What the hell are you talking about?"

"Dad leaving. He made me a promise he would always be there for me. But he wasn't. I used to think that if I had been a better kid he would have stayed."

Lanie froze, her large pale form a mountainous silhouette in the night. She took a deep breath and exhaled, pausing to think. "No, Spring, you weren't a bad kid. I'm sorry you think that."

"Then why, Mom? Why did he leave?"

Lanie dropped the cigarette, still only half-smoked, and stamped it out with her foot. She hoped Sam wouldn't wash it away with the hose in the morning. "It wasn't you. Hell, it wasn't me. Some men aren't fit to be tied down to one place. Or one person." Lanie looked at Spring and squeezed her hand. "I'm sorry, baby. I wish I could tell you more. Fortune tellers don't really have all the answers, you know? But I do know it was never you. You were his girl."

Lanie leaned over in the chair, her face in her hands, and for the first time in Spring's life she heard her mother cry.

"Don't cry, Mom. It's going to be okay."

Sam lay in bed, head tucked under the covers. He didn't really have a headache. He just needed time to think.

So this was the reason Spring was acting so peculiar and unmanageable lately. This young punk kid who didn't know the first thing about life was here to take away all that he had worked for. Sam rubbed his temple as the image of John Smith appeared in his mind's eye. Something had to be done.

Not for the first time, he thought of packing it up and moving on. Maybe she wasn't worth all the trouble. But it was too close to the deadline. His grandmother's health was failing and he couldn't take any chances. If he played his cards right, he would inherit a library...an entire fucking library filled with more books than one dared to dream about, collected by his grandfather from all over the world. Endless knowledge that in the wrong hands could be squandered, or worse, lost. It was a modern day Alexandria and he wasn't going to let this kid ruin things. He would marry Spring soon and take her to see Grandma Rosary. She would grant her blessing and Spring would ask, on their behalf, for their inheritance.

In theory it wasn't that fricken' hard. But it sure was becoming that way.

He had to act and he had to act now. An idea popped into his brain and he quickly got out of bed before he could talk himself out of it.

Nineteen

1986

Ernest sat on the queen-sized bed, its mattress old and tired, sagging beneath his slight weight. Lanie hadn't been particularly pleased about this motel, but it was better than sleeping in the trailer again. Times were hard. People weren't coming to carnivals like they used to. Theme parks were all the rage and the news declared them 'safer.' This made Lanie indignant. In all her days on the road she had only seen two accidents. Granted, one of them had taken a man's legs, but that was still a pretty good track record.

"We can't keep doing this, Lanie." Ernest sighed.

Lanie tried to ignore him as she manually flipped through the channels. Almost all static. Nothing was ever fucking on!

"You're insane," she hissed, trying not to wake the girls. Chloe and Spring lay motionless on the twin bed, spooned up together for warmth. She could hear them breathing, the deep restful inhalations of the sleeping. "You don't just walk into a bank and take money. It's stupid. And illegal."

Ernest smirked. "It's a small-town bank. I've been there a dozen times over the last few years. The security guard is basically Don Knotts. I get the money and we run away to Mexico and live like royalty."

She looked at him, her mouth agape. One thing that TV had taught her was that criminals always get caught. "Ernest, I've followed you all these years, but I can't do this. We have kids to think about. We can't be on the lam!"

Ernest punched his hand into the bed, trying to put a hole in the soggy mattress. It hesitated but bounced back reluctantly. "We are already on the fucking lam, in case you haven't noticed! Half the f'ing carnies are 'on the lam!.' I didn't join because it was 'fun,' goddamnit. I'm tired of running. I just wanna get enough money and settle down. This is my only fucking shot. Can't you understand that, woman?"

They had been arguing about this for a week now, and Lanie thought he would forget about it, the way he forgot about most things. But he seemed insistent. She slumped down on the bed and placed her fingers between her eyes, trying to ease the pressure that was building in her head. He was serious. He really wanted to rob a bank.

"Ernest," she said. "I love you and I want you to be happy. If you aren't happy here you need to go and find what gives your life meaning. I had always hoped it was me and the girls, but I see now it's not. I love you and wish you well, but I can't be any part of this." Lanie looked at her husband, absorbing him, knowing this might be the last time she ever saw him. He said nothing in response as he grabbed his duffle bag, already packed. He walked to the girls' bed and blew them each a kiss and then made his way to the door. He was really going. He smiled at her, opened the door, and left.

That was the last she heard from him, until a few weeks later when he made headlines in a local newspaper for attempted robbery. He was now serving many years in state prison.

When the girls awoke that next morning she told them their father had gone to see a sick relative, but when Spring saw her father on the newspaper as well, she turned to Lanie with a look that said she hated her. And it was three months before Spring said another word to Lanie, or anyone, for that matter.

Lanie lay naked on the top of her bed, three fans blasting air over her body. She had always looked forward to this time of life, the transition from motherhood to crone-dom. But her ascent into sage-hood wasn't going as smoothly as she had hoped. Besides the hot flashes and the strange cravings and the weird fluctuations in libido (she would never admit this to a single soul but one day she had even found Sam appealing as he was stirring something in a bowl), there lay a nagging feeling deep down inside of her.

She didn't feel like a woman anymore. Her eggs were hatched. She was on the other side now, beyond the line that separated the fertile from the unfertile, those who could produce and those whose time had passed. She would never have another baby again. Ever.

She willed up memories of Chloe and Spring when they were infants, tiny bundles of pink flesh, wrapped up like flower bouquets in knitted blankets. They smelled so good. Well, most of the time. And they looked up at her with something akin to godliness as they suckled her, wrapping small fingers around her own. Even her grandchildren did not show her that much love. No one had ever shown her that much love––the love of a child in its first years of life.

She squinted, trying to wring out the few memories of her own mother, but like a dried up lemon, nothing was there to juice. She had left Lanie in foster care when she was six and Lanie must have purposely destroyed any images she had of the woman. Either that, or she was getting senile.

"It all changes when they grow up," she said, returning her attention to Spring and Chloe. "All that admiration, gone in the wink of an eye the first time you forget a holiday." Lanie rolled onto her side, letting the fans beat against her back. The air hit a mole (that must be new) and created a peculiar pulsing sensation. "...We're all judge and jury of our parents."

An image of Spring's face in the dark beside her, asking if she had really been a bad kid.

There was a knot in her stomach, a memory knocking, wanting to be let in. Lanie tried to clear her mind and practice her meditation, but this one was insistent.

"Your father couldn't handle you, and neither can I." She had said this once, when Spring was in the throes of adolescent rebellion. She hadn't meant it, of course. Hadn't even remembered it until Spring had asked about their father earlier. The problem with words was once you said them you couldn't take them back. They hung in the Universe forever like wet sheets that never quite dried.

The real truth was that she wasn't able to cope with raising two daughters on her own. And the fact that their father was never, ever coming back, and she might be alone for the rest of her life. For all her hellraising about women's lib in the 60s, she hated to admit that being without a man was the scariest thing she could ever imagine.

"What I'd give for a do-over, learn a real trade, set a good example for the girls." Lanie gritted her teeth. The mole on her back danced in the wind. Maybe she should get it looked at. "I'm too old to cry over spilt milk now," she said, reaching out to stroke her pig. His plastic, hairless body gave her some odd comfort. It wasn't a baby, or even real, but it was...something.

It was going to be a long night. She wished she had more of Jason's insomnia medicine, but it was gone the first day he had dropped it by. Sleep. She needed sleep.

She was about to shut her eyes and give it a try when a flicker of pale light in the window caught her gaze. At first she almost ignored it, thinking it was just a ghost. But this ghost had an awfully big head. She squinted in the dark to make it out, and then her eyes grew large as saucers.

TWENTY

"Pookie, wake up. Pookie?"

Spring pulled the pillow over her head in an attempt to drown out Sam's voice and go back to sleep. Sam hastily removed the pillow and the room was suddenly flooded with light. She had been in a dark, dreamless sleep and wasn't ready for the morning quite yet.

"Sweetie, I don't want to alarm you but there's a strange man in our house."

"What?" Spring sat up, dropping the pillow back onto the bed and pulling the sheet to her chest. "Is Mom alright?"

"I don't know. I saw him in the kitchen and tiptoed back in here to tell you."

"What did you want me to do about it?" she asked. Sam was the man. Why wasn't he handling this?

He spread his palm helplessly and looked at her.

"Good, God. Fine. I will get up and face the rapist. Better me than you." Spring tied the sheet around her chest and crept towards her bedroom door. Sam tiptoed behind. "Got your cell?"

"No. I dropped it when I saw the murderer."

Spring grunted and opened the door, careful not to make any noise. Sam stood behind her at a safe distance. She squinted down the hall but could not make out anything. "I don't see anyone."

"He's in the kitchen. Hurry before he tries to steal the new espresso maker!"

Spring picked up the tail of the sheet and proceeded down the hall. Floor boards creaked beneath her feet.

"Careful, Pookie," Sam whispered encouragingly.

Sam had been right. In the kitchen, drinking from one of Lanie's coffee cups, sat a man. His face was turned from her but she recognized the odd shape of his body even in the dimness of the morning light.

"Mr. McClure?"

He jumped. "Oh, dear. I'm sorry. I was trying to be quiet. Lanie told me to wait out here while she showered."

"Lanie let you in?" Spring looked to see where her mother was, half expecting her to be duct taped to a chair.

Mr. McClure lowered his eyes, feigning interest in a sugar cube as it dissolved in his coffee. His hairless head gleamed in the early light of the morning. "Yes. Last night."

"Last night? Why, was she hurt? Are you hurt?"

Mr. McClure dipped his pinkie into his cup and stirred but did not say a word.

"Oh my God. You don't mean?" Spring shook her head to get rid of the image that was trying to form.

"I'm afraid so. Lanie and I had adult relations."

"Sam," she called, her voice raspy and dry. She needed support. He had run back down the hall. Why was he never around when she needed him?

"Don't be alarmed. We used protection. I was very clear on that." Mr. McClure held up a cellophane wrapper with a picture of Casey the Condom smiling back at her. "I might be past my prime but Lanie appears quite fertile."

"Sam!" Spring felt dizzy and she stepped back, tripping over the sheet. She fell crashing down hard upon Lanie's wind up pig. The pig let out one last grunt before dissolving into a pile of gears and springs.

"Your mother is a lovely woman," Mr. McClure said, standing. He walked to where Spring was and offered his hand for support. "She made me see things I hadn't seen in years."

"Hell, I saw something I hadn't seen in years too," Lanie clucked, shaking out her wet hair as she trundled into the room wearing nothing but a bath towel fastened around her bosom.

"I need air," Spring said, shaking away Mr. McClure's hand and crawling towards the door.

"Oh, come on. Ain't like we aren't all adults here."

Spring turned to see Lanie plant a kiss on Mr. McClure's cheek.

"...Mr. McClure's a guest, and we should treat him as such."

"Name's Bob," he said, his thin lips turning up into a smile at Lanie. "And you've already treated me better as a guest than I've ever been treated."

In all the years since her father had left, Spring had never seen Lanie with another man. She hadn't even flirted. And now...an overnight guest? "How did this happen?" Spring regretted the words the second they were out of her mouth. She wanted no details.

"Turns out Bob here is our peeper." Lanie nodded to Mr. McClure who blushed under her gaze. "He thought I had kidnapped his cat. Turns out, he was seeing my pig." Bob chuckled in the background and Spring was still confused.

"His cat ran off a few weeks ago," Lanie went on. "And he saw me petting something and assumed it was his kitty. We worked it out last night and then I invited him in for coffee."

"Coffee is my favorite hot beverage," Mr. McClure added, smiling sheepishly at Lanie. "After your mother apprehended me..."

"What?" Spring pictured Lanie throwing the man down, cuffing him like he were on an episode of *COPS*.

"Well, she saw me in the window and needed to make sure I wasn't a pervert. After she caught me, we figured out there had been a terrible misunderstanding. And all is well that ends well." Mr. McClure sat his coffee cup down and straightened his tie. "I must confess though, I did peer a little longer than necessary."

Spring's fingers locked onto the doorknob but she could not open the door.

"You okay?" Lanie asked.

"No. No, I'm not okay. You don't date for 20 years and all a sudden you're having sex with a man you've never met before in *my* house."

Spring pulled herself upright, adjusting her sheet so that Mr. McClure, the peeper, would not be getting any more free looks.

"Oh, we've met before," Lanie winked. "Bob and me shared a past life. I was a Gypsy slave girl and he was my master."

"No," Bob corrected her, shaking his head. "That wasn't a past life. That was our role play from last night."

"Oh yeah." Lanie smiled wickedly, batting her eyelashes.

Spring finally collected herself and found her way outside for air. But the air was hot and dry and not a bit of relief. "Fucking Arizona," she muttered.

Sam stood at the entrance to the bathroom, watching Spring splash water across her face. "Our home has become a den of iniquity and sin," he said, raising his eyes to the heavens. "Allah will not be pleased."

"Fuck, Sam. I'm not pleased either. But she's a grown woman. Who am I to say she can't have sex?"

Sam shuddered. "Well, that's not our call. But she needs to do it someplace else. He has a house. Let her do it there."

"For once, Sam, I completely agree with you."

Spring sat on the couch a very long time, a phone in one hand, a broken toy pig in the other. Lanie was sitting outside with Bob, tickling his pointy chin. She had never seen her mother so flirtatious, even with her own father, and the sight was unnerving. Spring thought about closing the blinds to block the sight, but she could hear their pillow talk everywhere in the house.

She dialed the number.

"Hey, Debs, this is Spring. I can't come in today. I'm feeling kinda sick." A pang of guilt stabbed at her, but she willed it away. It wasn't a complete fabrication. She *had* been sick this morning, after all.

"What? Oh, Spring, don't do this to me. Kimberly is acting really strange. She keeps circling me and asking me if I've ever considered getting highlights?"

"Sorry, Debs. I haven't taken a sick day in a long time and I need one. I mean, I really, really need one."

"Okay." Debbie sighed into the phone. "But I'm getting someone else to deliver the news...there's no way I'm telling that woman...hey, Becca, wait up. Okay, Spring, gotta go. Feel better."

Spring hung up the phone. In the kitchen, Lanie and Bob were trading Eskimo kisses. Spring went into her bedroom, where Sam was fixing his tie.

"I'm not going to work today," she said.

He shifted his gaze from his own reflection to hers.

"Why not? You can't let Kimberly bully you forever."

"I really need a break, Sam. I'm running on empty."

Sam turned to look at her and Spring detected a note of concern in his eyes. "Pookie, if you use up this day you won't have another for when you really need it."

Spring grunted in frustration. "I could use some support here, Sam. Not a lecture. You aren't my..." She let the word hang in the air.

"What, Spring? Finish out that lovely sentiment, please."

"Father."

Sam paused, narrowing his eyes. He almost spoke, caught himself, and started again. "I never meant to act like your father. But sometimes you act like a little girl. I need you to be aware of that."

Spring nodded absently and went into the bathroom and returned with a brush. He was being condescending, but she would think about that later. She had more important things to attend to now.

"Why do you need to comb your hair to hang around the house?" Sam raised an eyebrow suspiciously and stopped grooming himself while he waited for her answer.

Spring considered carefully what she would say.

"I have some errands to run. And I want to look respectable." Spring knew she had answered right. Being respectable was one of Sam's top priorities.

He snapped his fingers and dashed for the closet. "I know exactly the little number you should go with. You haven't even tried on the navy pants suit with the gold embroidery."

"It will make me look like a cruise director."

"It will make you look," he corrected, holding it up against his frame. "...Snazzy."

Spring grunted but obliged. She would acquiesce to anything, if it would shut him up. The suit was uncomfortably warm, too tight in some places and too loose in others, but Sam seemed to like it. Once she dressed and got Sam's nod of approval, he left for work. When she was sure he was gone she picked up the phone and dialed.

"Trevor? It's Spring. I really need to see you today. Are you free?"

Spring drove around the city for several minutes before heading to the apartment building where Trevor said he was staying. She wanted to gain focus and clarity before seeing him. If she had learned one thing about men, it was that they ran at the first sign of drama. When she had finally calmed herself enough, she headed in the direction of his address and cringed.

This was the apartment building where John Smith said he lived.

"Of course." Spring put on her sunglasses, tied her hair up in a ponytail, and sat in the car, wondering what to do next. She prayed like hell that John wouldn't see her. She had no idea what apartment he lived in. For all she knew, the two roomed together.

Spring surveyed the apartment. It was an old, well-cared-for, brick building. The lawn was short but lush and must have cost the owner a pretty penny in water bills to maintain. The property sat in stark contrast to the shiny, metallic dwellings that surrounded it.

Spring reached into the backseat and pulled out a dress, a flowery number Sam despised. Ducking down into the seat she shimmied out of her pantsuit––not an easy task, as it clung needily to her body. She discarded it onto the floorboard of the passenger seat. Spring slid the roomy dress over her head and sighed deeply, feeling more like herself. After a brief face check in the rearview mirror, she left the car and headed up the three flights of stairs to the floor where Trevor said he lived. As she scanned the hallway she heard a whistle behind her and jumped.

"You are lucky I'm a gentleman," a familiar voice said and Spring turned to see John behind her.

"Don't you have a job?" She glowered at him as she quickened her pace, trying to make her way towards apartment 314. Any friendship she had felt for him that night at her house dissipated in her embarrassment over being caught slinking off to see Trevor.

"Nope. I got let go a few days ago. Turns out I'm not Penny Saver material." He smiled good-naturedly, shoving his hands into his front pockets. "You should be nicer to me, young lady. I could save you a whole lot of embarrassment."

Spring turned to regard him, raising an eyebrow. He was toying with her. She thought about kicking him but doubted that would help her much. "What now?"

John backed away, grinning. "No, no. If you don't want my help, far be it from me to offer my services. I was trying to be a nice guy, but you don't have much interest in those do you?" He turned and started walking in the opposite direction, mumbling and shaking his head.

Oh Jeez. She wasn't sure if he was still playing or she had hurt his feelings. Why were men such trouble?! Spring clenched her teeth and ran after him.

"Wait! John. Wait, I'm sorry. What is it?"

"Well," he said when she caught up. "The back of your dress is stuck in your underwear. You might wanna fix that."

Spring looked over her shoulder at her bottom and was horrified to see that he was right. Worse. She had forgotten to change into the slinky, sexy ones she had brought along and was still wearing the large white sacks Sam had purchased for her during his last shopping spree.

'Modesty panties' he had called them. If more young women wore them, you could mark his words, unwanted pregnancies would be on the decline!

She tugged the dress out of its undergarment prison with as much dignity as she could muster and gave him her cruelest scowl. "Every time I start to feel some humanity towards you, you have to go and be a jerk!"

"Hey now," he said. "I brought you your earring and I gallantly saved you from bearing your rather cute soul to the world. You could be more grateful." John smiled as Spring marched past.

At last she found Trevor's door number, made sure John wasn't still watching, and knocked.

"Who's there?" Trevor's voice called from the other side of the door. The sound of it made her jittery.

"It's me. Can I come in?"

Trevor opened the door wearing only a t-shirt and underwear, both of which had seen better days. His hair had that 'just woke up' look to it and he had facial hair that had probably been growing for the last three days. He scratched his head, yawned, and smiled.

"Hello, beautiful," he said, kissing her on the cheek and pulling her inside.

"Oh, God, Trevor. I've missed you so much. I'm sorry I couldn't see you earlier. It's just been hard with Sam and all. You forgive me?" She hugged him, latching on and taking in his scent. Expensive cologne and cheap beer.

"Of course." He lifted her chin and pecked her on the lips. Then he led her to his bed, which was right in the middle of his living room, its headboard positioned up against the wall. The sheets were askew and a remote controller lay on an uncased pillow. They sat on the edge and Trevor leaned over, picking up a bottle from the ground. He popped open the lid.

"Beer?"

"No thanks. I'm good."

Trevor nodded and leaned his head all the way back, sucking in half the contents in one swallow. He replaced the cap and placed the bottle back onto the floor.

"So, this is your place?" Spring looked around. Dirty clothes in piles all over the room. An adult film playing on the TV. A table with one chair. Spring was confused. He was living like a refugee. He used to stay in a large loft with expensive furniture and stainless-steel appliances.

"Yep. My castle. My father cut me off, so I had to cut back a little. You say one fucking thing about his girlfriend looking a bit like a horse and you're disowned for good, you know?" Trevor stroked his chin and looked around the room. "I'll be back in his good graces soon enough. It's just a matter of time before he drops the nag and moves on to the next filly." Trevor grinned and took another swig of his beer. "Anyway, I'm only here 'til fall, then I'm gonna head home, patch things up with the old man. I just needed some sunshine. Maybe I'll move here once things are settled." His eyes widened as he stared at her.

Spring nodded. She had felt that pulling many times as a child, especially when they traveled through colder climates. "You miss me, too? Is that one of the reasons you came back?"

Trevor looked puzzled for a moment and the corner of his mouth twitched. Taking her face in his hands he responded. "God, yes. Of course. I think about you all the time." He kissed her neck, his warm breath covering her, sending sensations she hadn't felt for a very long time down her spine.

"Mmmm," she moaned into his ear. "God, how I needed this."

"Me too, babe." His lips made his way across her cheek, past her nose, to her lips. They tasted like stale Miller Lite. Or Budweiser. She couldn't tell. Trevor pulled her up onto the bed, leaned her back, and straddled her. He lay his wonderfully muscular body over hers, draping her like a blanket. He kissed her chin, her cheek, her ear, one hand running his hands over her thigh, the other in her hair.

"Trevor," Spring said, in-between those tiny moments when his lips were not on hers. "You think about me a lot?"

"All the time." He spread her legs, burrowing his knees between hers. His hand moved from her breast to her knee, and then walked its way up her dress. She shuddered, feeling that rush of sexuality and love she had for the man. Nothing could ever be this good. Nothing. Ever.

"I think about you, too." She took his head and held it steady, looking into the green abyss of his eyes.

"We are good together. So good." Trevor's hand was on her thigh. "Let me make you feel things. Wonderful things."

"Trevor?"

"Yes?" His finger was looped around the elastic of her underwear, urging them down. "Terrible panties by the way, love. You're too young to be wearing these."

"Take me with you when you go?"

"Huh?"

"When you leave, take me with you? Please. If we come back to Arizona, that's great. But if we need to live somewhere else, I can do that, too. I grew up in the carnival. I'm adaptable. I didn't ask you last time until it was too late. I won't make that mistake again."

Trevor's eyes narrowed and he loosened his grip on her underwear. He pulled himself up onto his knees and let his chin fall on his knuckles.

Spring slid into a sitting position. "What's wrong?"

"I don't think my wife would like that. She's funny about that sort of thing. I guess we could ask her, though."

Spring blinked, drawing her knees up into her stomach. "What? Wife? Since when?"

Trevor twisted his body around, placing his feet back on the floor. He leaned forward, holding out his hands and counting on his fingers. "Three years. Maybe four."

Spring felt her temples pulse. *Three years? Maybe four?* "We were together two and a half years ago. You were married two and a half years ago?" She was on her knees now, ready to pummel him. He had been drinking. His math had to be off. It had to be a mistake.

"Yeah, that seems about right. What year is it again?"

"Trevor!" Spring flew from the bed and stood in front of him. He looked up at her like a puppy that had been caught digging through the garbage. "You told me you loved me. You told me you fuckin' loved me then. And you had a wife!"

Trevor squinted. "I'm sorry." His words felt sincere. "She and I have an understanding. As long as I don't bring them home..."

"Them? Fuck, Trevor. Them? Am I just one of them? Do you even fucking remember me?"

He stared off to the side, his eyes flickering with what Spring guessed were pieces of memory. The gears were turning, she could see, but it was work for him.

Her heart almost stopped beating. "Trevor. Tell me what you remember." A tear waited in queue, ready to slide down at a moment's notice.

He smiled coyly, a lock of his dark hair falling to his forehead. "Well, the good parts."

"The good parts? You mean screwing me right? That's all you remember?"

His brows formed soft C's over his eyes. They were gentle, but they told the truth. He didn't remember much of anything about his relationship with Spring two and a half years ago. His eyes broke her heart.

"You drank Piña Coladas. I remember that. Does that count for something?"

Spring said nothing but continued to stare at him, her mouth agape. He shrugged.

"I'm having a hard time remembering things these days." He went to touch her shoulder but she evaded him and stumbled from the bed. The tears fell. She tried to stop them but the dam had broken. Trevor stood up, putting his arms around her. "I really am sorry."

"Get away from me! You asshole! You goddamned asshole." Spring pushed him off, tripping over her feet as she backed away. She scrambled towards the door, her eyes stinging.

"I don't understand why you're so mad." He looked confused. "Didn't you have fun?"

"We were in love!" She was hunched over, choking. "We were in love, you moron."

"We were?" Trevor stared at a picture on the wall. Two little boys playing baseball. His eyes blinked repeatedly. "I'm sorry if I misled you. I need to work on that."

"You go to hell, Trevor Donnelly. I hate you."

"No you don't," he said. "You just told me you loved me."

Spring wrestled with the door, yanking on it. It was broken, like everything else she touched. Trevor stood, kicking through heaps of laundry, looking for clothes. She managed to escape before he could dress, and stumbled back down the three flights of stairs to her car. She turned the key in the ignition but it wouldn't start.

"Perfect!" she screamed. "That's fucking perfect."

On the radio a salesman declared that Casey the Condom would be making a special guest appearance at the Fourth of July Toyotathon.

"It was all a lie," she said, wiping her nose with the hem of the dress. Why didn't she ever have a Kleenex when she needed one? "The last two years of my life have been a lie." The realization washed over her like a wave bringing in ocean garbage to a pristine beach. It made her sick. She opened the car door and hurled, then quickly closed it again.

"God, I was stupid. I was so fucking stupid." She held her knees into her chest, rocking back and forth like a baby. People passed by her on their way in and out of the complex, but she didn't care. As far as she could tell, her life was over."

"You okay?"

She was startled by the voice and the rap on the door. She sat there for a moment, snot dripping down her nose, her hair clinging to it like lint on a sweater. She did not want to see him, talk to him, face him. Him or anyone. Ever. She tried to ignore his tapping on the window but he wasn't going to stop. If she could have started the car and put it in reverse, running over his toe, she might have. Finally, reluctantly, she rolled down the window.

"Go away." She wiped the snot from her nose with the back of her hand, and transferred it to her dress. "I've had about all I could handle from men right now. And I'm a mess."

John kneeled down to her level. "You look beautiful to me. You could never look anything but beautiful."

She forced a smile. She knew he was trying to cheer her up, but it worked. It had been so long since someone had actually worked on making her feel better. "Watch out for the puke," she pointed to the mess on the ground and he positioned his shoes on either side of the puddle.

"Noted. Car problems?"

"Won't start. Not sure what to do. I can call AA I guess."

"This might not be my place to say, but you don't look like you are in any condition to drive right now." He opened the car door and gently pulled her out, lifting her over the pile of vomit.

"Wait, I need to lock it."

"Anyone who is going to leap over your throw-up to break in probably needs whatever is in that car more than you do." John led her up three flights of stairs to apartment 354, a few doors down from Trevor's.

"You wouldn't happen to be a killer, would you?" Spring went inside and he motioned that she should take the only seat on an old blue recliner.

"Maybe. You never know."

"Good. When you are done with me will you visit apartment 314?" She smiled over the glass of milk he offered her.

"So, all these tears aren't about Sam or a car that wouldn't start. I should have guessed."

"No. They were for Trevor Donnelly, the man from the bar. I thought we were in love." She couldn't control her sobbing then, long slow wails that began deep in her chest and pushed their way out of her throat. Ethereal moans she almost didn't recognize. She fought for control, and finally steadied herself.

"Weren't you?"

"He barely remembers me. I built a whole fantasy around a man who doesn't even know my name. And get this..." Spring paused and took a breath. "He is married." Spring turned her head so that John couldn't see her face. She felt like someone had taken a fork and stabbed it into her heart. "God, I'm a fool." She buried her face in her hands, mourning the loss of a love that apparently never existed.

"There's no nobler reason to be a fool, in my humble opinion," he said. John stepped forward to touch her but she halted him with one of her hands.

"I'm okay. I'm okay." She took a deep breath. "Just feels like the Universe is out to get me."

John looked baffled. "The universe? As in God?"

"Yes. As in God. But more. Much more. Everything, I think. Lanie explains it better."

"Why would God, the Universe and Everything want to get you?"

Spring thought for a moment. "Karma. Something I did in this lifetime or the past. I'm not sure. To be honest I only half-listen to Lanie most of the time."

"Have you considered that maybe..." John began, rising from his spot on the ground and walking across the floor to where he kept a box of Kleenex. He pulled three from the carton and handed them to Spring. She dabbed her eyes and brushed the hair out of her face. He sat himself on the floor in front of her, looking up into her tear-stained eyes. "... Maybe the Universe has other plans for you?"

"Why are you being so nice to me?" she asked, her eyes heavy from crying. "I thought you didn't like me."

"Me? Not like you? Where did you get that idea?"

"Well. I haven't been able to give you any money and you were teasing me about my underwear in the hallway." Her face darkened with embarrassment.

John took a sip and thought a moment. "Don't you remember in elementary school where they tell you if a boy is mean to you it's because he likes you?"

Spring snorted. "I was educated by an Indian lady in an RV. And I always thought boys were mean in general."

"That tells me you must have had a lot of admirers." He looked away. "I like you, Spring. From the moment you wrecked my car and threw a wad of dollars at me, I have liked you."

Spring's brow furrowed as his words registered in her brain. "But you don't know me."

"I know I like the way you run up and down the aisles looking for things. The way you wear those holey dresses of yours yet they still look beautiful on you. The way your barrettes hang out of your hair. The way you smile. The way you talk. The way you tilt your head when you are thinking of something. I know all that. What more is there to know?" John sat up on his knees, taking her hands and pulling them around his waist, locked in his own. Their faces were very close. His lips were inches away. His breath was on her face.

She closed her eyes.

He dropped her hands and stood up. "I'm sorry. I can't do this to you right now. You are vulnerable and I won't win that way."

"Huh?"

"I want you, Spring. But I want you on your own terms. Not because some jackass a few apartments over doesn't have the sense to appreciate you. Or because you wanna get revenge on your little gay boyfriend. I want you because you want me."

Spring shook her head. "I think I'm going to get sick again." She stood up, turning in circles, looking for a door. "Where is your bathroom?"

John walked to a door, opened it, and turned on the light.

"I'm sorry. I really am." Spring tottered towards the restroom, one hand clutching her head, the other holding on to her stomach. She shut the door behind her. "I haven't been sick this often since I was pregnant with the twins," she said, emerging from the bathroom, wiping her mouth with the back of her hand.

"You sure you aren't?" he said.

"That would require sex, something I don't have." She laughed. "I need to go now. Thank you for the use of your bathroom."

He should have been a gentleman and escorted her out. Instead, he waited by the window for her to emerge from the building. She stumbled to her car, opened the door, lay her head on the steering wheel for a moment, before trying her luck with the engine. It started right up. She drove away. Maybe forever.

John took out his paints. One thing about being unemployed, he had time to practice his craft. He wanted to paint a picture of Spring, but he couldn't bring himself to paint her crying. Instead, he painted her smiling, happy, and in love. The way she should be.

TWENTY-ONE

Spring was relieved to see that Sam's car was not in the driveway when she returned home. She entered quietly, hoping to steer clear of Lanie, but there was no reprieve. Spring opened the door to find her mother and Bob engaged in some elaborate dance sequence. When Lanie leaned back, Bob leaned in, and then they switched.

"Hi, Spring," Lanie called in-between gyrations. "Okay, Bob, now shimmy..." Lanie shook her body and the top half moved in one direction, while the bottom half moved in the other. Bob tried to emulate her and ended up looking like a Rock 'Em Sock 'Em Robot.

"He's a great dancer," said Lanie and Bob beamed. His bow tie dangled from his collar and Spring tried not to think about how it got that way. "And he introduced me to something called Nine Inch Nails. Ever hear of them? Bob is taking me moshing next week. Sing one of their songs for Spring, won't you Bob?"

Spring tried to ignore Bob's yodeling and she made her way towards her bedroom.

"Sam's fit to be tied," Lanie called after, and Spring froze in place.

"Oh? Why is that?"

"I don't know. He was running around the house looking for the credit card and talking about the sins of Eve and then he left."

"Anything happen while I was gone. Besides you two?"

"Oh no. Bob just got here. Looked like Sam had the hemorrhoids to me. That's the way your father used to look when he got a swell up. I made him up some salve but he hasn't gotten home to give it to him yet. It's on the counter." Spring picked up a jar labeled Hemorrhoidal Helper. "Confidentially," said Lanie. "I'd watch out, Spring. That little man of yours is losing his grip on reality."

"What? Why?"

"If you ask me," said Bob, still gazing at Lanie. "He senses another rooster in the chicken coop. You never know what a man is capable of, if his territory is threatened." Bob's eyes gleamed and Lanie giggled.

As if Sam had been waiting for this introduction, the front door flew open and Sam's red face appeared.

"Well, hello, Spring. Nice of you to come home. Anything interesting happen today?" He was advancing toward her, his head poised in ram position, his hands clasped behind his back, a bag marked Discovery Store dangling from his fingers.

Lanie and Bob paused to watch, looking uncertain about what they should do.

"What are you talking about?"

"Oh, I think you know what I'm talking about."

"Spring?" Lanie was puffing up, and Spring knew her mother would step in if given the word.

"I'm alright, Mom. Why don't you go over to Bob's for a while?"

Lanie and Bob exchanged glances. Bob took Lanie's hand and gave it a delicate squeeze. "Perhaps we'd better go. I will make you some iced tea." Lanie gave Spring a worried look, but followed Bob out the back door towards the back gate.

Spring's heart thumped wildly inside her chest. *He knows about Trevor.*

"I followed you today. I saw you at that boy's apartment," Sam said. He continued to advance and Spring backed up against the counter. When he reached her he tossed a business card on the counter; the one John had left with his address.

"I don't know what you are talking about."

"Oh really? The boy who was here the other night to return *your lost earring*. Did you lose it in his couch cushion?"

Spring gulped. "John? You saw me with John?"

"Yes, my dear. I did. Now come clean and I might take it easy on you. Lie to me and you'll be sorry."

"I wasn't with John."

"I knew you'd say that. That is why I brought this!" Sam reached into the sack and produced a box labeled *Amateur Lie Detector Test*. "Now, sit down."

"You want to administer a lie detector test on me?"

"You have two choices. Take it. Or we are through."

Spring sat down obediently, her knees shaking as he hooked up wires to her arms and head. She didn't know why she was acquiescing like this. Why she was letting him lead this and have his way?

"Okay, three questions. Answer these three and I will leave you alone. Deal?"

Spring nodded, the wire near her eye pushing into her skull.

"First, we have to do a couple of test questions to determine the accuracy of your statements. These do not count towards your three. Is your name Spring Rainbow Ryan?" Spring nodded that yes, it was, but he gave her a look that let her know she needed to speak the answer. "Yes. My name is Spring Rainbow Ryan."

Sam looked to see how the machine measured that response and was satisfied with the answer.

"Do you have twin daughters?" Sam looked at her impatiently, wanting to hurry the preliminary questions along in order to get to the real ones.

"No. I do not have twin *daughters*." Spring emphasized the word daughters and Sam nodded.

"Good. This thing works. You pay a little more for quality. Okay let's make this official. Here we go. First question. Did you see John Smith today?"

Spring took a deep breath and looked at Sam. "Yes, I saw John today."

The bars on the detector moved and Sam nodded. "At least I know you aren't a complete liar. Next question-did you have sex with John Smith today?"

166

Spring shook her head at him. "No. No, Sam, I didn't. I promise!"

Sam scratched his head as he looked at the test. "Fine. Even if I know the true nature of woman you can't argue with science. Last question: did you kiss John Smith today?"

Spring wanted to fling the test at his potato head, but she calmed herself. She didn't want a false reading just because she was angry. "No. I did not kiss him. We talked. That's it. Happy now?" The lie detector confirmed that Spring was telling the truth.

Sam slumped into his chair, looking mystified. "Did you..."

"You asked three, that's all you get." Spring removed the wires from her body and threw them onto the table.

Sam was stumped. For a moment, Spring thought of confessing everything to him. Her shameless chase of a man she had loved years ago, but who no longer wanted her. But what was the use? The Universe, which was supposed to have given her at least one true love, had really given her none at all. The feeling settled over her like a soggy blanket on a damp night. She had been a fool to have believed that love, real love, existed anywhere other than fairy tales and romance novels. Heroes don't really come dashing in to save you at the last moment. Not when there were beers to drink and internet porn to surf.

She looked at Sam again and wondered what it would be like to spend her life with him. Certainly not glamorous or even romantic. But practical.

Sam smiled weakly, apologetically. "Sweetie," he said. "Then why did you go over to John Smith's apartment?" His eyes were large and hopeful. He was begging for a reason that made sense. Any reason and he would let it go.

"He left something here. I returned it."

Sam nodded. She was feeling guilty about her deceptions and knew he didn't believe her, but he would accept it. For now.

"I love you, Pooks," he said, hugging her to his side.

"Do you?" she asked, the question genuine.

"Of course I do. I may not love everything you do or wear or say, but

167

I love you. Fundamentally. And isn't that the most important part?"

Spring nodded and let her chin settle into his bony collarbone.

Spring, come home! Emergency!

Sam was texting her on the cell phone. Sam never texted her, stating that impersonal electronic communications was barbaric and uncivilized, and his message worried and annoyed her all at once. She was already late to work and she briefly debated whether or not she should call him. As she sat at the stop sign on her way to work, she spun her car in the opposite direction and dialed.

"What's wrong?" she said.

"Your mother's crazy, that's what's wrong! She keeps screaming about putting a curse on the neighbor. I would stay but I have to meet with Grandma Rosemary's lawyer today."

Spring put her foot on the gas and was home within the minute. Lanie hadn't put an actual curse on anyone in years and something must have really rattled her to make her want to do it. As she pulled into the driveway she witnessed Lanie running around in the front yard, still in her pajamas, pointing to the purple house next door.

"Mother, what's wrong?" Spring asked, trying to catch Lanie's attention as she darted hysterically about the yard.

"That witch is trying to take your kids!" Lanie bounced emphatically. "She can't have hers so she wants yours!"

"What? What are you talking about?" Spring lowered her voice in an effort to calm her mother down. "No one's going to take Blaine and Shane, Mom. Understand?"

"I'll put a curse on you so big it will make Armageddon look like a trip to SeaWorld!" Lanie hollered to the house next door, then turned her attention back towards Spring. "The She-Bitch wrote the state and said you were an unfit parent, living in a sinful household. The state worker was here earlier. I saw the letter! Who else do you think would do that?"

Spring considered the boy's teacher, Ms. Droll, and even Jason.

"I'm not the most popular woman in the world, Mom. It could have been someone else. Let me talk to her okay? Before you do something you may regret."

Lanie nodded, a nod that was out of breath and labored, and Spring wanted to hug her mother. She was crazy but at least she cared. Spring strode towards the neighbor's house and knocked carefully on the door, not believing that anyone would answer. But after just a few low taps the door swung open and Mistress Zara spread her arms out to greet her.

"Come in."

Spring was not sure what to expect inside, but she guessed it would resemble the sock motif in the front yard. Instead, the home was neat, clean, and simple. Except that there were pictures of a little boy––the same little boy––everywhere Spring looked. Many times, even the same picture. A blue-eyed, tow-headed, angelic child, a few years older than her own twins. Spring guessed it was Zara's son who had been killed in a car accident.

"Mistress Zara," Spring began, hesitantly. "Did you write Child Protective Services and tell them I was an unfit parent? My mom thinks you did. And if you did, can you tell me why?" Spring looked around the room, the blue eyes of the child watching her every move. It unnerved her. Mistress Zara said nothing. A familiar-looking black cat hopped on Zara's lap and purred contentedly as she stroked it. Spring tried one more time.

"I know I'm not conventional. But I do try and do what's right for my kids. They have food. They have a roof. They have some stability. I just wanted to show you for myself that I'm normal. Kind of. And I love them."

Again, there was only silence and the purring of the cat. Spring realized that Zara was not the writer of the letter. The lady could barely communicate. Spring stood up and nodded an apologetic farewell as she made her way to the door.

"I didn't write the letter." Zara spoke, scarcely more audible than the purring cat, as Spring's hand slid over the doorknob. "I know what it's like to lose a child. I wouldn't wish that on anyone, even your crazy mother. Tell her that."

Spring met Zara's eyes and noticed they had changed. The cataracts that had seemed to cloud and block them had moved aside for a moment. Spring could see the violet beauty of her eyes and witnessed for a moment the woman she must have been years ago, before some reckless driver took her son. Spring nodded, an understanding from mother to mother. Mistress Zara, in that moment, could possibly be the sanest person Spring knew.

"He was beautiful," she said, scanning the pictures on the shelf nearest her. "You were lucky to have him in your life."

"I still am," said Zara. "He comes by every night and we play Parcheesi."

"It was her, wasn't it?" Lanie asked, fanning herself by the pillar that held the front porch up. She had her T-shirt tied up in a knot near her breasts, exposing her abdomen, and sweat trickled down every available inch of her belly.

"No, Mom. But I think you two could actually be friends if you gave her a chance."

Lanie snorted, uninterested, and Spring got back into her car.

"Oh, by the way. I think I know the whereabouts of Bob's cat. I don't think she's ready to come home anytime soon, though."

Lanie glared at Zara's purple house as Spring drove away.

When Lanie had finally calmed down after what Spring called her 'episode,' she stretched out on the sofa, flipping through the channels until she found *The Young and The Restless*. She marveled at the way the actors stayed the same age, decade after decade. No Egyptian Pharaoh had been so well preserved.

When she had called Bob to tell him about the whereabouts of his cat, he had been very upset. She could hear the little man wheezing through the receiver and she did her best to comfort him. What he needed, she had told him, was a new pet. Something smart and obedient, that couldn't leap fences to look for greener pastures. Perhaps a pot-bellied pig.

He was averse to the idea at first, but when she explained to him her End of Days theory, he, being a practical man, saw her logic. That warmed her heart. She was beginning to grow very, very fond of him.

Lanie tried to watch her soap but it was annoying. The plotline had not changed at all since she had last watched it, well over a decade ago. She turned down the volume and went for her tarot deck. She had a tickle in her throat. Despite her good fortune with Bob and the pig, there were still problems. Spring was an emotional wreck. Someone was trying to take away the twins. And Sam was one shell shy of the nut farm. Lanie shuffled the deck, said a quick prayer to the Universe, and pulled out a card. A real witch only needed one.

A young woman sat shackled at the feet of a terrible horned monster. The woman had the key to her chains but refused to use it. The Devil card.

Lanie scratched her head and asked her spirit guides for advice. But they were unusually silent today.

Spring drove this time with Sarah in the passenger seat, carefully stitching away at the tattered Casey costume. "Wonder if Betsy Ross looked as intent as you do?" Spring teased.

"If Betsy could sew condoms, the whole history of our country might have been changed," Sarah answered thoughtfully, sucking on her finger where the needle had pricked her.

"I think I'm going to run away," said Spring, rolling through the backstreets of Phoenix. The little gas tank on her dashboard blinked red indicating that she would soon be out of fuel. She ignored it.

"Take me with you," said Sarah, her tongue sticking out of the corner of her mouth in concentration. "I'm beginning to have serious doubts about my life, lately. I dress up like a prophylactic for a living and I caught my husband with another woman...and neither thing phases me. Something is seriously wrong here."

Spring gasped, shirking her attention from the road to Sarah. "Albert and another woman?"

"Yep. In the parking lot of the Burger Barn. I was in the drive-thru and I thought, hey, that looks like Albert. Then I thought, hey, that *is* Albert...and up popped the head of this other woman. I didn't even flinch. All I could think was, 'good, at least it saves me the trouble.'"

Spring shrank back. "It didn't bother you?"

"Well, I also thought, 'that son of a bitch better not have spent my money to buy her a burger,' but other than that, no, not really." Sarah shrugged and continued to sew. The needle and thread was not really working on the rubber, creating more tears in it than it resolved. "Look, Spring, all done." Sarah held up the costume for Spring to examine, and the poor thing was stitched up so badly Spring couldn't contain her laughter.

"We will have to rename him Franken-Penis," Sarah said, throwing Casey into the back seat. "Who knows, maybe Kimberly won't notice?" said Sarah, and both women laughed.

Spring pulled into the office parking lot. "I need a few minutes. Cover for me?"

Sarah nodded. "Take your time. I will keep the beast at bay. After the few days I've had, Kimberly doesn't threaten me at all."

Spring circled the block several times, dodging in and out of midday traffic. It was hot but she didn't turn the air conditioner on. It seemed like too much effort. "Fuck!" she said, slamming her open palms against the steering wheel. "I'm such an idiot. What did I think would happen when I ran into him? Did I really think he would confess his undying love for me and beg me to marry him?"

Yes. Yes, as a matter of fact you did think that.

Spring pulled into a city park and watched as small children played in the sprinklers while their mothers chatted with one another, shading themselves from the sun with newspaper. She didn't remember one time that she had played in a sprinkler as a child. What had she done as a child? Traveled the country with her crazy mother on the carnival circuit. Rode Ferris wheels. Ate corndogs. Babysat her little sister. Watched her father leave. But she didn't remember any parks. She had visited 48 states and they had never, ever been to a park.

Where the fuck were all parks?

She was tempted to get out, run with the children through the sprinklers, splash the women with their overdone hairstyles, reclaim her childhood, and scream to the Universe that although it had taken her one true love from her, she wasn't going to give up. She was going to fight.

You're not going to lick me!

She wanted to challenge whoever the hell was in charge. She would be goddamned Scarlett O'Hara. Adversity bubbling out the bazoonga, and she a cool-headed shot that would as soon kill someone who tried to take from her as look at him.

But she was not Scarlett. Scarlett's strength came from caring for herself. The cruel, heartbreaking truth was that nice girls were not heroines. Nice girls sacrificed their lives for other people, allowing someone else be the protagonist in their story.

Spring thrust the car into reverse and headed back to the office to face Kimberly.

Spring had not seen Kimberly since the Monday following Sarah's accident at the parade. She had called in several times the previous week and mercifully, on the days she had come in, Kimberly had been away at a training workshop. But Spring could not delay the meeting forever. The day of reckoning had come.

Kimberly, of course, was livid. Her hair, though not attached directly to her head, had the good manners to stand on end for her. "What have you done to Casey?" Kimberly held up the costume for Sarah and Spring to inspect, and Sarah had to stifle a laugh. "That was an eight hundred dollar puppet you blew!" With that Sarah could hold it in no longer and burst out laughing while Kimberly scathed in response.

"We tried our best to fix it," Spring said. "What did you want us to do?"

Kimberly snarled and Spring watched the woman's entire scalp crawl. "You get to explain this to Jane," she said, snapping her fingers at the women. "I'm not."

Sarah, finally calmed enough to respond, crossed her arms and gave Kimberly a flippant look. "No, Kimberly. You explain this to Jane. I'm done with this whole nutty place." She grabbed her purse, as casually as if she had announced that she were going on her lunch break, and left the room, leaving Spring and Kimberly to stare at one another, open-mouthed.

"Did she just quit on me?" Kimberly asked, and Spring shrugged, her eyes following her friend as she disappeared down the hallway. "Nobody quits on me." Kimberly moved quickly to follow Sarah, leaving Spring in the office alone.

Kimberly reappeared a few minutes later. "She quit. I can't believe she quit." Kimberly walked over to her desk and stared at the monitor that was not turned on. "I guess you get to play Casey from now on. Lucky you."

You don't have to go." Spring tried to convince Sarah as she packed all of her belongings into a box. "...You could transfer. Or appeal directly to Jane." Spring couldn't lose Sarah. They had become close over the last few weeks.

Sarah tossed a photo of her and her husband into a garbage pail by the desk and stopped to look at Spring. "You know, for someone as smart as you, sometimes you just don't get it, do you?"

Spring shook her head. "What don't I get?"

Sarah took Spring's hands and shook them. "Sometimes we have to stand up for ourselves even when we think we might lose everything." Sarah looked out over Spring's shoulders to where the sun had cast a loose beam on the floor, illuminating a spot on the dirty carpet. "I need a change, and I need to make it now before I'm one of those women who watch the shopping channel twenty-four hours a day to compensate for all the emptiness." Sarah released her hands and looked out the door, down the empty corridor. "Besides, it's not just for me anymore." Sarah's face softened and she patted her tummy.

"You're going to have a baby!" The truth registered in Spring's brain and she felt stupid for having missed the signs. "Albert's?"

"Unfortunately. Call me anytime. I love you."

Sarah gave her a quick hug and Spring trembled as she realized this would be the last time they would be together at *Teens in Trouble*.

Then Sarah gathered her half-empty box and walked out of the office, leaving Spring feeling very, very alone.

Spring left the office early, claiming stomach pains. Kimberly, still speechless from Sarah's departure, didn't try and stop her. Spring drove randomly around the city, zigging and zagging across lanes, no destination in mind. It wasn't until she was actually in the parking lot that she realized that she had been heading here all along. She looked up at where she guessed his window was and thought about her last meeting with Trevor. A pang of sadness shot through her. Without thinking she got out of the car and raced up to the third floor, her clunky heels tripping her on every other step. Taking a deep breath, she knocked, three times.

"God, I'm happy to see you," she said, falling into his arms. His hair smelled like cheap shampoo and his breath like beer. He caressed her shoulders as he kissed her cheek.

"I'm happy to see you too. Thank you for giving me another chance."

TWENTY-TWO

John's first reaction was of disbelief. But when she fell onto him, letting her warm tears soak through the thin fabric of his Wal-Mart T-shirt, he put his arms around her and held her. All his misgivings about his feelings for her vanished the second she melted into his arms.

"I'm so sorry," she said at last. Her nose was running and her eyes were small and red. He led her into his apartment and closed the door behind her, offering her a tissue.

"You don't see many bachelor guys who have a box of tissue handy," Spring laughed, blowing her nose. "You must be used to rescuing damsels in distress."

John said something about her being the only damsel he wished to share his tissue with and she smiled. He directed her to sit down at his table. He had been painting chess pieces and he cleared them away for her.

"You play?" she asked, picking up and examining some of the finished pieces. He normally did not like anyone touching his things. Even his brothers had called him 'Stingy Johnny' as a child when he refused to let them play with this toys, but he didn't flinch as she looked over one figurine after another. The revelation pleasantly surprised him. He could share anything with her, he thought, and happily.

"Yes. I'm not good, but I enjoy it."

John watched as Spring fingered a knight, painted gold and purple, and twisted it around in her fingers. "I love the little horsies," she said. "The way they move about the board in their own unique way." Spring twisted the end of her hair and nibbled on it, staring at the board. For a moment she was Alice, lost in the looking glass.

"Not me," said John, removing a castle from the board. "I like the straightforward manner of the rook. No scenic routes. No hidden agendas. Always knows where he is going."

He handed the rook to Spring and watched as she rolled it over in her palm. Then she placed the two pieces side by side and smiled. "And yet, they both have the same goal. Good metaphor for life I suppose."

Usurp the King, John thought, and decided not to share that thought with Spring. "Indeed."

"I'm sorry about coming here and disturbing you," she said. "I didn't know where else to go."

John pulled up a chair next to her and took one of her small hands. It took every ounce of strength he could muster not to press them to his lips, but he wasn't about to do anything that might make her dash out. "I'm just surprised. I kinda thought you hated me."

Spring laughed. "Me? Hate you? I'm sorry I gave you that impression." She tilted her head and her large blue eyes looked at him with such incredulousness John wondered if he had imagined their last few meetings. He might learn to love a woman but he doubted he would ever understand them.

He continued watching her as she sat quietly, waiting for her to speak again. He watched as she looked away at an image that flitted outside of his window, and he took the opportunity to take her in completely. She was curvy and strong and for a brief moment he wondered if he could lift her up and carry her to his bed. He had never done that to a woman before.

She caught him staring and he moved his eyes back up towards her face. "What are you thinking?"

"I'm thinking I should probably work out." He smiled and she laughed. God, what a laugh.

"This is going to sound really strange, but John, is there someplace I can lie down? I really need to sleep right now. It's been that kind of life."

John placed one hand on her back and the other on her hand and helped her up, leading her to his bedroom. Wishing he had picked his clothing up from the floor, he managed to kick his underwear beneath the bed before she noticed them. "You can rest here. I won't let anyone, or anything, bother you. I promise."

He watched her stumble to the bed and crawl in, like a little girl who had been kept up too late. She lay curled up on her side and he pulled the sheets and blanket up to her chin. Kissing her forehead he whispered, "I will be right out here if you need me."

She nodded and he left as quietly as he could, leaving the door cracked open in case he needed to go to her.

He sat on his recliner and muted the volume on the television. He could hear her breathing, strong and steady, slowly replaced by a quiet snoring. He had never known that girls snored and the thought made him smile.

No one had to tell John Smith that he was in love. Though he had never been in love before, he was as certain of the feeling as he was his own name. As he leaned back in his recliner he thought his life might be perfect if she stayed tucked into his bed for the rest of her life. Even if she never left the bed, and he was never allowed to go to her in the way he ached for, life would still be pretty damned good. He looked back over at the knight and the rook and smiled before falling into a hazy sleep.

"Hey, Beautiful. You awake?"

Spring blinked slowly and paused to feel her heart beat. It was so loud she could hear it in her ears. She turned slowly towards the voice, her face red, her eyes apologetic. He was lying next to her on the bed, his face inches from her own.

"Hi," she said, smiling weakly. For a moment she remembered what she must look like, her hair wild and uncombed, her mascara smeared across her cheeks, her eyes red and swollen from crying, and panic took over. But when he smiled back she knew she was okay.

"It's late. I wasn't sure if I was supposed to wake you, but I thought

I should."

Spring shot up. *It's late?* She was sure she had slept no more than an hour. As she looked at the clock on the bedside table, she knew that she was in trouble. It was after eleven and she had not been home.

"I gotta go. Sam is probably worried sick. And Lanie, too. Oh, God." Spring jerked herself out of the bed, letting the blankets fall to the floor. "Where's my shoes? I lost my shoes."

John pointed to her shoes by the bedroom door, neatly arranged by an invisible hand.

"Thank you," she said, slipping into them. "You've been a great friend to me. I really needed this."

"You going to be alright? I can drive you home."

"No. I'm okay. I need to make up a story. Sarah's last day at work party. That will work."

Spring felt John study her as she straightened out her clothes. "You could tell him the truth. It was innocent."

"Tell Sam the truth?" Spring almost choked on this. "Obviously, you don't know Sam." Spring patted down her hair, grabbed her purse, and was about to leave the room when she noticed something. A framed picture by the bed. It wasn't a photograph. It was a drawing done in charcoals. A drawing of her.

She walked towards it, not quite believing what she was seeing. When she got to it, she picked it up. Sure enough, it was her face. But more beautiful. "You do this?" She turned to see John. He had his hands shoved into his pockets and he was looking at the floor. He nodded but wouldn't meet her gaze.

"John." She put the picture down and walked around the bed to him. "John, that's the most beautiful thing I've ever seen." She wrapped her arms around his neck and pulled herself into him, as tightly as she could. She could hear his heartbeat.

"I worked on it while you were sleeping. You're the most beautiful thing I've ever seen," he said simply, looking down at her. "It's all you, Spring. Not me."

Spring wasn't quite sure how it happened but without warning their lips met. His were warm, and firm, and strong. "Oh, God," she moaned as he pulled her close. "You're a good kisser. God, you feel good."

"So do you," he said back, between the urgent meetings of their mouths.

His passion surprised her. She felt a need she hadn't known she possessed wash over her. It was stronger than she had ever felt for Jason, or even Trevor. The desire to meld with this man. The more she kissed him, the closer she needed to be to him. It was never close enough.

"I want you," John whispered, his hands finding their way under the back of her shirt. She felt him tug on the hooks of her bra. Her body warmed, responding. One of his hands found her breast and she moaned again, louder. A primal moan that startled her. And it broke the spell.

Spring stepped back, out of his arms. "No. No, John. God. What just happened? I shouldn't be here. I have to go." She grabbed her things and ran out of the building. Sam was right. She was acting like a Jezebel. How could she explain this to him? John stared after her, looking confused, but he didn't try and stop her as she made her way to the door.

As Spring drove home, she knew that she would be in more trouble than she could handle. Sam would be up, waiting for her, and might possibly give her another round on the lie detector. But this time she had done something. She had kissed John Smith. Worse, she had liked it. She was an engaged woman and she was running around town like a common harlot.

It was my last fling, she told herself, as her neighborhood came into view. *Before I marry Sam.* Those four words came back at her like a punch in the stomach.

Before I marry Sam.

Sam was indeed waiting for her. He sat on the rocking chair on the front porch, rocking like a man who had been keeping accurate time of how long his fiancée had been missing. She could see the whites of his eyes against the darkness of the night and she shuddered. She braced herself for what would come next, but as she made her way towards Sam, she realized that he was not going to confront her. He sat quietly looking at her, like a wounded child, and a wave of compassion fell over her.

"I'm sorry I was gone," she said, sitting down on a concrete step. She leaned over to pluck a blade of dry grass from the lawn and bit on the tip, crunching it between her teeth. "The marriage thing. And work. I needed a break from life. I should have called you."

Sam sighed letting his shoulders sag deeply into his back.

Spring noticed a gold shopping back sitting primly on his lap. "What's that?" she asked.

"I got you a little something." He handed her the bag, which was surprisingly light. Spring reached in and pulled out the gift. It was silky soft and smelled good, like lavender. She held it out to study it under the porch light. A burgundy-colored nightgown, about four sizes too large for her.

"The salesgirl helped me pick it out," he said. "I told her that my fiancée was about the same build as she was, and she thought this would be perfect."

Spring imagined the salesgirl was the size of a small duplex.

"Go in the house and try it on sweetie. I bet you will look beautiful in it."

Spring bit her tongue to avoid saying anything hurtful about her gift. This was her penance for her shenanigans. She took off her shirt and pulled the nightgown over her head as Sam's jaw dropped in protest. As he frantically checked to make sure none of the neighbors were watching, Spring checked her reflection in the windowpane. She was reminded of old cowboy cartoons where the bad guys walked around in barrels to conceal their nudity.

"Oh, Pookie. You look beautiful," Sam beamed. "You can wear that on our honeymoon. It's perfect."

Spring smiled, offered him a peck on the cheek, and went inside.

In the next room, Lanie couldn't sleep. She rummaged through her vials, bags, and drawers looking for some of Jason's magic sleeping herbs. Despite what Spring had said, Lanie had no objections to natural remedies. If it came from Mother Earth it had to be okay.

She puckered her lips thoughtfully when she realized she was out. She'd finished the last of it off during her last lovemaking session with Bob. The thought of the two of them snuggled up together made her smile and she entertained the idea of walking to his house for a midnight session.

"No," she said to herself. "The poor boy needs his rest." She grinned wickedly as she thought about how he had begged her to take it easy on him.

Lanie slipped quietly down the hall and rummaged through the medicine cabinet. "Hmmm," she said, turning the bottle of the twin's Ritadate over in her hands. "...May cause drowsiness."

Lanie took a few, followed by a swallow of water from the sink, and headed back to her room. Once inside, with the door safely locked, she went to her closet and groped around on the top shelf with her hands until she found the shoebox, hidden quietly behind the collection of Frank Sinatra and Burl Ives albums that she'd never found the heart to part with. She had lost so much in her life. She couldn't lose Frank and Burl, too.

She hadn't opened the shoebox in years, and sifting through it for the first time in over a decade made her feel like she was reaching into another dimension––another life she scarcely had memory of anymore. One hundred and fifty-six letters from her ex-husband sent from his twenty years in prison. No one knew about the letters. Not even her daughters. Why she had kept them, she never knew. Maybe she liked the idea that someone out there loved her, even if that someone was a sorry son of a bitch who walked out on wives and children.

Lanie puffed on her cigarette and held the smoke inside her lungs as she read the one on top of the pile.

My Dearest Elaine,

I think about you every night and day. I will never be able to tell you how sorry I am for leaving you and the girls. It is the biggest regret of my life. But I will come back to you when I am worthy. I promise.

Ernest

"Mother fucker," she said during an exhale and crumpled the letter, tossing it back into the box with perfect precision. "Bastard liar." She kicked the shoebox, sending it sprawling across the room, dumping its contents in a path across the floor. She remembered a story told to her by an old Indian woman who ran the corn dog machine. The Trail of Tears. Lanie couldn't recall what the trail referred to, but as she looked at her line of letters, she understood...something.

Lanie had waited for him. For days. For weeks. For months. For years. Each letter promised his return, but he never made it. She had been holding onto a box of empty promises.

There was a hollowness in her chest and it was associated with an emotion she couldn't identify. She snapped her fingers, trying to name the feeling. *Loneliness?* No. She was not lonely. *Loss?* Getting closer. *Regret?*

Yes, that's right. She was feeling regret.

Lanie had never had a moment's regret for anything she had ever done, but she was feeling it now. Regret for the lost time she had spent mourning a man who couldn't make it back to her and who hadn't loved her enough to stay with her in the first place. She crawled alongside the letter trail until she straddled the empty shoebox. She peered inside and saw Ernie's face. Or what she thought it looked like. She could hardly remember any more. Time had taken his eyes, his smile, his hair. Time had taken the crinkles she thought she remembered forming around his eyes. Time had distorted him into a menagerie of images, some real, some made up. She was a crypto-zoologist, chasing Bigfoot. What was she holding onto again?

Standing was difficult. She heard things creak in her body that probably shouldn't be creaking, and wondered if she was doing the right thing. She could keep the letters. These were more than ink and paper; they were a testament that someone had once loved her and that she had loved them back, however misguidedly.

She had loved. She had been loved. Could she do it again?

If you had the faith of a mustard seed, you would see that anything is possible. The words came to her and she wracked her brain to remember who had quoted this. Big Bird? It didn't matter. It was true.

She gathered the letters and went into Sam's work area. One by one, she began to shred them. Suddenly she stopped. A white envelope with a Cinderella sticker caught her eye. The one Ernie had written to Spring that Lanie had never given her.

"Oh well," Lanie said. "Time for her to face the truth, too."

She tucked the envelope into her waistband and shredded the rest. It hurt like childbirth, but then she remembered the way Bob touched her, talked to her, made love to her, and the pain became butter over toasted bread. That hole in her chest seemed to fill up too, and she clutched her chest, to hold onto it.

"Goodbye, Ernie," she said, kissing the last letter and releasing it into the shredder. And she was surprised to find that no tears fell.

185

TWENTY-THREE

Sam held the phone to his ear, a constipated look on his face as Spring walked, messy-haired and blurry-eyed, into the kitchen. The patio door opened and Lanie entered the living room, followed closely by Bob.

"Look, Bob's a dad!" Lanie pointed to a fat, pink creature cradled lovingly in Bob's arms.

"Mom. Is that a pig?" Spring shook her head in disbelief.

"Of course, it's a pig," Lanie said. "I knew I should have taken you to the zoo as a child."

Lanie led Bob and his pig back into her bedroom and Spring heard the click of the lock behind them.

"Your mother isn't allowed to have pigs in the house," Sam said, placing his hand over the mouthpiece. "Go tell her."

Spring smoothed her hair into place. "You tell her. I'm late for work."

Sam scratched his head. "I've got other things going on right now. I guess we can deal with this later."

Spring paused. Sam wasn't normally so complacent, especially about things he found repulsive. "Is everything okay?"

Sam listened to someone speaking on the phone for several moments before hanging up. He placed his hand on his forehead and made his way to a dining room chair and plopped himself down, staring absently at the wall in front of him.

"It's Grandma Rosary. Her condition is worsening. They give her a few days. Week tops." He scratched his chin thoughtfully, running his fingers across his new stubble.

"Oh, Sam! I'm so sorry." Spring wasn't sure what to say to make it better. She knew how much he loved the woman who had basically raised him since his mother's divorce.

"That's why we have to get married right away, Pookie. It's her dying wish." Sam shifted his gaze from the spot on the wall to Spring. "You are all I have left."

When Spring entered the lobby of *Teens in Trouble,* Debbie was crying at her desk.

"Debbie, what's wrong?" Spring asked. "Kimberly try and scalp you?"

Debbie shook her head and dried her face on her shirt. "No. Not Kimberly. It's Roger. He's...he's called off the wedding."

"What?" Spring crouched low so that she was eye-level with her friend, who sat hunched over in an oversized, black, office chair. "What do you mean, called it off?"

"He says it's too much. He thinks I'm more invested in planning our wedding than in being his wife." Debbie stopped crying long enough to sigh dramatically and a pile of invitations fluttered from the desk onto the floor. "Maybe it's true," Debbie sniffed. "But is that so wrong? I've always had this fantasy of my wedding day. I just want everything to be perfect."

Spring allowed Debbie a few heavy sobs before speaking. "Debbie, if you love him, fight for him. But remember, marriage is for life. It lasts long after the wedding day is over."

Debbie nodded. "I know." The phone beeped and Spring could see that it was Kimberly's line. "It's probably for you," Debbie said, wiping her nose with the back of her hand. "She wanted to see you the moment you got in. I'm sorry."

Spring stood up. "I'll be back in a bit, hopefully in one piece. If I disappear, call the police. I didn't run away."

"It's Friday," Kimberly said. "I want my answer."

Spring stared at her boss but said nothing.

Kimberly picked up a tube of red lipstick from her desk and applied it perfectly without looking in a mirror. Spring felt envy at the feat. "I'm not giving you my hair," Spring said. "This is extortion."

"Wow. You got balls. Maybe hanging out with the penis has done you some good," Kimberly said, tossing the lipstick into an open desk drawer. "It still doesn't change anything."

"I could go to Jane," Spring countered.

"You could," Kimberly agreed. "But let's just say I have Jane wrapped around my finger." Kimberly winked and Spring felt a wave of disgust wash over her.

"Fire me, then. Let me get unemployment and move on with my life." Spring crossed her arms.

"Deliberate misconduct will not get you unemployment benefits, young lady."

"Let's see what the unemployment agency says about this," Spring shot back defiantly, surprising herself at the force of her words.

Kimberly said nothing but stared at her in shock, obviously taken aback by Spring's newfound courage.

"You know what, Kimberly?" Spring continued, unable to stop herself. "I got an even better idea. I quit."

Kimberly regained her voice. "You're not serious."

"Aren't I?" Spring turned towards the door and Kimberly caught her arm.

"Spring, you can't go." Kimberly's voice was shaky. "If you go, who is going to wear the condom outfit?"

Spring gave Kimberly a smug smile. "Well, think of it this way. If you are in costume no one's gonna see that bald head of yours." Spring broke away and marched out the door to deliver the news to Debbie.

"It's not going to be the same without you." Debbie said.

"You will be fine, Debs. Besides, it's a temp job, remember? This was never supposed to be your career."

"I thought about what you said and you were right. I will fight for him."

Spring gave Debbie a warm smile. "I will miss this place. At least what it used to be like before we went Hollywood. Too bad you weren't here then. It was a good place to work." She hugged her friend. "Let's keep in touch."

"I never thought you'd be the one to blow up," said Debbie. "Somehow, I thought it would be me."

Spring laughed. "So did I."

Spring drove straight to Chloe's. She knocked at the door three times and was about to give up when her sister answered, wearing nothing but a towel.

"Oh, thought you were the mailman," her sister said, sounding disappointed.

"Since when do you greet the mailman wearing a towel?" Spring asked, stepping into the house.

"Since when don't I?"

Spring sat on the couch and Chloe lazed across from her on a well-used chair. Scented candles placed ceremoniously around the living room were the only source of light and some New Agey music, probably left over from Lanie's days, played romantically in the background. "What's up, sis? You don't grace me with your company often. Something's wrong."

Spring looked up at the ceiling and noticed for the first time that it was popcorned, an odd contrast to Chloe's sleek and stylish lifestyle.

"I don't know who I am anymore. This isn't the life I planned. I quit my job. Mom's got a pig. I kissed a man I hardly know. Trevor doesn't remember me and Sam wants us to get married…"

"Wait a sec," Chloe interrupted. "Did you say Mom got a pig?" Spring's lip began to tremble and Chloe caught herself. "I'm sorry. I wasn't being very sensitive."

"All I ever wanted was a normal life. Is that too much to ask?"

Chloe sighed and offered her sister a half smile. "We had a unique childhood. The only glimpses you ever got of normal were from the windows of the houses we passed on our way from one town to another. Or from TV shows." Chloe came to her sister and draped her arm lovingly around her. "But you know that isn't real. None of its real. It's all an illusion. Perfect marriages, perfect homes, perfect children, perfect hair. Perfection is a game we play because we can't bear to let others see us as we truly are. You, my sister, are normal. It's the rest of the world that's crazy."

Spring looked up at her sister and felt a wave of love rush over her. "You mean it?"

"Yes. People envy that about you. You wear torn dresses and cry in public. You don't talk in that annoying nicey-nice voice to your children. You admit you're in debt. Your hair is always a mess and sometimes your shoes don't even match. You show your humanity and it is a sweet, endearing thing. Don't knock it."

Chloe smiled at her until a *ding-dong* at the door caught her attention. She ran to answer it, one hand still fastening the towel in place. She returned with a package. "Toys for the bedroom," she smiled, holding up the plain brown box. "What's really normal, Spring, is what we hide from the world."

Spring spent the rest of the afternoon with Chloe. She was reluctant to see Sam and to tell him that she was now without a job. As she pulled into her driveway she saw him, watering the lawn in white sneakers, black socks, a striped button-down shirt, and a pair of long denim shorts that flared at the hips, giving him an oddly pregnant profile. His thumb covered the mouth of the hose so that he could control the flow of the spray. When he saw Spring, he waved with his free hand and turned the water off at the spigot.

"Hi, Pookie. Just tending to things that need tending to." Sam kissed her on the cheek as she got out of the vehicle. Behind her, she heard a familiar rattle she recognized as Jason's van. She skirted out of the way as he pulled in.

"Mommy!" Shane and Blaine shouted, tumbling out of the double-doors in the back of the van. There were two sleeping bags lying on the floor of the vehicle and Spring decided not to ask if they had been sleeping in them while Jason drove.

"Hello, beautiful," Jason said, as the boys ran in dizzying circles around them. Jason put the crook of his arm around Spring's lower back and guided her to a private spot on the opposite side of the yard. She could feel Sam's eyes burn into her back. "...We need to talk."

"One moment, please, Jason. Take the boys to Lanie. I need to speak to Sam real fast."

Jason nodded and rounded up the twins, herding them indoors.

"I don't like him," Sam said. "The sooner we can get rid of him the better. Ever think of giving him full custody?"

"Sam!"

"I was joking, Pookie. Relax." But Sam's eyes were still on Jason, watching him intently as he made his way into their home.

"Sam. I did something today. Something I'm afraid you aren't going to like."

Sam turned his full attention to Spring. "You went and saw John."

"No!"

Sam fanned himself, relieved. "Then whatever you did couldn't be that bad. Try me."

Spring fidgeted a moment. "I quit my job."

"What?" Sam threw open his arms in a gesture of incredulousness. The sun hit his bald spot, funneling a deep beam of light into his head and Spring worried he would fry.

"I couldn't take it anymore, Sam. They are crazy. And now that Sarah's gone and Kimberly wants me to be Casey, well, I just couldn't go back." Spring leaned against her car defiantly and looked out over the endless horizon of tract homes. With the exception of Zara's home, each was an exact replica of the last.

"Well, that's just dandy. And how do you suppose we eat?" Sam's hands reached down to comfort his belly as if it was already sensing the impending hunger pangs.

"We aren't destitute. You still have a job. We have enough to pay the bills. We may have to cut down on the luxuries for a while."

Sam's body began to quake. His whole body convulsed and Spring wondered if he were having a seizure.

"Sam? You okay?"

Finally, he composed himself and carefully formed the words. "What kind of luxuries were you thinking of cutting out exactly?"

Spring thought for a moment. There was no easy way to say it. "Coffees. Trips to the movies. Books."

The last word registered across Sam's face, turning it the color of toothpaste. He turned and paced the length of their newly-watered lawn, hands clasped over his head like he were about to surrender to the cops. "It's so nice of you to put things into perspective for us. So very fucking nice of you." Sam stopped in front of his car and fished around in his front pocket until he produced his keys. "I'm going for one last coffee before the apocalypse."

"Sam. Why are you so upset? You are going to get an inheritance soon?"

"That doesn't help me today, does it?" Sam slammed the car door closed and started up the engine while Spring watched him drive away. She thought she saw him flip her off but she couldn't be sure.

"What's got his panties in a wad?" Jason asked, emerging from the house, his tan hands tucked lazily in his front pockets.

"Oh, that's Sam. He gets flustered sometimes."

"What you need, my dear, is a laid-back man." Jason smiled playfully at her. "One who doesn't freak out on you at every little thing."

"A laid-back, employed man would be nice," she teased.

"No such thing. Guess you are out of luck."

"Maybe I'll be a nun, then. I'm already getting nun in the morning and nun at night." Spring snorted, remembering her father telling that same joke to his carnie friends. The thought made her smile now that she understood the meaning. He must have been teasing though, because she was sure that Lanie had quite the appetite even in those days.

"You're in a good mood. Guess it's the perfect time for us to have a little chat." Jason stepped in closer and Spring tried to ignore how he made her feel. Her hormones seemed to be going crazy lately. Maybe she should go to a doctor.

"What do you want, Jason? It's been a long day and if you have more bad news I'd rather you commit me now, please."

"You're growing testicles, Spring. That's good. One person in a relationship should have a pair." He laughed and Spring elbowed him in the ribs. "I miss you, you know?" He didn't speak again and she didn't respond. It was a statement, not a question.

She missed him too, at times. You didn't have children with someone and go through the trials of pregnancy and the pangs of childbirth and the joys of diaper-changing without missing that person who had been there with you. And in truth, he hadn't been a bad boyfriend. He was simply someone she couldn't count on to start a life with. A cloud above them shifted into a dozen tiny shapes before stretching itself into a thin line and disappearing.

"I've known you a long time, girl. I can tell when something's bothering you."

Spring turned towards him, observing the way his long brown hair hung perfectly around his face. The ends were dipped in honey. Women spent hundreds of dollars to have hair like that. It didn't seem fair.

"Jason, do you ever wonder how we got here?" Spring focused on a tall blade of grass, bending to the weight of three beads of water. She watches as one bead melted into the next, and all three pooled at the base.

"Well, I drove the van."

Spring smiled and rolled her eyes. She missed him more at times like this. "We used to have dreams. I was going to save the world and you were going to be a famous musician."

Jason nodded thoughtfully. "I haven't given up on my dream." Jason pointed through the van window to a guitar that sat fastened securely in the backseat. "Have you? Jason's lips formed into a thin smile, revealing dimples she forgot he had. She wanted to kiss him in that moment, but not because he was sexy. She wanted to kiss him because he was Jason.

"I hate to change the subject," he said, breaking the spell. "But I want to talk to you about the boy's education. I'm tired of the teachers telling us how bad they are. I think we should give home-schooling a shot."

"Jason. You live in a van!"

"Yeah, well, no one's perfect. But I heard about this thing called un-schooling. It's like home-schooling but you don't do anything. So the boys could travel around with me, seeing different things and experiencing the world, but I wouldn't be teaching them, so it would be legal." Jason tapped his right index finger to his temple to indicate the brilliance in this plan.

Spring shook her head. "Jason. I don't know what the hell you are talking about. I gotta go." She had almost felt a kinship with Jason again. Almost.

"We wouldn't have to worry about schools and social workers and what-nots. At least think about it, okay? And you may want to find out what kind of drugs Lanie's taking. It's nothing I've given her. It might be menopause, but I doubt it. I've known some crazy menopausal ladies in my time, but she's just...nuts."

194

Jason got into his van and cranked the engine three times before it decided to turn over.

I sure can pick them, Spring thought, and wondered if being a nun was an option for a woman who had given birth to twins, slept with men who didn't love her, and consulted spiritual advice from a woman who lived in her spare bedroom.

Lanie had been cleaning for hours, but no matter how much she swept, dusted, mopped or shined, it wasn't clean enough. She had, in fact, scrubbed one spot on the carpet for so long that she had worn through the fibers and could see the padding beneath.

"Why won't this spot go away?" She cursed the spot and the two boys, which she guessed were earthbound spirits, blinked at her and dashed away.

"Grandma's crazy," said one of them.

"Yep," replied the other.

Her daughter entered the room. Lanie knew it was her daughter intuitively, but somehow the person walking through the door didn't match up to her memories. When had her daughter grown boobies?

"Mom? You okay?"

The words sounded distant and muffled, like someone talking to her through a glass door. Lanie had to pay close attention to make sure they were coming from the daughter's lips and not from inside her head.

"This place is filthy. We live in filth!" Lanie scrubbed the spot again, tearing through the padding. The daughter came over and placed a hand on her shoulder. Lanie slapped it away. "Go get your father and tell him we're out of elephant ears."

Her daughter's eyes opened wide and she scurried away. Hopefully to get some goddamned elephant ears. How could they run a show without elephant ears?

"Did you hear that?" Lanie turned her head. Sirens. She was sure it was sirens. Where were they coming from? Lanie ran to the window and peeked outside, down the row of homes that looked so much alike she was sure she was hallucinating. "The fuzz is coming. Everyone hide your stash."

"What's Grandma doing?" asked one of ghost children.

The sirens were coming from the other direction, too, and Lanie left her watch at one window to check another. They were everywhere! "Don't let them see you. Plead the Fifth. Confess nothing. It's our constitutional right to stage a sit-in!"

The daughter walked over to her again. "Mama. Did you take anything? Did Bob give you something?"

"Take? Did I take anything? I'm not a thief. I don't care what those pigs say." Lanie began shaking and swatting at the little crawly things that were converging on her body. They came out of nowhere, tens of thousands of little black balls with legs. "The bugs. They are all over me. Spray me down with Raid."

"Mom? Mom?" The daughter snapped her fingers. She ran down the hall and Lanie could hear her open a drawer or cabinet. She returned with an orange bottle without a cap. A pile of pills were in her hand.

"Mom, the pills in the cabinet. Did you take some?"

"Pills? That reminds me, I need to call Wayne Newton." Lanie looked around for the phone.

"Mom, did you take some of these pills?" The daughter's droning voice seemed to be driving the bugs away. She had a talent after all, thank God.

"No." Lanie tried to remember. The bugs were receding as she gained a moment of clarity. "Yes. I took them to help me sleep. Only, they didn't seem to work."

The daughter spun around, talking to the two little blurs that whizzed by, then spun back. "Mama. Come sit down with me, okay?"

Lanie was panting, burning up, hotter than the Sahara desert, but she took her hands and followed.

"Boys!" The daughter called and two children appeared. "Grandma took some of your special pills, so we have to keep an eye on her, okay? Those pills are only for you boys. They make everyone else sick."

"They make us sick too, mama," said one of the boys. "Daddy said so. He threw ours out."

The daughter slapped both hands to her cheeks. "Okay. Mommy needs to go next door and get Bob. You guys keep an eye on Grandma."

They nodded and the daughter ran out the back door.

"Mr. McClure. It's Spring. Are you there?" Spring rapped on Bob's door. She could see him through the window of his front room, but apparently he didn't hear her. He was preoccupied with his broom and new pig. After a few more minutes of pounding, Bob came to the door. He was wearing a white, button-down shirt, a red bow tie, and a blue pair of jeans.

Spring wondered, not for the first time, what it was he did for a living.

"Sorry, Spring. Was doing some cleaning. Your mother was right about the pig. They aren't filthy at all. As matter fact whenever I drop lunchmeat little Buttermilk here devours it right up. It's cute, even if it is cannibalistic." Bob snorted and the pig snorted back.

Spring looked around. This was her first official visit to 'Bob's House.' Everything was white. The floors, the walls, the furniture and the appliances. Not even a throw pillow for color. But against the alabaster backdrop were clocks. Hundreds and hundreds of clocks. Clocks of various shapes and sizes perched on shelves that ran the perimeter of the main room. They ticked and tocked and cuckooed in perfect unison, except for one that sat on the kitchen table, which missed a tick here and there as if suffering from a heart murmur. So Bob was a clock man. Spring half-expected to see an army of Elves huddled around a work bench creating master works of clock art.

"Mom's not doing well. She got into the twin's Ritadate and she's acting kinda funny."

A large clock struck behind her and Spring jumped. Bob nodded and removed a leash from a hook on the wall and positioned it around Buttermilk's neck. The pig oinked twice in protest, but followed Bob obediently.

"Oh dear," Bob said, wringing his hands as he followed in a half-trot through Spring's backyard. "I'm so worried about her I could spit."

When they arrived, Bob dropped the leash and ran to Lanie who was lying on the couch with her hand over her forehead. The boys were attending to her, wiping her down with paper towels and Lysol. When they saw the pig they dropped their cloths and dashed after Buttermilk, sending him scurrying under the table.

"Are you okay, my love?" Bob settled himself on the couch, cradling Lanie's head in his arms. He kissed her cheek and stroked her hair. "I don't know what I will do if something happens to you. Please be okay. Buttermilk needs you."

Lanie smiled in response. "My sweet little man." She managed a stroke over his face.

"Mama," Spring said, fishing around her purse for her cell phone. "It's gonna be okay. I'm going to call 911."

"No! No hospitals. I hate hospitals. It's full of nothing but germs and dead people. I lived through the 60's, I can live through anything." Lanie turned her head back to Bob and smiled adoringly up at her boyfriend. "Don't let that crazy book-licker come near me."

"Bootlegger? Who's bootlegging, mama?"

"Book-Licker. The little bald man that masturbates to Dante. Can't he get a *Playboy* like everyone else?"

Spring shook her head. Her mother was really going crazy. "I'm going to call the Poison Control Center," she said. "Mama's worse than I thought."

Bob looked at Spring sympathetically. "She's right. I saw him caressing a copy of *War and Peace* when I was checking to see if my cat was here. I was so disturbed I almost didn't come back."

Spring scrunched her face together and let it go for now. Buttermilk oinked hysterically in the background.

"Why don't you take the boys for a while?" Bob suggested. "This is probably a traumatic thing for them to witness. I can take care of Lanie and will call you if anything happens. But I think the worst of it is over." He blotted Lanie's face with his shirt cuff and she smiled adoringly at him.

"Are you sure?" Spring looked from Lanie to her boys. Blaine was tugging on Buttermilk's tail while Shane was trying to ride him.

"Quite sure," Bob said and Spring ushered the boys out the door.

"My cell number is on the fridge, and so is her doctor if she gets worse," Spring hollered as she left and Bob nodded absently.

Spring wasn't sure where she should go. The park? Chloe's? The mall?

"We want McDonald's!" the twins chanted, bouncing up and down in the back seat. Spring glowered at them in the rearview mirror.

"I already told you that your McDonald's days are over." She fiddled with the radio, settling on a classical music station to calm her nerves.

"Where are you taking us, Mommy?" Shane leaned forward as far as his seat belt would allow him. "Are you selling us on the black market? Daddy says you can sell white kids for a lot of money in Mexico."

Spring shook her head. "No, I'm not selling you on the black market. I can't believe your daddy told you that. What else does he tell you?"

"If you can't sack it, go home and whack it."

Spring almost hit the car in front of her. "Okay. That's enough." The boys giggled in the back seat and she could see Blaine sign something to Shane who nodded.

It wasn't until that moment that Spring knew exactly where she was going. Her car drove on its own accord and Spring surrendered to it. A few minutes later she pulled into the parking lot of John Smith's building.

Spring didn't need to knock on the door; the boys did it for her, their small fists pounding away like tiny hammers on a drum. When John answered, Spring smiled and hugged him so tightly she worried she was hurting him. John's arms hung limp at his side a moment and then he hugged her back, patting her and kissing the side of her cheek.

"These must be your boys," he said, as the two pushed past him and into his living room scouring his apartment like pirates on a quest for hidden treasure.

"I'm sorry. I was sent away for a while. Long story." Spring plopped into his recliner, noticing for the first time that John's usual blue jeans were replaced by Khaki pants that looked new.

"Not a problem," he said, looking up at a clock on the wall. "They got names?"

The boys gathered at his kitchen table, which was canopied with paints and chess pieces. "No, boys, no," Spring called out to them, but John was one step ahead of her, scooping up the pieces before they could pop them in their pockets. "The one in the red is Blaine, and the one in the *Party Like Its 1999* shirt is Shane. Or, as Sam likes to call them, Thing One and Thing Two."

Once again, John glanced at the clock and Spring realized he must be late for something.

"Oh, God. I'm sorry. You have someplace to go." Spring felt her face redden with embarrassment. What right did she have to assume that John would be here waiting for her whenever she needed him?

John looked at her and she felt a thud in her heart that was so loud she was sure he had heard it too.

"I'm going to make a quick call and then I'm all yours. There is nowhere else in this entire world right I need to be right now."

"I'm not ready to go yet," Spring said, watching Blaine and Shane wriggling under a blanket on the floor. They looked so sweet as they slept that Spring felt a wave of maternal love wash over her.

"Don't," John said. He was sitting on the floor watching TV, a large bowl of popcorn in his lap. "Stay here forever, if you like."

Spring laughed. "If only things were that easy." She caught him looking at her and she shifted away. Something about his stare made her uneasy.

"What is there to go home to?"

"Well, there's Sam. And Mom."

"They are both grownups." John scooted forward, leaving the popcorn bowl behind him. One of the twins rolled over, but did not wake up.

"But I'm getting married, John."

"Is that what you want? Do you really want to marry this man?"

"Everyone wants to be married. It's the American dream." Spring pulled her knees up into her chest and thought about the question. "He loves me," she said after a long pause.

Too long. John reached over and brushed away the strand of hair that had fallen in her face. She missed that strand of hair. It was the only thing that stood between her and John. Her and utter vulnerability.

"Does he?"

"In his way, I think he does." She sat with the thought, letting it roll around in her head like dice in a Yahtzee Cup, until it meant nothing at all.

"Come outside with me," John said, pulling her up by the hand. He led her to his back patio through a set of clear glass doors.

He had a nice setup on his patio. Two plastic chairs and a small round table. A half-read fantasy book perched lazily atop the table. But it was the view that struck her. From his third-story apartment building he could see the world––or at least got a very good glimpse of it. Blocks and blocks of city. The mountains against the horizon. Paradise Pub.

"This is nice," she said, meaning it.

He could be alone here. A luxury Spring never had anymore.

"I miss home," he said, looking up at the sky. The moon was full and bright, playing court to the few stars that had decided to make an appearance that night. "In Indiana you can see so many stars they all kinda blur together. In the city, with all the light and pollution, there are only a few visible ones. Makes me kinda sad."

Spring squeezed his hand and followed his gaze. "It's amazing isn't it?" she asked. "The Universe is so large, so vast, so...unquantifiable, and here I am, a tiny speck of nothing, consumed in my own worries. It's almost pitiful."

"You," said John, turning to look at her again. "Are anything but pitiful. You are a child of the Universe, not a speck." He lifted her chin and their eyes met. His blue eyes became almost as dark as the night behind him.

"I want to be happy, John. Why is it so hard?"

John's fingers traced her face, from her cheekbone to her chin. It sent shivers down her back. "We all want to be happy, Spring, but very few of us ever achieve it. I wonder why we bother at all."

"Don't be cynical, John. Lots of people are happy."

John lowered his head and kissed her. It lasted only a moment. Their lips hardly met, barely parting at all as they came together.

"John, stop," she said, her voice no louder than a whisper.

But he wasn't going to let her go. He took her head and pulled her to him, kissing her deeply. "Are you happy now, Spring?" he asked, his tongue rolling around hers, searching for more of her. She could feel the longing inside him. His need.

"Yes," she breathed between kisses.

"I love you, Spring. I love you so goddamned much..." He pushed his lips onto hers. His fingers dug into her shoulders. "Tell me you love me, too."

"I...I..."

John released her mouth, and lifted her chin. He looked into her eyes. "Tell me, Spring."

"I'm so confused. There's Trevor. And Sam. God, what about Sam?" She started to panic. Sam was probably worried sick about her at this very moment. She had left her cellphone in the living room. He could be calling her right now.

"He doesn't love you, Spring. Not the way you deserve to be loved. I could see that after spending a single hour with him. How can you be so blind?" John shook her, ever so slightly, before letting his arms drop.

Spring shook her head. "Let's pretend for one little moment that I did have feelings for you. Then what? Are you prepared for what that means? That means taking me on, and my boys, and my mother. Are you prepared for all of that at your age? You don't even have a job, John."

"I just want a night with you for now. One step at a time. That, I'm prepared for."

Spring felt her jaw tighten. Of course he wanted a night. That's all any man wanted.

"Mommy, my tummy hurts." One of the boys called to her beneath the blanket.

"I think it's time I go home."

John turned from her. She could see his reflection in the glass door, his mouth was drawn down and his eyes were hollow. "Yes. Sam will be waiting."

John was making breakfast. He hadn't gone to sleep yet, and he had no intention of going. Sleep would bring dreams, and dreams would bring images of Spring. Spring with Sam.

As he fried his eggs he felt a pang of guilt for not meeting Amy the previous evening. He should have called her. He prayed that someday she would forgive him. He hoped she hadn't sat out in the parking lot too long, waiting for him. But there was no chance he was going to miss being with Spring, even if it meant an eternity in hell for all the sins he'd commit in the process. He hadn't showered, either. He wanted her scent on him as long as possible and when he breathed in deeply he could still catch glimpses of her in his mind. She was so beautiful it almost killed him. He knew he should have talked her into staying, but after he mentioned having her for a night, her mood seemed to have changed.

Of course he wanted her for a night. But there was more. He wanted her for a day, and a night, and the next day, and to see where the road led them after that. She was the mother of two kids, and that carried a heavy weight. He didn't want to fail her. She deserved more than that.

He flipped the eggs and broke the yoke in the pan. That was good. He wasn't in the mood for runny eggs, anyway. He needed something solid, something he could hold onto. Even if it was a breakfast food. He served himself a plate. The eggs were overdone and the bacon had been burned during his daydreaming, but he couldn't taste it. All of his senses were still focused on the memory of the night before. He had thought before that he had loved her, but after holding her last night, he knew for certain. And he knew, in the deepest part of his heart and soul, that he wanted her to be happy. Even if it meant letting her go back to Sam.

After breakfast he opened up a recently-purchased book on mountain trails of the Southwest. Arizona was renowned for beautiful hiking trails and scenic peaks, and he had not explored a single one of them. As a matter of fact, in his month in the city he had not done a single thing worth writing home about...*except falling in love with an engaged woman, but that was a letter Mom wouldn't want to get.*

"Some adventurer I am," he sighed.

The mountains of his childhood seemed a million miles away. *You can leave, you know?* This wasn't the first time he had this thought. Pack it up and go home, back to cornfields and Pete and the VFW and his family. A place where he wouldn't be alone.

Yes, you will.

Yes, you will.

TWENTY-FOUR

Sam skipped his prayers, knowing with utmost certainty that Allah would understand. Instead he spent the morning tidying his den, making room for all of the new books that he would soon inherit.

As soon as he married Spring.

He tightened his grip around the dust rag as he thought about the situation. He just had to keep his head. They would be married. And soon.

Why did Grandma Rosary have to be such a religious freak, anyway? To her, The Ten Commandments were not just suggestions, they were laws to be followed, and heaven help the soul who didn't believe as she did. It was a wonder he had come out normal at all. He still hadn't told her he was no longer practicing Catholicism. That would have to wait until after the wedding...or maybe never tell her. Let the old woman be happy in her final days, he thought, as he dusted and arranged his books. He was jostled out of his thoughts by the snorts and whimpers of a pig and a steady, annoying, rap at the back door. He could pretend not to notice, but that would only call Lanie out of the woodwork.

His first order of business, after the matrimonies, was in getting rid of the terrible trio.

"Well, hello, Bob!" said Sam, a smile pulling itself tautly across his face. It hurt to stretch his lips that far, but he held it, fighting back the curl of his upper lip.

"Good to see you, neighbor," said Bob, bringing Buttermilk inside. "I do hope Lanie is feeling better. We worried about her all night, didn't we, sweetie?" Bob bent down and gave the pig a peck on the cheek.

Sam felt goose bumps rise up all over his body. He wasn't sure what he hated worse, watching Bob kiss the pig or watching Bob kiss Lanie. Both were equally unnerving.

"I'll check in on her," Sam said, glad for the reprieve. He knocked quietly on Lanie's door, and hearing no answer, opened it enough to peek inside. "Lanie?"

Lanie sat cross-legged, palms up, eyes rolled into the back of her head. Candles of various colors flickered around her. She seemed to be in a trance. He was about to leave the room, and tell Bob she was sleeping, when her eyes snapped open suddenly.

"Sorry to interrupt your devil worshipping. Your boyfriend is here. And so is Bob."

Lanie pursed her lips together and let her hands fall into her lap, shaking out her frazzled red hair. After a moment of collecting herself, she spoke. "I know what you are doing, and I suggest you rethink things before karma kicks you in the ass."

She picked up a card and flicked it in his direction.

It flipped and whirled in the air before landing gracefully beside him. Sam stooped to retrieve it, knees groaning in protest. *The Tower*, it read ominously. It was a tall, mortar building being struck by lightning. Bodies with arms flailing and *Oh Shit* faces plunged out of the windows and to their deaths. Charming.

"Don't worry about me, Lanie," he said coolly. "I've got everything under control."

Sam tossed the card into the air and watched it flutter down, tumbling over itself, only to land face up on his toe. He kicked it off dismissively, gave Lanie one final look and left her bedroom.

Your time is coming, old woman.

TWENTY-FIVE

Spring sat on the cold, metal folding chair, wishing she had worn a pair of pants instead of a skirt. Though it was blistering hot outdoors, it was like the arctic tundra inside the store. There were others with her—bored, chilly patrons looking for a great deal. She resisted the urge to crawl into a fetal position and fall asleep across three of the empty seats while she waited for Sam. A woman twirled the dials on an old television monitor that was bracketed to a wall. She flipped through the channels and grunted when she realized the only station it received was the local news, only partially visible through the static lines.

"Non-profit organization, *Teens in Trouble,* is under fire today," reported a blond newscaster, "After mascot, Casey the Condom, allegedly threatened a woman with office supplies at a local strip mall..."

They cut to a clip of a giant penis brandishing a pair of black-handled scissors near a woman with long, flaxen hair.

"Ta-da!" Sam emerged from the dressing room, dressed in black and white from head to toe. "What do you think?" he asked, adjusting a bow tie.

The hairs on his head stood up straight as if in salute. The material was shinier than any tuxedo material Spring had ever seen. It certainly did not fit him right. It was an inch too short in the arms and legs and too tight across the chest.

"It's got quite the sheen to it," she said, shielding her eyes.

Sam smiled and nodded approvingly. "That's not even the best part," said Sam. "Watch this." Sam scurried back into the dressing room and returned with a shiny, matching top hat and a black lacquered cane. "See?" he said, leaning on his cane and tilting his top hat over his left eye. "I know you like the men in those old movies, so I wanted you to have your fantasy."

He did a little heel click and almost fell over on the dismount.

Spring's mouth fell open as she struggled to find the words.

"I knew you'd love it, Pookie. To heck with renting. I think I'm going to buy it. Ring it up, Charlie." Sam snapped his fingers at a thin fellow who bustled obligingly to the register. When Sam was sure the salesperson was out of earshot he whispered. "Don't say anything, but I think they made a mistake on pricing. It's only $69.95."

Sam looked around the room, not at all affected by the cold blast of air that swept through the space. In fact, he was practically flushed.

"We can get you a dress, next. Charlie was showing me a darling pink taffeta number that would look so good on you. It's even got a hoop skirt. You could be Scarlett O'Hara for our wedding and I could be your Rhett."

Sam bowed chivalrously, his top hat tumbling from his head and rolling towards a chubby adolescent boy who was sucking down an ice cream cone. Sam shot the kid a warning look and snapped it before the child could lay a sticky finger on it.

"Here, check this out." He handed Spring a folded piece of paper that had been tucked inside his hat.

"Are those bells sewn in around the collar?" Spring looked closer at the ad.

"Yes! Southern Bell. Get it?" He elbowed her in the ribs. "You'd look so beautiful in that, Spring. Maybe we can even dye your white pumps to match it."

"Sounds good, Sam. But not today, okay? I'm pretty tired." Spring took Sam's hand as they made their way out of the store.

His fingers suddenly gripped hers very tightly.

"Isn't that Trevor?" he asked, staring in the direction of a café across the street. "If it's not, he looks exactly like the picture of the guy you keep in your wallet..."

Spring swallowed. It was Trevor. He sat staring into a coffee cup, mindlessly ignoring everything that was going on around him. His hair was disheveled and his clothes had been thrown on haphazardly, but he looked sober.

Spring caught her breath as Sam pulled her into the car.

Sam yelled the whole drive home. Spring tried to tune most of it out but he wasn't going to let up.

"Trevor?" Sam ran a red light. "What the hell is he doing in Phoenix? Have you seen him yet?" When she didn't answer he shook his head. "Isn't that just dandy!"

"You could be more understanding. I was in love with the man." She reached to turn on the radio but he caught her hand and closed on it tightly.

"Was? Or are?"

Spring shrugged, freeing her hand from his. "You don't choose who you love."

This ignited Sam. "Oh, that's right. You are so evolved you can love a whole herd of men at once. I forgot." Sam removed one of his hands from the wheel, holding up fingers to count. "How many studs are in Spring's little man-harem? Let's see...there's Trevor. John. Me. Jason, when he chooses to show up. Any others I ought to know about? I bet we can rack up a few more before the wedding if we really work at it."

"You're overreacting." Spring pulled at her hair in frustration.

"Am I? If anything, I think that I am under-reacting. All I can say is that you are very lucky we don't live in a country where betrothed women are punished for adultery."

Spring crossed her arms defiantly. "Well, by all means, feel free to move to one, then. Better yet, marry a woman no one else would ever look at. Then you wouldn't have to worry."

This caught Sam off-guard and he said nothing else the entire ride.

"I gotta bad feeling about this," Lanie said. She and Bob were cuddled up on her mattress, his unclothed body fully resting on hers. She played with the little hairs on his back, letting them curl around her finger as he shivered with delight.

"Now, now, Lanie," Bob cooed. "She's a grown woman. You have to let her make her own mistakes."

Lanie sighed and watched as Bob's body rose and fell. "I know. But I think marrying Sam will be the biggest mistake of her life. I mean," Lanie whispered in case anyone was listening. "...Half the time, I get the feeling he don't even like girls."

Bob chuckled and bit her neck. "He needs to take a crack at you, then." Bob's breathing progressively deepened until Lanie knew he was asleep. She stroked his cheek and smiled.

"I'm sorry," Lanie whispered to the Universe.

Why couldn't there be do-overs like in her video games? You fuck up a video game and you restart, no harm done. But in life, you were stuck with whatever muck-ups you created and sometimes it just plain sucked. Sometimes the only thing you could do to get through was to pretend they never happened, because if you acknowledged it, even for a moment, it could destroy you for the rest of your life. The guilt choked her and she reached for a cigarette for salvation.

"You know smoking's bad for you," said Bob, stirring from his sleep.

Lanie was surprised to find that she was not annoyed at this remark. In fact, it was comforting. Bob looked at her with his beautiful hound-dog eyes.

"I want you to be around for a very long time."

Lanie nodded and crumbled the cigarette in her palm. She could go another hour without one. Maybe two.

"There's something I need to ask you," Bob said, digging his elbows into her flesh in order to prop himself up. He smelled so good. Such a wonderful blend of cleanliness and raw masculine energy. She wanted to take a bath in that scent, perfume her body from head to toe with the essence of BOB.

"What's that, darling?" Lanie stroked the little grey hairs on his head. They were soft as cotton candy.

"Do I make you happy?"

Lanie thought for a moment about all the things that made her happy. Ice Cream. Matlock. Nude beaches. Santana. But none of these made her as happy as Bob. Bob had his own category of happy.

"Yes. You make me very happy."

"Good," said Bob, falling back upon her breast. "That's what I wanted to know."

Lanie listened to him snore as he rode the waves of her body. She could listen to him snore forever, she thought, and resisted the violent urge to squeeze him.

Twenty-Six

1982

Spring felt the hand break loose, felt her own slide from his like the untying of a bow on a Christmas present. She stood on tiptoe, craning her neck to peer over countless heads that separated them. But they all looked the same. Flappy faces and striped shirts. One nameless customer melding into the next. She twisted sideways, slithering in between two women large enough to work as fat ladies if Bernice ever found a fella (which Lanie insisted would never happen). No man wanted a woman who weighed twice as much as he did. And there was no excuse really, now that Jane Fonda had put out her video tapes.

The sun set the midway ablaze and Spring was careful not to touch anything metal. But the rides still whirred, ticked, tottered and clanged, paying no attention whatsoever to the heat. Make us stop! They challenged the elements in the cities they visited. But nature gave way to the carnival. Even the earthquakes in LA were not powerful enough to stop those who came in droves to experience The Bob Cat Show. Folks took their chances, foolish or not. It may have even added to the thrill.

Spring passed Donny and Falco, the old-timers who'd been on the circuit since the 1930s and liked to let everyone know it. They raised their cigarettes towards her and continued their conversation.

"Fuckin' Reagonomics…"

"Problem is we don't use real freaks anymore."

"…Ain't no one believing in headless ladies since cable tel'vision."

At last she saw him. "Daddy!"

She pushed through the crowd, bumping into a girl about her height and knocking her snow cone to the ground. She stopped to help the girl. She had been saving up the pennies she found and could probably buy her another. But her father was still moving and she didn't want to lose him again.

"Daddy!"

She tugged on the tail of his denim work shirt and the man spun around. Her heart sunk. He was too bushy and old to be Daddy.

"You lost, little girl?" The man stooped down to get at her eye-level and Spring wanted to touch his mustache, but she wasn't allowed to talk to grown men. Except for Roy the Strong Man, whom Lanie insisted was compensating for something and harmless as a tsetse fly.

Before the bushy stranger could ask her more questions, she darted away.

The carnival was a maze of concession stands, information booths, roller coasters and dime toss games set up differently for each town. Some places liked to have the food near the entrance, while others preferred the games. Spring tried to remember where each of Daddy's booths were located, and she ended up backtracking several times. She was always able to find her way back to the center, as Marta, who ran the cotton candy stand, insisted on playing the Candy Man song in a continuous loop. It made for big headaches but easy navigation.

A popsicle stick fastened itself to the bottom of Spring's shoe and she succeeded in kicking it off, only to find an ice cream sandwich wrapper stuck to her other. Spring scowled and wondered if people would continue to litter if they knew it was she and Chloe who got to stay up late to clean.

Spring stopped at the Ferris wheel and began to cry. She would never find her father. He was gone and the next time she would see him would probably be on the back of a milk carton. Chuck, the Ferris wheel man, who smelled like boiled eggs, noticed and nodded in the direction of the ladder climb game.

And there was Daddy.

She should have remembered. Daddy had been spending a lot of time there training the hitchhiker girl who was running it. Daddy liked to say he was showing her the ropes, but Lanie said it was because the girl didn't wear any panties when she climbed the ladder. Spring suggested that maybe they could buy her a pair, but that put Lanie in such a foul mood that Spring never brought it up again.

"Darlin! Why are you crying? Come to me." Daddy's arms were open wide. Spring ran towards her father, barreling through anyone unfortunate enough to be standing in her way. Her father received her with a big hug and spun her high in the air.

"You left me!" she accused, wiping her nose on his flannel shirt before he sat her down.

Daddy smiled and twisted the ends of her long hair in his hand. "I didn't leave you. I would never leave you. You are Daddy's girl." He looked at her for a long time and his blue eyes looked bluer than she had ever seen them.

"You promise?"

"I promise."

Spring took his hand and they made their way together towards their trailer. Lanie was waiting with soup and hotdogs as Chloe shoved pork and beans up her nose. Spring lay her head on her father's lap while he munched Fritos.

Chloe spent the afternoon with Spring, shopping for a wedding dress. Sam had given her two-hundred dollars to *go wild*. He wasn't keen on Chloe shopping with her. He considered Chloe a bad influence, but he relented when she had threatened to go alone instead.

"Does he not understand that the only wedding dress you will find for that price is going to look like something from *The Rocky Horror Picture Show*?" Chloe asked as they left their third shop empty handed.

"I don't think it matters what I wear," Spring said. "Sam's reserved a place in line at some chapel, and it's not like anyone will see us. We are spending the night in Sedona and then he's whisking me away for a romantic honeymoon at Grandma Rosary's house in Eggshell."

"An Eggshell Honeymoon," Chloe clucked. "Living the dream aren't you, sis?"

"I like this one," Spring said, ignoring her sister's comment as she pointed to a short, floral sundress in the next store. Spring found her size and examined the price tag. "One twenty-nine. Perfect."

"Sam's gonna be pissed," said Chloe, as Spring emerged from the fitting room. Spring twirled and the skirt flared up in compliance, revealing a hint of her thigh. "So you get my seal of approval."

The girls took Spring's package and made their way to a corner café. Spring had offered to buy Chloe lunch with the remainder of her wedding dress money.

"You don't have to marry him," said Chloe as she picked through her salad, spearing a cherry tomato and popping it into her mouth. Her sister's brown eyes misted and Spring saw a sincerity in them she wasn't used to.

"It's too late, Chloe. The wheel has been set in motion."

Chloe chewed, considering. "You aren't going to lose the kids just because you aren't married. This isn't the Biblical days."

"It will make things easier on me. And Mom. And Blaine and Shane. I'm tired of struggling. It's all I have ever done."

Chloe's face reddened, and Spring wondered if her famous temper was going to make an appearance. "You'd rather settle than struggle?"

Spring turned her head and caught the image of a young couple holding hands outside. They were smiling at each other. Laughing. Looking into each other's eyes. The woman stood on her tiptoes to kiss the man and he held the small of her back as their lips met.

"Ever have moments like that with Sam?" Chloe asked, pointing her fork in the direction of the two lovers.

"No," Spring said, feeling the ache of the honesty.

Chloe pressed on. "Ever had moments like that with anyone?"

Spring took a drink of water and swallowed. You couldn't cry and swallow at the same time. A little trick the man who ate swords had taught her.

"Dad's never coming back, Spring," Chloe said, putting her fork down and leaning across the table. "You gotta stop replacing him."

Spring was stunned. "I'm not replacing Dad. That's not what I'm doing."

"Really? You get one guy who was a deadbeat. One who abandons women. And now a guy who treats you like a child. Roll them all up and who do you have?"

"Shut up, Chloe." Spring's fingers tightened and she attempted to keep her voice steady, but her words were shaky and staggered. "You don't know what you are talking about?"

"Don't I?" Chloe's own voice trembled. "I know you think you've lost your perfect love, but there is no such thing as perfect. Perfect only exists in fairy tales. So, you didn't end up with Prince Charming. Does that mean you run away with the toad? Even if he does promise you a castle?"

Spring stared at her sister for a moment, not sure how she should respond. She wanted to be more like Chloe. Wild. Reckless. Free. "You make things sound so simple."

Chloe winked at the waiter as he poured more water. "Sometimes things really are that simple."

Jason was there when she pulled into the driveway; sitting in the van, tapping his fingers on the dash in time with Lynard Skynard. The sun beat down hot, searing the lawn and withering what few plants existed, but Jason seemed unaffected by the heat. In fact, he looked comfortable. "Hey, babe," he said as she got out of her car. "Good to see you."

"How do you tolerate this heat?" she asked, fanning herself with one hand and tying her hair up in a knot with the other.

"I love the cleansing purge of the sun. The heat is nature's enema."

He smiled lazily, revealing surprisingly white teeth for a man who most likely did not own a toothbrush.

Spring smiled, relaxing in the presence of an old friend, until she smelled a suspicious aroma wafting from his vehicle. "I thought you gave that up," she said, crossing her arms.

Jason shrugged. "Hey, it's from your garden. Your mom gave it to me." Spring looked in the direction of her house and shot an unseen Lanie a dirty look.

"Got the boys ready?" he asked. "I think I'm gonna take them to the hemp museum in Northern California this weekend. Everything there is made out of hemp. It's the first lesson in my home-schooling curriculum."

"Jason. We need to talk."

Spring circled the van and climbed into the passenger's seat. Jason sighed in anticipation of a lecture. "Is this a nagging session? Because you know I don't get into the nagging sessions." Jason reached to adjust the volume on the radio, but Spring got to it first and clicked the knob to the off position.

"What's gotten into you? Are you taking your mother's estrogen pills or something?"

Spring glowered. He had a way of making the anger rise up in her. She took a moment to calm herself and then began. "Jason, things have to change. Blaine and Shane need better parenting than we are giving them. Unless we want to end up on the news someday then we..." She fanned her hand between the two of them, to motion that they were in this together. "...We need to fix this."

"You *are* on something," he said, a smile crossing his face. "Right on. Just don't do it in front of the boys. That's all I ask."

Spring gritted her teeth and tried again. "No, Jason. This is about the boys. They have no stability. You *live* in a car."

"Van," he corrected.

"A motor vehicle at a campground for hippies. That's their home, half the month. You don't discipline them. They don't have a schedule.

They don't have any rules or boundaries. No wonder they are screwing up in school."

Jason shifted uncomfortably in his seat. Spring braced herself for his reply. "Now listen here, Little Miss Prim and Proper. Just because you've sold out doesn't give you the right to lecture anyone. What rules do you have for the boys?"

Spring thought for a moment. She hadn't meant to put this all on him but that's how it was coming out. "God, Jason. I hate to say this, but I agree. It's not only you. It's both of us." Spring took a deep breath in and began to sob. "They are going to take Blaine and Shane away. Lanie was visited by a social worker. I know I'm a sucky parent who can barely keep her own life together let alone the lives of two children, but I love them. They've given me stretch marks. They've kept me up all night. They've given me a patch of grey hair..." She pointed to a spot on her head where she had noticed three white hairs seeding up recently. "... But I love them so much. I can't lose them, Jason. They are all I have. We have to fix this."

Jason appeared flabbergasted. He glanced from Spring to the lawn outside of his window, and back to Spring. He tapped his knee thoughtfully and Spring could see that he was considering. Something. The moment was broken by the sound of Blaine and Shane rushing from the house. Spring slid out of the seat. "We could look into taking parenting classes together. For the boys."

Blaine and Shane dashed to the truck, their arms in the air, smiles on their faces. "Daddy!" they cheered as Lanie followed behind, complaining that they had broken the last working video game controller in the house.

Jason scratched his head with one hand, while opening the door for the boys with the other. "Yeah. Maybe. But let's do baby steps, okay?"

Spring nodded and buckled in the twins.

He leaned over and whispered in her ear, "I didn't smoke anything today either, if that's what you are worried about. I threw out Lanie's shit. It's terrible. Whatever she is using for fertilizer should probably stay in the cow. What you smelled is from a lady friend I gave a ride to."

"Bye, boys," Spring said, blowing them kisses. They waved and bounced, protesting their belts.

"Let's talk next week, okay? You listen to me, and I'll listen to you. We've got to make this work." Jason saluted her with two fingers as he drove away.

Spring watched them go, feeling a sense of pride for the father of her children she wasn't used to, interrupted promptly by Lanie.

"Is it okay if Buttermilk moves in for a few days? Bob's gotta go out of town next week and the airline refuses to recognize pigs as service pets."

Spring shrugged. "Sure, Mom. Why not?

Twenty-Seven

Sam packed into his duffel bag a pair of jeans, a button-down shirt, a top hat (which folded down, accordion-style) and a shiny, black tuxedo. Spring watched the event through the mirror of her vanity as she combed her hair for bed.

"I heard you got your wedding dress." Sam zipped his bag and looked at her with a glint in his eye. Spring nodded and busied herself with a knot. Her hair was always tangled. Maybe she should have donated it to Kimberly.

"...I guess it's bad luck for the groom to see it, anyway," Sam sighed when he realized she wasn't going to speak of it, and went to retrieve his copy of *Bride Magazine*. He flashed her a photo of a teal gown, trimmed with peacock feathers. "Oh sweetie, I hope you got something like this," he said, tapping the page with his long, thin fingers.

Spring imagined them probing specimens on some intergalactic space mission. Maybe that was why he was so fond of the tuxedo; it was made from the same material as his mother ship.

"I'm going to bed now," he yawned.

Spring blew him a kiss and left the room, almost tripping over the pig that was right outside her door. "Mother," said Spring, peeping into Lanie's bedroom. Lanie was playing the new video game Bob had dropped off for her. "Please keep a better eye on the pig."

"You're the one marrying him." Lanie cackled as she pounded on the controller buttons. Buttermilk rummaged through the wastebasket, oinking in protest that there wasn't anything worth eating. "Isn't he the cutest thing you've ever seen? I'm not sure I could eat him after all."

Spring smiled. "I guess it would be hard to eat something you love."

She reached down to stroke him and he nuzzled her hand in an offer of friendship.

"Damn it!" Lanie tossed the controller as the words *Game Over* flashed across the television screen. She hefted herself off of the floor and waddled into the hall. "Guess you're going through with it," Lanie grunted.

Spring followed and noticed that her mother seemed to be losing some of the girth in her rear.

"Yep. Tomorrow's the big day. Might as well get it over with. What else can I do?"

They were in the kitchen and Lanie opened the patio doors. A cool breeze caught the ends of Lanie's hair, causing it to float around her shoulders like a gypsy witch in a movie. In that moment, she was almost beautiful. Another movement caught Spring's attention and she turned to see Bob's bare head in the back yard, illuminated by the moonlight like a light bulb in a dark closet. "I thought Mr. McClure was out of town?"

"He isn't leaving until Sunday. We thought we'd give Buttermilk a chance to adjust to his new surroundings for a few days." Lanie's eyes found Bob's figure as he scuttled towards the door. "What a man," she shivered.

"Do you love him, Mom?" Spring never took her eyes off of Bob as he weaved his way through Sam's cactus garden in the dark. He was quite adept at navigating dangerous yard work and Spring wondered where he received his training.

"I used to think you only got one chance at true love, my darling. But the Universe is a pretty big place, don't you think?" Lanie opened Spring's hand and placed an envelope in her palm. Lanie patted it closed. She then turned to scooped up Buttermilk and greet Bob. They embraced, becoming one mass of Lanie, Bob, and pork.

Spring glanced at the paper as she stepped into Sam's library; a section of the den where Sam stored his most beloved books. He had given her a shelf of her own and her twenty or so volumes seemed insignificant next to his vast collection. She searched the titles until she found her copy of *Wuthering Heights*. It was the only hardbound she owned. She took it from the shelf and sat down on the floor. After glancing down the hall to make sure she was still alone, she opened the envelope Lanie had given her and removed the letter inside, tucking it into the book to read. Her body quivered as she read the words.

My Dear Spring,

First of all, I want you to know how much I love you. I know that may be hard for you to believe, after all this time, but it's true. I didn't mean to leave you. It's a long story but it starts with a man who thought he was nothing and wanted to prove to the world he was something. And it ends with a man who realized he had everything he wanted but only learned this after it was too late. Please stay strong and true to yourself. You are a remarkable girl who will someday be a remarkable woman. Settle for nothing less than extraordinary. I'm with you. Forever.

Daddy

Spring re-read the letter several times before folding it up into a tiny square and tucking it into her bra. The house was quiet, save the tick and tock of Sam's grandfather clock. She listened to it mark off the seconds, like one of Lanie's doomsday countdown devices, telling her the end was nigh. When the clock struck three, she realized that she was getting no sleep this night. The sun wasn't up and John probably wouldn't be either, but she had to try. This might be her last chance to talk to him. Ever.

John hadn't heard from Spring since their kiss on his patio, days before, and he had been worried sick. He wasn't sleeping. He hardly ate.

The only thing that kept him from falling over the edge completely was his art. He painted constantly now. He had found his muse.

When the phone rang, he almost ignored it. It was probably Amy again, yelling at him for standing her up. In retrospect maybe he should have gone out with her. Then he wouldn't be sitting home alone like an abandoned puppy.

"Hello?" he answered, realizing he should invest in the $1.99 a month more for caller ID. John was surprised to hear that the voice on the other end was not Amy's, but Spring's.

"John? I'm sorry. I didn't mean to wake you up. I just needed to talk."

"Spring? What's wrong?" He could hear the sadness in her voice, the hesitation between words, the labored breathing.

"Are you upset with me?" she asked.

"Don't be silly, Spring. We are friends. You can call me anytime you need to. Okay?"

She did not answer.

"Okay?" he repeated more urgently.

"Okay," she said finally and he breathed a sigh of relief. He paused a moment to make his voice sound soft and relaxed. He didn't want to scare her away. "What can I do for you?"

"I don't think I can see again."

"What do you mean? Why can't you see me? We are friends right?" He was beginning to panic. What was going on?

"Yes...I mean no...I mean yes," she said, her voice no louder than a whisper. "John, I'm marrying Sam in less than twelve hours. I thought you should know."

"Spring, it's okay. It's going to be okay, I promise. Just...just don't stop seeing me. We are friends. That's all. We kissed and it never has to happen again." John wanted to reach through the phone and grab her and pull her into his apartment with him.

"But John. This is the truth. Do with it what you will. Take a hammer to it and pound it into the ground afterwards. The truth is, I think I love

223

you. And I'm not sure how this happened." She stopped for a moment and John thought he lost her. But then she spoke again. "Lanie said you get one chance at true love. So I thought we were safe. But Lanie says she was wrong."

John's heart stopped beating at that moment. *Time of death: three eighteen on a June morning.* He took in a long breath and let it go.

"Stay right there," he said. "I'm coming to get you."

"You can't," she protested. "Sam won't let me see you."

"What do you mean Sam won't *let* you?" John demanded. "You are a grown woman. Sam can't stop you if you choose to see me." There was a silence on the other end. He wasn't going to let it end like this. "I'm coming over, and you can't stop me, Spring. Do you hear me?"

"Okay. Come over. But don't knock on the door. I will meet you outside."

John sped towards Spring's house. It was dark, but dawn would come quickly. He ran every red light, letting the thought that he had never run a red light filter into his brain and then flitter away. He had to get to her. He needed to hold her, even if it was for only a minute. And he needed to make her promise to take care of herself.

She said she was getting married tomorrow. *Tomorrow? Why tomorrow?*

He sighed in relief as he turned on to her street. Even from a distance, he could see her, the ghost girl with the wild blond hair and a flowing white nightgown. She stood out against the dark like a sheet flapping in the wind. He pulled up beside her and could see the dark circles around her blue eyes. She looked so fragile standing there, he was afraid she might fall over, or crumble away like part of last night's dream.

"Hi," she smiled, climbing in. She had an aura of sadness around her.

"Hi," he said, driving away from her house, from her neighborhood, from her life. He wished he could carry her away to a brand new one. "Where to?"

"I'm sorry to do this to you," she said, pulling on a strand of her hair.

She looked like a little girl in his passenger seat as her chin trembled. He took her hand and held it tightly, kissing her fingers, steering with his free hand. He wished he had something to say.

"There's a park nearby," she said, looking out her window. "I found it the other day, when I was out rambling." She forced a laugh that turned into a cough.

John turned as instructed and discovered a small park with a man-made mini-lake. Another thing he missed about home. Natural water reservoirs. He pulled into the empty parking lot. Before he could even turn off the ignition, Spring escaped from the vehicle. She glided towards the lake and he wondered if she would walk right into it. He caught up and grabbed her by the hand. She didn't protest and the two stood side by side at the water's edge, the moon falling behind them.

What should he say? If words escaped his lips they might be cruel or accusing. Or worse. Pitiful. John bent down, found a pebble in the grass, and skipped it across the lake. It hit the water four times before sinking to the bottom, a trick his dad had taught him. The last time he had done it was the day of the funeral, but in this moment it felt right and natural and not at all disrespectful to his memory.

"I've only seen that done in movies," Spring laughed, picking up a pebble and attempting to do the same. Hers clunked straight to the bottom. Her lower lip poked out and John smiled. He wanted to kiss that bottom lip, to chew on it, to feel every part of her mouth. He had to pick up another stone to get his mind away from the thought.

"You don't have to do this," he said, casting another stone.

Spring tossed a handful of pebbles into the lake. She hit a sleeping goose who shot them an angry look and swam away. "Yes, I do, John. You wouldn't understand."

"The white picket fence idea is overrated, Spring. Don't buy into the garbage they sell you on TV."

"Easy for you to say. I'm guessing you grew up with a home, two parents, and a dog. I didn't have those things. I want that for myself. I want that for my kids. Is that too much to ask?" She wiped the dust from her hands on the hem of her nightgown and turned to face him.

John's face tightened. He clenched and unclenched his fists, a habit carried over from his younger days whenever the subject of his family arose. "In spite of my 'normal' appearance I was not raised in the *Leave It To Beaver* lifestyle you seem to believe. My parents were great. Mom baked pies. Dad went to work each day." He paused, wondering why he was telling her this. It was a subject he never talked about. "But then Dad got sick," John choked, strangling on his own words. He bent over to pick up another stone and sent it skimming across the surface.

"...For almost a year, I watched him lying on the couch, getting smaller and weaker by the day. We never talked about it. I'd come home from school and he'd say 'Hi, John, how was your day?' And I'd answer fine, and that was that. And then one day I came home and nobody was there. Grandma came to get me and I stayed with her for three days and when I went back home, Dad was gone and Mom wouldn't come out of her bedroom." John spread his palm. He wished he had something to focus on, something to keep him from crying in front of Spring. Then he looked and saw that she was crying herself.

"I shouldn't have told you," he said. "I'm sorry."

"I didn't know..." She looked up at him, her chin quivering.

"No matter how hard we try to control our lives, we can't control everything. I guess that's what I really wanted to say." Morning was imminent and John knew his time was limited. When the sun made its appearance, all of this would turn to dust and he might never see her again. Before he could remind himself that he was breaking his promise, he kissed her.

"Come with me," he whispered into her ear. "I can make you happy."

She shook her head, even as she kissed him. "It's not just about me, John."

"I love you," he whispered, brushing the hair out of her ear with his mouth. "You told me you loved me, too."

"Yes. I love you." She looked up at him, her chin set with defiance. Her eyes had a faraway look to them. "...But it ends tonight."

John released her and made his way angrily back to his pickup truck, leaving her tottering behind. For a moment, he considered letting her find her own way home. But it was he who had broken the vows, not her. He dropped her off near her house without saying a word, just as the first rooster crowed from a purple house where socks were hung from trees.

Spring tiptoed across the room, racing the first beams of sunlight that seeped in through the window. Guilt stabbed at her as she saw Sam's face, pale in the moonlight. She caught a glimpse of her own face in the mirror and stopped momentarily to study it. The reflection staring back looked alien to her. The features were the same, but there was an emptiness of expression to it. She was sure that same face hadn't existed during her stay with John in his apartment.

Sam is the best thing that ever happened to me.

She challenged her reflection, daring it to contradict her. Sam stirred behind her. Spring climbed into bed and felt Sam's bony body beside her. She missed the feel of John already. She pushed her pillow into her head to drown out the images.

"Hi, sweetie," Sam said, rousing from the bed and heading to the bathroom. "Did I wake you?" He didn't wait for an answer. "Lanie seems back to her normal self." Sam laughed, pulling up his black socks so that they were perfectly aligned with one another. "Told me she's working on a voodoo doll of me. Your mother's a kook, you know it? But a lovable one."

Sam tossed the towel into the hamper, blew Spring a kiss, and left the room.

"He knows." She mouthed the words. And tried with all her might to go to sleep.

She hadn't realized she had slept so long, or so deeply. She awoke to Sam, elbows propped up on the edge of her bed, smiling dreamily.

"Wake up, sleepikins," he cooed, stroking her cheek. She tried to swat him away and he chuckled. "Wedding day jitters, Pooks. I have them too." He helped her up and escorted her to the bathroom where he encouraged her to look her finest. Beethoven was playing joyfully in the bedroom as she dressed. When she emerged, hair half-secured in a ponytail, wearing flip-flops and her wedding dress, Sam handed Spring her suitcase. She took it without question, knowing Sam would have everything she'd need for her honeymoon packed inside.

"I still don't like the dress," he said, as he surveyed her. He was dressed in his tuxedo, resting against the door. He spun the cane in his right hand, his feet crossed at the ankles, posing like Mr. Peanut. "...And I packed your pumps so you can change before the ceremony. But it's not like anyone is going to be taking pictures."

Spring smiled an agonized, close-lipped smile. She wondered if he could sense her distress. But he didn't seem to notice.

"Okay, we're off," he said, seizing the top hat from a hook on the wall. "...Off to our brand new life."

Lanie was sitting on the couch, stroking Buttermilk and sipping a Slim Fast. When she saw Spring and Sam in their wedding gear, she clicked her tongue. "So it's off to the altar for the two of you?" Buttermilk grunted in his two cents and Lanie gave him a soft squeeze on the ear.

"We are," Sam said, tipping his hat.

"I thought you may be too tired, Sam. After you spent all last night on the phone. Who was that you were talking to? Some book broker in Mesa?"

"Book broker? What book broker?" Spring said.

Sam glowered. "That doesn't concern you, Lanie." He pushed Spring towards the door. "You shouldn't be such a busy-body. Curiosity killed the cat."

Lanie huffed. "If that was the case, I'd be dead many times over. But mark my words. The Universe has its eye on you."

Spring shook her head. "Let's just go," she snapped. "Before my legs give out."

Sam took her bag and carried it to the car. "Remember the vastness of the Universe!" Lanie called out as the door shut behind them.

"This is going to be so much fun, Pookie!" Sam fiddled with the radio dials, settling on a station that was playing the Beach Boys. He sang along, mucking up the words to *Help Me Rhonda*. "Next stop, Sedona!"

He pulled onto the freeway and accelerated, going much faster than the law allowed. He rolled down the window and offered a wave to the biker couple that rode alongside them. The wind caught his top hat and sent it tumbling down the freeway. Spring turned and watched it become a speck of black, shiny dust.

"Oh bother," he said, annoyed, but uncharacteristically shook it off. "By this time tomorrow we will be on our way to Grandma Rosary's as Mr. and Mrs. Samuel Thomas Wayne."

Spring digested the news. "Sam," she said, watching the line of the road ahead. "Do you realize we've been together this long and I never knew your middle name?"

Sam nodded thoughtfully. "There's a lot we will get to know about each other in our life to come." He reached across the seat and patted her knee. "So much to see, so much to do. It's exciting!"

Spring watched the markers count down the miles to Sedona as Sam howled along to *Blue Moon*.

John hadn't slept at all. Not a wink. He tried a couple of times, but gave up and gave in to what was left of the night. Spring was getting married. Today. John knew he wasn't the smartest guy in the world, but it didn't take a genius to figure out that this would be the greatest mistake of her life. His eyes scanned the living room, stopping at a bundle of multi-sized paint brushes on the table. He grabbed a beer and set up his easel. He had to capture the image of last night. Commit it to canvas before it was gone from his memory forever. His hand moved. Brush. Stroke. Dot. Brush. He was surprised by how fast he worked. The picture that took shape was effortless. Beautiful. He hated to take credit for it. It didn't seem to be his.

A knock at the door startled him and he dropped a brush, sending droplets of white across the grey linoleum. "Coming," he mumbled, offering one final glance at his creation before dragging himself towards the door.

"This is for you," said the big-bellied man John recognized as his landlord. He brandished an envelope in his right hand. "I'm not the mailman, so please tell your friends what apartment number you live in, so I don't have to play delivery boy again."

John received the letter, shutting the door before the man could say more. It was addressed to JOHN SMITH. John fished the Leatherman from his jeans pocket and used the knife accessory to slice open the envelope.

Dear John,

Please leave me alone.
I do not love you. You were just a project for me.
I need a man who can take care of me. Not a boy.
If you come near me again I will be forced to call the authorities.

Spring

John reread the letter several times. He turned it over to see if there was more, but the back was blank. He sank into the wall, not knowing what to do. He could take her leaving. He could take her marrying Sam. But he could not stand the thought that she didn't love him. He wanted to scream, cry, break things, hurt things. He wanted to fuck the shit out of something. He had never experienced this feeling. This primal helplessness. He was an animal. He turned his attention to the girl in the painting. Her lips were parted as she looked at a boy. Him. Her eyes were wide. Intense. Truthful. As he stared at it he realized that something wasn't right. The words in the letter weren't right. His mind rolled over. He had to think now. Madness could wait.

John breathed deeply, letting the memory of last night engulf him, until he felt the truth of it. This wasn't Spring's doing. Sam had written the letter. John crumpled the paper and shoved it into his pocket.

Spring might be marrying Sam, but she loved him. He would give her the wedding gift. Then he would set her free for good.

TWENTY-EIGHT

Lanie sat on the couch, flipping through channels, pausing at the ones selling promises of youth and sexual prowess. She heard a knock on the back door and smiled as she saw Bob's head peeping into view. That man was all the youth and sexual prowess she needed.

"I've decided not to go on my trip," he said, stepping in and adjusting his bow tie. He was wearing a long-sleeved shirt and she wondered how he fared so well in the Arizona heat. The man never sweated. "I'd miss you way too much."

Lanie popped up from the sofa and hugged him so tightly she thought he might break.

"Careful," he warned. "You might crack a necessary part."

"I've got a question to ask you," Bob said, straightening himself and looking into Lanie's eyes. His tone deepened turning her warm.

"Sure, Bob, shoot," she said, hoping they'd be done with the talking soon, so they could move on to the smooching. He had one of those tiny bow mouths that were so popular in the silent films of the twenties and she needed to kiss it all of the time.

"These past few weeks have been the happiest in my life," he began, pausing to clear his throat. "I've been a bachelor all my life, never giving much stock to love. I mean, you can't quantify love, right? How do you know it exists? But here you are." He motioned his arms up and down like she were the grand prize in *The Price is Right*. "And I wanted to ask if you, well, if you and Buttermilk would…"

The knock at the door startled Lanie and sent Buttermilk scrambling. Lanie watched Bob's small frame slump. She scurried to the door, promising Bob that he would have her full attention once she sent their visitor on his way.

"It's store boy!" she exclaimed, seeing the young man before her, a smile spreading across her face. "John, right?"

"Yes, ma'am," John said, as she pulled him inside. He looked thinner than the last time she had seen him. Poor guy needed a home-cooked meal.

"Don't step on the pig," she warned him. "It's real this time."

"Is Spring here?" John looked around the house, craning his neck to peer down the hall.

Lanie clucked her tongue. "No. She's getting married today. Didn't you know?"

John sighed. "Yes, ma'am. I did." John scratched his head in a defeated fashion. The poor boy had it bad, Lanie thought. "I'm gonna get something out of my truck real fast," John said after a long pause. Bob moved towards them and placed his arms protectively around Lanie's waist. The couple watched as John jogged to his truck and returned with a large picture.

"This is my beau, Bob," Lanie said when John returned, chastising herself for not introducing him sooner. John nodded a hello.

"Can you see that Spring gets this?" John handed the picture over to Lanie. She looked at it and gasped.

"This is the most beautiful thing I've ever seen!" Lanie marveled at the use of color and light. She pushed it towards Bob so that he could see. "Did you do this?"

John nodded. "Normally, I'm not this good. But Spring...inspires me."

Bob pushed his glasses back onto his nose and focused his attention on the painting. "I must say, that is a haunting scene. Who is the young lady by the lake?"

Lanie patted Bob on the head. Men couldn't be counted on to notice anything. "That's my daughter! Can't you tell? Looks exactly like me."

Bob leaned in closer, squinting through his glasses. "So it is," he acknowledged. "Simply marvelous."

"I'm gonna go now," said John, pushing his hands through his hair. "I need to go home, drink six beers, and fall into a very deep sleep." John turned to leave, but seemed to think better of it. "Oh, and see that Sam gets his letter back." He pushed his hand into a pocket and delivered a letter with fancy scrawl into Lanie's hand.

"This is from Sam?" she asked, turning the letter over in her hand. She saw that it was signed from Spring, but that was not Spring's handwriting. No woman had writing that fancy.

"Yes, ma'am. I want him to know, that, well...I know."

Lanie was about to ask more questions when the thought occurred to her. "The social worker who came to the house and told us the boys would be taken away...she showed me a letter. It was written in this type of handwriting, on this type of stationary! Sam!" Lanie smacked her head. Here she was chasing witches when there was a warlock at work. "What a bastard!"

John looked confused but Lanie smiled reassuringly. "You're the knight!" she said, bouncing up and down.

"Huh?" The poor boy looked like he had just been caught sneaking into the women's changing room.

"From the cards. You are her Knight of Cups."

John looked at her; his face as empty as her ex-husband's wallet. She shifted her considerable weight from one foot to the other and then dashed out of the room, returning with the tarot card.

"I did a reading for Spring awhile back. And this came up. It's you." Lanie gave him the card. John stared at it for a while before handing it back to her.

"I admit, it does look a bit like me," John said. "But..."

"A bit? Boy, that's the spitting image of you! Why didn't I see that before? I'm way out of practice." Lanie clucked her tongue, wondering if she should take some internet classes or something to brush up. Bob checked out the card and nodded his agreement. When Lanie saw that the boy wasn't going to say anymore she sighed. Why was she the one who always had to fix everything? "You're in love with her, right?"

He nodded.

"And you know as well as I do that marrying that man will ruin that girl, right?"

He nodded again.

"Then let's go get her before she makes the biggest mistake of her life."

John drove Bob's red '67 Mustang, trying to drown out the Metallica CD that Bob insisted was great traveling music. Buttermilk sat buckled in beside him and Lanie and Bob shared the backseat, making out like teenagers. He hoped that they didn't pass any cops along the way.

"Where exactly is the chapel?" John asked. They had been driving through Sedona for the last forty-five minutes and Lanie offered nothing as far as directions. He heard the heave of her shoulders rise and fall in a shrug. "You don't know where your daughter is getting married? How could a mother not know these things?"

"I try not to concern myself with things of the material world," Lanie answered, tickling Bob's ear.

"We could ask a local," Bob suggested. "Surely this town can't have that many chapels?"

John nodded, cursing himself for not having his laptop. He pulled into the parking lot of a building that advertised itself as a Tourist Center.

"Hello, sir," said the smiling man inside. The place was a conglomeration of crystals, dream catchers, Indian fetishes, and brochures. John ducked to avoid being hit by a bird that flew freely about the store. "Can I help you?"

"I need to find local chapels that might perform weddings," said John, leafing through a brochure. "I have a friend who is scheduled to get married today, and I'd like to be there."

The man scratched his head and his eyes focused on some object outside the window. John turned in that direction but did not see anything. "We have several chapels here in town, sir. And several more outside of town. Might take us awhile to narrow it down."

John sighed and wondered if he was supposed to offer a bribe like he had seen in the movies.

"There's the Chapel of the Rock," said the man, holding up a finger. "The chapel of the Red Rock, The Chapel of the Supreme Rock, The First Chapel of the Red Rock, The Unquestionable Chapel of the First Red Rock, and the Red Rock Chapel of Hope and Forgiveness."

John scribbled them down on the back of a brochure.

"Now, all of those are on Red Rock Chapel Drive, of course. But if you head north, you will find the Chapel of The Sun. The Sunset Chapel of Devoutness. The Chapel of the Sun Gods. The Chapel of Those Who Think the Sun Gods are Heretical. And the Chapel of St. Donald McRonald..."

"You're making these up."

"Now, if you head west, you will find..." The man went on as John left the building.

"Sir!" The man followed, calling to him through the door. "Might I interest you in a timeshare opportunity while you are in town? You get a free night's stay and a chance to interview a group of dolphins who believe that in the last days, all humans will have to convert to blowhole breathing."

"Any luck?" asked Lanie, who was walking Buttermilk. Bob was hunched over, following the pair with a small shovel and a plastic baggie. John ignored her and got in. "Guess we drive around and see if we spot their vehicle," she said.

It was as good a plan as any.

Sam and Spring sat in a pew awaiting their turn to be married. They had arrived late because Sam insisted they check out the shops the moment they entered downtown Sedona. There were so many bookstores and coffee houses that Sam commented, this must be what Paradise was like, minus the virgins. Luckily, Pastor Paul was a generous man who would never turn away a couple with big dreams and fifty-five dollars. Spring listened as Pastor Paul performed the rites for a young couple ahead of them.

"There are gonna be times when you want to cheat," said Pastor Paul, eyeing the young man who stood before him. "Lotsa times. When your wife starts looking old and her boobs swing like monkeys on a rotting vine and you lose your hair and want to feel young again." The couple in front of them exchanged worried glances. "But don't. Don't you do it. You don't get into heaven by pulling your pecker out whenever the urge hits you." He shifted his gaze to the woman. "Or by flashing your firm breasts at truckers at three in the morning."

Sam turned to Spring and winked. "I'm not worried about that, Pookie. Your breasts aren't that firm."

Pastor Paul proclaimed them man and wife and the couple disappeared behind a curtain for pictures and shrimp cocktail. The next pair stood and Spring felt a wave of nausea wash over her. "I have to get something from the car." She needed the valium she had snatched from Lanie's purse.

"No." Sam stopped her. "Just a few more minutes. Then we can get whatever you need."

"And don't forget to put the toilet seat down," Pastor Paul advised. "Keep your makeup on when you go to bed. And a little oral goes a long way."

Spring turned to Sam. "I don't think I can do this." She grabbed his chin and forced him to face her. "It's not right. We don't love each other." Though Sam remained perfectly composed, a storm brewed behind his eyes. He pursed his lips together and clicked his tongue against the inside of his cheek.

"Next," said Pastor Paul, beckoning to Sam. Sam motioned for the couple behind them to take their place, then returned his attention to Spring.

"What do you mean, you don't think we should?" His face was taut.

"I don't love you, Sam. I've never loved you. I'm sorry. I really am. I wanted to love you. You were normal and stable and there for me. All the things I thought I needed. And you were getting the inheritance..." Spring looked down, avoiding Sam's gaze. She had never felt so ashamed. "And Lanie told me I only had one shot at love, anyway." Tears begin to form and she fought them back. She clenched her fists together and stood up straight.

"I don't love you, either," Sam hissed, grabbing her arm as he stood up beside her. "But I didn't invest two years of my life for you to call it quits like this. You are going to march down this aisle and marry me. Do you hear me?" He pushed her out of the pew and ushered her into the aisle. "In five minutes," he whispered, digging his nails into her wrists. "You *will* be my wife."

Spring felt light-headed and the room began to spin. She heard Pastor Paul pronounce the couple in front of them man and wife and Sam shoved her forward.

"Dearly Beloved," began Pastor Paul, and Spring could hear no more.

TWENTY-NINE

The clock on the dashboard said 3:20 and John was certain he had missed his one shot at stopping Spring from marrying Sam. He had made several loops through town and had not seen their vehicle. He turned his car around and headed back in the direction of Phoenix, flipping on the radio to drown out the sounds of Lanie and Bob's slurpy kissing in the backseat. The newscaster announced that parts of Arizona and Nevada were going to have severe thunderstorm warnings until Monday at 10 a.m. He hoped he had shut his windows back home.

And then he saw it. A giant billboard with a picture of a white-haired man holding the Koran in one hand and the Bible in the other.

The Sedona Chapel of Infinite Knowledge. Three miles east of town. Exit 211.

"We got it!" he said, spinning the wheel in a wild arc.

"You sure?" Bob asked, unbuckling his seat belt and leaning forward.

"Better be," John said, putting his foot on the gas.

Spring and Sam emerged from the chapel, the sunlight forcing them to squint. A bird squawked overhead and Spring marveled at the beauty of Sedona. It was a vivid, Technicolor red and thirty degrees cooler than Phoenix. She wished she could stay. But Grandma Rosary was dying, and there was not much time. As they sloshed towards their car Spring thought she saw a familiar vehicle speeding in their direction. But it couldn't be.

"What the..." Sam's voice trailed off as they watched the Mustang peel into the parking lot. In the vehicle were three humans and one barnyard animal. Spring recognized them all.

John was the first out, throwing open his door and racing towards her, the car's engine still running. Lanie, Bob, and Buttermilk followed. "Spring!" John panted. "God, I'm glad to see you." He reached for one of her hands and held it in his. "I'm sorry I'm too late. But I had to let you know something."

Spring exchanged a look with Sam. "John, why are you here?"

"I love you, Spring. I love you more than the stars, and the moon and the sun and the rain and all that other corny stuff I've heard them say on the Oxygen Channel."

Spring looked at Sam who was rolling his eyes.

"You deserve the best, Spring. You're beautiful and funny and smart, and no, that's not normal. That's a beautiful, amazing, anomaly. You deserve so much more than a *normal* life."

Bob and Lanie were nodding behind him.

"Look buddy," said Sam, pushing John back. "It's been a long day and we want to get going, okay?"

John held his ground. "I'm not asking you to come with me," John continued, ignoring Sam. "That's way too much to ask. But I love you enough to want you to be happy." John pulled Spring into his arms and hugged her. "You deserve everything, Spring. Settle for nothing less." He kissed her on the cheek and let her go. "I guess that's it, then," John said. "I had to tell you."

"You came to save me." Spring smiled as the truth sunk in. "You came to save me!"

"Someone had to do it," Lanie said.

Spring gave the trio a disappointed look. "That's where you are wrong." She held up her left hand revealing a ring finger without a ring. "Ta-da! Sam and I didn't get married."

John did a double take. "You're not married?"

"Nope. Still single. I just couldn't go through with it." Spring smiled.

That same smile that had disarmed him in the grocery store.

"Any other suitors I should know about?" John pecked at the pebbles in the ground with the toe of his shoe.

"Just one," Spring grinned, pulling him in by the shirt collar.

"Can we get out of here? The suit is starting to melt onto me." Sam tugged at the tux which was clinging to him like saran wrap.

"I have one more thing to do," Spring whispered to John. "And then I will come back to you. Can you wait here?"

John nodded and watched as Spring and Sam drove away. Even as he watched her go, his heart soared.

"You know," said Bob to Lanie. "This *is* a marriage chapel."

Lanie arched her brows. "What are you saying, mister?"

"I bet they have an open slot, since the Sam/Spring wedding didn't work out. It would be sad to waste it, don't you agree?" Bob adjusted his bow tie and Lanie grabbed his face between her hands and kissed him roughly on the lips.

"That's the most beautiful proposal I've been given," Lanie said, leaping into his arms.

Somehow, John marveled, Bob managed to stay standing.

THIRTY

When Spring returned, John was still standing outside of the chapel, his hands shoved deep inside his pockets. Lanie and Bob were nowhere to be seen. She could feel John's eyes on her when she kissed Sam on the cheek. "The right woman will come along," Spring reassured Sam. "I promise."

Sam laughed. The first sincere laugh Spring had heard from him in a very long time. "Oh, I doubt that, honey." Sam looked out over the red mountains and let out a weary sigh. "Guess you can get a ride home?"

"I'm sure I can. Take care of yourself, Sam. I will keep all of your things safe until you can come back for them."

Sam nodded and before Spring could open the door he leaned over and hugged her. "Thank you. For everything."

Spring watched as Sam sped away towards his new life. She felt bad about the deception but it really wasn't hurting anyone, she decided. And everyone would end up happy.

"Hi stranger," she said, walking towards John. She had removed the rubber band from her hair and blond strands swung lazily around her face. "Fancy meeting you here."

John smiled, drawing in a long breath. "I must be in heaven. The most beautiful place on earth and the most beautiful girl in the world. Doesn't get any better than this."

"Heaven minus the virgins," Spring teased.

"Huh?"

"Never mind." She reached up and grabbed his neck, nuzzling it with her lips. "Sedona is beautiful isn't it?" Spring turned to face the red mountain ranges that dominated the landscape. "Too bad we can't stay."

John jingled coins in his pocket. "Why can't we?"

Spring threw her head back and laughed. "You're crazy, John Smith, you know that?"

John tilted her chin up, so that their eyes locked. "I'm serious. We're both unemployed. Nothing to really bind us anywhere. Think of what the fresh air would do for the boys."

"I guess Jason could park here just as easily. Though I might have to give him extra gas money." Spring wrinkled her brow and thought. "What would we do?"

"Well, if you can throw caution to the wind and let your life unfold as it will, then Spring, my dear, we can do anything we want."

Spring smiled and the sun touched her face. Yes. They very well could. "I still can't believe you came all the way out here to save me," she said, leaning her head on his shoulder.

John kissed her on the top of the head. "I had to. How else was I going to collect the twenty bucks you owe me for this week?"

Lanie and Bob emerged from the Chapel of Infinite Knowledge, giggling like high school sweethearts. "Guess what?" said Lanie. "I got hitched."

Spring squealed and embraced her mother, falling into the warm folds of her flesh. Then she went to Bob. "Hurt her and you deal with me."

"Hell with that," said Lanie, flexing. "Hurt me and you'll deal with me." Bob beamed and tenderly patted Lanie's behind.

"Not a bad way to spend a Saturday," said Spring as they stood in the shadows of the red mountains.

"Not a bad way at all," agreed John. "And who knows," he whispered so softly into her ear that she almost didn't hear it. "Maybe someday that will be you and me in the Chapel of Infinite Knowledge."

Spring turned to whisper back. "Not a bad way to spend a life."

Buttermilk snorted.

EPILOGUE

Forging the marriage certificate was easy and ingenious. Sam was surprised that Spring had come up with that herself. Why hadn't he thought of that before? And as much as he hated to admit it, it was a decent thing for her to do. She didn't ask for anything in the deal, just that they part ways on good terms and he get those bobble heads out of the house as soon as he was able to.

They had picked up the stationary at a local shop, created their own certificate from a printer at a cyber café, and stamped it with a seal stating that the couple were now certified Reiki healers. His grandmother would never know the difference.

When he presented it to Grandma Rosary she was beside herself. "You got married! Oh, thank God. Now you will go to heaven." She hugged him as hard as her bony arms could hug him, and for a moment Sam felt a stab in his gut at the deception. But it was making her so happy, and would make him happy in return, so he pushed the feeling away.

"In the top drawer of my bureau is the key to the building where I've kept the books," croaked Grandma Rosary. "Your grandfather built it himself, and I didn't have the heart to move them. I hope they bring you much happiness."

Sam had to check his own heart to make sure that it was still beating. "Thank you, Grandma. I love you." And he meant it.

The building sat on the far side of his grandmother's property. It resembled a large white barn. Sam's pants tightened as it came into view. He felt like an archeologist who happened upon some great discovery that had been lost for millennia. He wished that he had not let

Spring talk him out of the Indiana Jones hat and whip set they saw in the Discovery Store.

Sam waved at the landscapers along the way, who appeared to be leaving for the day. He could only hope. This would afford him some privacy while he sorted through his treasures.

His fingers trembled as he pushed the key into the old, rusty lock. The place had probably been sealed off since the time of his grandfather's death twenty years before. After some minor protest the doors swung open and Sam fell to his knees.

"Oh sweet mother of Buddha," he said, feeling richer than King Solomon.

The room was large, perhaps as large as his own house, and twice as tall. Each wall was lined in shelves––shelves housing hundreds, perhaps thousands, of books. All hardbound and glorious. A tall ladder was fastened to a rail that spanned the perimeter of the space, making navigation among the tomes easy for those who weren't afraid of heights.

He picked up a book that had somehow fallen to the ground. It was covered in dust; Sam had to blow the cover clean in order to read the title. *A Christmas Carol*. First edition. Signed by Dickens. His legs felt sticky.

Thunder boomed in the background and Sam saw a flash of lightning that coincided with the darkening of the sky, as if God had turned off one switch and turned on another. He looked at his watch. It was going to be full darkness and night soon and he knew he should leave, come back the following day when he had sunlight on his side. But he couldn't go. Not yet. He had waited too long for this.

He raced to his car and opened the hatchback. He ran to and fro, carrying whatever books he could shelter in his arms. When the rain began, he tucked the books beneath his shirt to protect them.

"Fuck me," he said, when his car was full, but the storage unit was still overflowing. "I guess I'll rent a U-haul." Sam shut the doors to his car as water fell in thick drops all around him.

As his fingers inserted the key back into the lock, he was suddenly reminded of the portrait of God and Adam in the Sistine Chapel. God breathing life into Adam. A shock jolted through him and he collapsed, reaching for books as he fell through a hole in the Universe.

"I'm not sure what he's saying," said the joweled one who kept trying to offer him a towel. "He's been blubbering like that since we woke him up."

Sam looked at the man and his lips tried to form the words *Fucking Idiot* but all he could muster was bu-bubu-bumm-bum.

"T'aint never seen no man sleep through a storm like that," said the skinny sidekick who was wearing overalls with so many patches Sam could hardly see the denim beneath.

"That weren't no nap he was taking, you ignoramuses. He was hit by lightnin'. Why you think he's smellin' like burnt toast?" This was the fat one who had a few years, and pounds, on the others. "Lewis will know what to do. Lewis always knows what to do." His lackeys nodded dumbly. The three turned their attention to a dirt road, awaiting the mystical Lewis.

Sam looked at the building behind him for the first time since his awakening. The doors were swung open and there were books everywhere. A few were charred. Most were wet. Everything was ruined. Armageddon had come. But only to the storage house.

"Gone," he wept, picking up book after book and watching it turn to mush in his hands. "Everything. Gone."

"Hey, he said something," said the skinny one, nodding encouragement. "Good boy. Goooood boy." He reached down to pat Sam's head and Sam swatted the hand away.

At last, a newly-painted yellow station wagon came into view. Sam watched as a face appeared behind the wheel, belonging to a round man with large, square-shaped frames balanced precariously on his blunt nose. The three yokels cheered in unison and Sam wished that Allah had taken him when he could have. Lewis emerged from his car carrying a brown leather briefcase. An expensive one from the looks of it.

"I'm Lewis," said the man slowly, stooping to meet Sam's gaze. He seemed familiar. "I am here to help you." He touched the small of Sam's back to show that he was non-threatening. Sam nodded and took the handkerchief the man handed him.

I'm not sure there is anyone who can help me, thought Sam, his lips not quite ready to form a sentence of that magnitude. Instead Sam buried his head into his hands and sobbed.

"There, there," said Lewis. "I'm going to take you to the hospital and see that you get proper medical care. Then I will request that you be released to me and I will help you through this trying time. I'm a lover of books myself."

Sam nodded, blowing his nose.

"I know you've suffered a loss but your grandmother tells me the books were insured. That's got to be some consolation."

Sam looked at his library that sat in ruins. His life's dreams lay fallen like the city of Gomorrah after God's wrath. He sniffed twice.

"I'm gonna set you up for therapy twice a week until the crisis is over. It will be okay," Lewis said, lifting Sam's chin to meet his eyes. Beautiful, gentle, warm eyes.

In a moment, all of the books that had been lost were forgotten. Sam nodded and the man squeezed his hand. When Sam squeezed it back he knew that everything really was going to be okay after all.

6 Months Later

Spring drove down the highway, smoothly merging into the right hand lane of traffic. She smiled and nodded at familiar faces that she passed. The boys sat buckled in the seat behind her, talking excitedly about their second-grade field trip to the Sedona Art Faire.

"Where are we going, Mommy?" Blaine asked, craning his neck to see evidence of familiar landscape. Towering red rock formations on either side of the car formed an interesting corridor and Spring smiled to herself. The scenery of the land never failed to amaze her.

"Home. I wanted to try out a new route."

"That rock looks like the one in John's paintings," Shane said, pointing to a smaller mound alongside of the road.

"They all look like the ones in John's paintings," Blaine laughed and Shane nodded in agreement.

Spring found her exit and pulled onto a narrow rocky path right outside of town. The boys bumped in their seats. Spring stopped the vehicle in front of a row of three trailers that sat on a large plot of crimson sand.

In front of the middle trailer, Lanie and Bob were engaged in an elaborate, snake-like dance while Buttermilk watched from the porch. "It's my boys!" Lanie stopped dancing and turned to face the twins, opening her arms wide to receive them with a hug.

"Grandma!" they said in unison, covering her cheeks in kisses. Bob adjusted his glasses and smiled warmly before nodding at Spring.

The door of the far right trailer swung open and Jason emerged, carrying a guitar that had lost one of its strings. "Hey, beautiful," he said, winking at Spring as he settled on to the steps of his front porch. "Want to hear me play Sister Goldenhair? I've been working on it all day."

Spring smiled. "Not now, Jason, but maybe tonight. I'm sure your sons would love to hear, though." Jason shrugged and began to pick away at the instrument. Bob took Lanie's hands and twirled her around as the boys patted Buttermilk.

"I'm gonna go for an hour," Spring hollered out to Jason and her mother who nodded in response. "But I will be back to feed the twins dinner." Spring ascended the three steps into the first trailer and made her way to a small card table near the kitchen. On it sat a stack of mail that Spring quickly sorted through and stuffed in her purse. She hopped down the stairs and into her car. "Bye, then. See you in a bit."

It wasn't a long drive. Within five minutes he was within view. Her face warmed as she took him in, leaning against his truck, arms relaxed and folded across his chest.

"About time you got here," he said, his eyes twinkling. He opened an arm for her and she settled into the nook.

"Sorry, had to drop off the twins. They said your stuff was quite the hit at the fair today."

"Yeah, tourists never get tired of rock paintings, it seems." The sun had settled itself behind a large chunk of rock, casting an ethereal orange illumination in all directions. "Wish I had brought my paints."

"I can't wait 'til it's built," Spring said, turning her attention to the frame that was beginning to look like a building. "I've never had a home."

"You have one now. Maybe next we build you your very own park."

"I can't believe books are worth that much," Spring said, recalling the insurance check Sam had endorsed and sent to Spring shortly after disappearing.

A bird chirped in the distance and Spring sighed contentedly. "Oh, I forgot. We got mail." She produced two letters from her purse. She handed one to John and took the other for herself.

"We're invited to a wedding," said John, showing her the invitation in his hand.

Spring read the names Amy Strick and Trevor Donnelly and shook her head. "How in the world...? He told me he already was married!"

"Well, not anymore, I guess," John chuckled. "...Although soon to be again. The Universe is a very strange place, Spring. I don't doubt anything. What does yours say? Good news I hope."

"It's a letter from my parenting classes." She carefully opened the envelope and read the letter several times, thinking there was a mistake. "John. They want to hire me. As a counselor."

John took the letter and studied it. "They know a good bet when they see it, Spring."

Spring tightened her lips and turned to face him. She tilted her chin up in his direction. "I love you, John Smith."

John took her in his arms and kissed her forehead. Spring could smell the strong scent of his soap when she was so close to him. "I love you too, Spring Ryan Smith."

The rock stole what was left of the sun and they watched it disappear into itself, surrendering to the Arizona night. "Of all the things I've ever painted," John said. "Nothing can ever match the beauty of a moment like this."

Spring closed her eyes and wrapped her arms around his waist. "Nope. Fairy tales are best left up to writers, I think."

"I agree, Spring. I agree."

ABOUT THE AUTHOR

April M. Aasheim was the second oldest of six children, and spent her childhood living with her mother and her stepfather, traversing the Southwest, and following one 'get rich quick' dream after another. Though her travels were interesting and often brought her into contact with colorful and fascinating people, April longed for a *normal* life. Her early adult years were spent working as a preschool teacher, a social worker, and a community activist. She was also a wife and a parent. During this time she started writing about her life and the people she met. She also realized that there was no such thing as a normal life.

April currently lives in Portland, OR where she is happily married and trying her hand at gardening. She has published several short stories and is working on her second novel, *Maggie Maddock and the Witches of Dark Root*. She maintains an active blog about her adventures as a suburban housewife at aprilaasheim.blogspot.com.

Bruce County Public Library
1243 Mackenzie Rd.
Port Elgin ON N0H 2C6

CPSIA information can be obtained at www.ICGtesting.com
Printed in the USA
LVOW08s0222281114

415887LV00001B/273/P